The GILDED GIRL

ALYSSA COLMAN

SQUARE FISH
Farrar Straus Giroux
New York

For my husband, Dan,

who makes every day magical

SQUARE FISH

An imprint of Macmillan Publishing Group, LLC
120 Broadway, New York, NY 10271 • mackids.com

Our books may be purchased in bulk for promotional, educational, or business use. Please contact your local bookseller or the Macmillan Corporate and Premium Sales Department at (800) 221-7945 ext. 5442 or by email at MacmillanSpecialMarkets@macmillan.com.

Library of Congress Control Number: 2020910185 (hardcover)

Originally published in the United States by Farrar Straus Giroux
First Square Fish edition, 2022
Book designed by Aurora Parlagreco
Square Fish logo designed by Filomena Tuosto
Printed in the United States of America by LSC Communications, Harrisonburg, Virginia.

ISBN 978-1-250-82053-2 (paperback)
3 5 7 9 10 8 6 4 2

AR: 5.5

The GILDED GIRL

The Kindling

DECEMBER 1905

Izzy watched through a crack in the door as the young ladies in the parlor burst into flame. Sparks that began at their fingertips drew up their arms like long silk gloves as the girls took their places on the dance floor. The Kindling Ceremony had begun.

Heat radiated out of the room and Izzy's eyes stung from the smoke. The headmistress went down the line, touching her diamond ring to a ring on the right hand of each girl. They murmured something with each touch. The unheard words were like kerosene to the flames, but Izzy knew the words were something far more powerful—they were magic.

The newly installed electric bulbs had been turned off, so the only light in the parlor came from the students themselves as they moved in synchronization through the elegant, secret dance that would give power to their magic. Izzy had never seen a ballet, but she thought even the best one in the world couldn't be more beautiful and challenging than this. She swallowed her fear and tried to memorize every detail.

The pair of teachers hovered by the wainscoted white walls, wringing their hands as they watched the flames grow around their pupils' bodies. Two years of work had gone into preparing for this moment, but now they could do nothing except circle the room in their long black dresses like watchful mother crows. Izzy had thought the magical flames would hurt, but the ten pupils kindling wore looks of intense concentration, not pain.

Outside the windows, the sky was the dusky gray of winter twilight. Magic tingled in Izzy's boot-polish-stained fingertips as each of the young ladies raised a clean hand with a gemstone ring. Red rubies, green emeralds, blue sapphires, and purple amethysts shone in the firelight. The girls twirled in perfect synchronization while the flames circled them like dancing partners.

If they passed the kindling, they'd each be awarded a shiny diamond ring at the party after. That way, everyone who saw it would know they were one of Miss Posterity's Diamond Girls. Only the elite were allowed to go through the Kindling Ceremony to secure their magic, and among them, everyone said the Diamond Girls were the finest graduates of any girls' kindling school in New York City.

Izzy shifted nervously but kept her eye pressed to the crack between the double doors. She should go back to the kitchen before anyone saw her, but she couldn't tear herself away.

In unison, the girls turned around and around, moving their arms with a casual elegance that took years of practice. The red and gold flares encircling them lit the awed faces of the onlookers. Izzy was too enraptured to hear the footsteps approaching behind her.

"What are you doing here?" Cook's rough hand pulled her back by the shoulder. "You're not supposed to be watching that."

Izzy glanced at the doors. "I wanted to see how—"

"Ignorant girl." Cook's shiny face was red with anger as she pointed at the parlor door. "What they're doing in there isn't for the likes of you and me."

"It's not fair." Izzy clenched her hands into fists at her side. Small eddies of wind whipped around her ankles, ruffling her apron and servant's uniform. "Why do they get to kindle their magic and the rest of us get nothing? We're the ones who need it more."

"'Cause that's the way things are and it's time you learn to accept it. When the Kindling Winds blow in

December, every twelve-year-old's magic either snuffs or kindles. There's no middle ground and no option for folks like us." Cook frowned at the tiny tornadoes of dust whistling across the tile. There was a flicker of something in her eyes. Envy, maybe. Izzy wasn't sure. "Your magic will snuff out next year, just like mine did. It gets easier to be around them after that, you'll see."

Izzy's gaze drifted back toward the doors. The steps of the dance played in her head. "I could try to kindle when my time comes next year. I think I could remember how to do it. Bits of it at least."

"You'd better hope you don't. The mistress will turn you out if she hears you talking about it, or she might report you to the police. Is that what you want?" Cook leaned closer. Her breath was sticky-sweet from the chocolate they'd set up for the post-ceremony celebration. "It's too dangerous."

"I'm not afraid of her."

Cook scowled. "Do you have any sense in that head of yours, girl? You *should* be afraid of her, but it's not only that. People have died trying to kindle wrong." Cook patted her on the shoulder and Izzy flinched. She was used to smacks, not sympathy from Cook's hand. "Best to forget it, I say. This is the way the world is and there's nothing you can do about it."

The swirls of wind around Izzy's ankles blew out like a reluctant sigh.

Cook motioned her forward. "Come on. Back to the kitchen where you belong. The shrimp aspic needs plating before the party. Those Diamond Girls work up an appetite with all that burning."

From inside the parlor came the sound of polite applause. It was over. Now there would be another batch of spoiled Diamond Girls who'd never know a day without magic. They'd go on to high school and learn how to use their newly kindled magic while Izzy would remain a lowly servant, doomed to watch her magic snuff out next year.

A flare of envy surged in Izzy's heart. Those wealthy girls had everything. The magic that tingled in Izzy's veins was the only thing that was truly hers. Despite what Cook said, she knew keeping it was worth any risk.

She wouldn't let her magic snuff out. Somehow she would find a way to kindle it next year.

Sparks flickered from her fingertips as she followed Cook back to the kitchen.

ONE

Miss Posterity's Academy for Practical Magic

JANUARY 1906

Emma

When the golden motorcar drew to a stop at the corner of Sixty-Fourth Street and Fifth Avenue, Emma thought there must have been a mistake.

"Are you sure we're in the right place?" she asked, even though the brass plaque on the iron gate insisted this was indeed MISS POSTERITY'S ACADEMY FOR PRACTICAL MAGIC.

"It's the right address." Papa checked the paper in his hand and then squinted through the ice-frosted car window.

Every other house on the street was brightly colored, as befitted the mansions of New York's Gem Row, but Miss Posterity's looked as if someone had inserted a black-and-white photograph in its place among the snowdrifts. The heavy front door and trim were lacquered in black, but everything else was dark gray. On the left side of the house, a round turret pointed at the sky like an accusatory finger.

The corners of Papa's hazel eyes wrinkled with amusement. "I say, what a fine example of a Queen Anne Victorian house. Excellent condition, though the color palette is admittedly odd." He nudged Emma with his elbow. "Don't you like it?" Worry lines creased his forehead.

She scrambled for the right words. "It's lovely. Very serious looking."

"Well, learning magic is a serious business." He tapped the tip of her nose. "Oh, don't look so glum, darling. It's only for a year." Papa tucked the paper back in his jacket pocket.

Emma grabbed his arm before he could open the door of the car. "But the other girls my age have been here for a year already. What if I don't fit in?"

He puffed up his chest with pride, looking not unlike one of the pigeons strutting in Central Park across the street. "How many times do I have to tell you? We Harrises don't fit in—we stand out!"

That was exactly what she was afraid of. She fidgeted with a gold button on her pink coat. The coat had been a present from Papa when they'd arrived in New York two days ago, and like everything else in her life right now, it felt strange and new.

"Emma." Papa laid his solid hand on hers. "They will love you. You are perfect, just like your mother."

She swallowed hard. Her mother had died of a fever when Emma was a baby and Emma had studied every scrap of information about her mother's life like it was a blueprint for her own. Mama had been an artist with beautiful magic and seemingly infinite grace and poise. In Papa's stories, she was kind to everyone and never struggled to keep her temper in check, not like Emma did.

Emma squared her shoulders. Perfect was a lot to live up to, but for Papa she would always try.

The rose quartz in her necklace flashed with magic as she turned her coat dark blue to match Papa's. It wouldn't last—children's unkindled magic lasted only a moment or two but it made her feel better.

The driver turned around from the front seat of the car. Emma had forgotten he was there. As soon as her focus wavered, the magic faded and her coat shifted back to pink.

"Excuse me, sir," the driver said. "Are you getting out or should I drive around the block? We seem to be drawing an audience."

Indeed, a small crowd had gathered across the street. Even on the fashionable Gem Row, a golden car was a sight to behold. A woman walking a purple-spotted Dalmatian was so busy gawking that she nearly collided with a streetlamp. Several street sweepers gaped, their pushcarts and brooms temporarily forgotten behind them. On the corner, newsboys in knickers craned their necks to see who might be inside.

"Thank you." Papa donned his silk top hat. "Let me get that for you, darling."

He climbed out and clapped his hands. The gem in his pocket watch glinted with magic and the snow turned into a bright red carpet that unrolled across the sidewalk. She forgot about the onlookers as he held out his hand and helped her down to the street.

Emma faced her new school. She'd known her kindling year was coming ever since she was seven and golden sparks had shot from her fingertips, signaling that she was capable of magic. Now she was here, newly twelve and a soon-to-be Diamond Girl. This year, she wouldn't have to learn arithmetic or geography, or any of the normal subjects she'd studied with her tutors. Kindling schools taught only magic.

There were a lot of expectations riding on a young lady when she went to kindling school. The first and foremost was that she would kindle. Children who failed were sent elsewhere and were rarely spoken of again. But Papa's greatest expectation for her was also Emma's dearest wish—to join him at the family magitecture business. She had spent her whole life traveling from city to city, learning from him as they went. Yesterday, he had taken her on a tour of New York's recent magitectural projects. They had gawked at the skyscrapers, including the triangular Flatiron Building, which rose on Twenty-Third Street with the aid of steel beams and carefully balanced magic. Papa had even arranged a private tour of the construction site of the massive central library on Forty-Second Street. One day, father and daughter would design beautiful buildings around the country together, just like father and mother did before Emma was born. There were quite a few steps between now and then—first kindling, then high school and university, but today was the first day of her expected future.

Emma hadn't yet told him about the secret plans she'd been drawing up in her notebook for the most beautiful house of all—the house they would one day build for themselves. After years of living in temporary rentals while Papa designed houses and elaborate buildings for other people, Emma thought it was high time they had a home of their own. She hoped Papa would agree when he saw her design. Then she could finally stay in one place long enough to make real, lasting friends. She felt the weight of her dreams and Papa's expectations resting on her shoulders as she walked up the freshly shoveled path to the front door.

The driver followed them, his valet hat and face hidden behind a pile of shopping boxes and Emma's traveling trunk. The trunk wasn't heavy—Papa had enchanted it to weigh no more than a handbag. The rest of her things had been shipped there by train and she was excited to see her books again. She always missed them when they were on the move.

"Anything else, sir?" the driver asked when they'd reached the front porch.

"We can manage from here, thank you," Papa replied. He flipped a coin and the driver caught it. "But be back in an hour. I have a train to catch."

"Yes, sir." The driver tucked the coin in his pocket and headed back to the car.

A tightly coiled brass rosebud hung on the heavy black door instead of a knocker. The plaque below it read:

PLEASE BLOOM FOR ASSISTANCE.
[ALL OTHERS USE REAR DOOR.]

"Charming," Papa said with a chuckle.

He touched the rose, infusing it with magic, and its

brass petals bloomed to reveal a sparkling diamond at the center. Somewhere deep in the house, a bell rang in answer.

Papa rolled his shoulders back and Emma copied the gesture. Had Mama felt this nervous and excited when she'd gone away to school? There were so many questions she wished she could ask.

Sensing her hesitation, Papa placed a protective hand on her shoulder. "All right, my girl?"

Before she could answer, the door creaked open and a pointed nose poked out at them. Its owner was a woman with hair so blond it was almost white, and which she wore in a poufy bun atop her head. "Yes? May I help you?"

"Hello," Papa replied. "We're here to see Miss Posterity. I'm George Harris and this is my daughter. She's to be a student."

"The Harrises at last and as lovely as I pictured you. Welcome. I'm Miss Posterity."

Emma blinked. This was Miss Posterity? She had been expecting someone sturdily built and graying, rather like the building itself. But the headmistress was petite and only a few years older than Papa. Her tightly corseted waist and high-necked white blouse were the height of Fifth Avenue fashion and her floor-length black skirt swished in a no-nonsense manner.

"Please come in." She opened the door wider and motioned for them to follow.

Emma stepped inside and nearly gasped out loud. The foyer was higher and wider than she would have thought possible from looking at the outside of the house. A crystal chandelier hung over the checkered black-and-white-tile floor that extended down the hall straight ahead of them. The walls were light gray at the top with white wainscoting panels along the lower section. Ahead, a white carpet ran up the center of the stairway. Both twisted around to a landing like a balcony box at a theater, before disappearing into an unseen upstairs. Everything about it felt rich, lush, and magical. Emma felt her own magic respond and it was all she could do to keep from sparking right there and embarrassing herself.

"This way, please." Miss Posterity opened the double doors to their right. "The girls are not normally allowed in my private office, but we'll make an exception today. It's one of the few rooms that are anchored."

Papa paused his inspection of the wainscoting. "Anchored? You're in for a real treat then, Em. I haven't seen an anchoring enchantment since my school days."

She had no idea what he was talking about. Anchored? Was the house a ship?

"Don't worry, I've anchored Emma's bedroom. Mustn't have our best room floating about!" Miss Posterity laughed.

Emma grinned like this was indeed a great joke and not a completely baffling statement.

They entered Miss Posterity's office, again decorated entirely in black and white. Emma looked around for a ship's anchor that would explain everything, but there was only a pretty wood-framed sofa facing two armchairs across a low, narrow table and a sturdy black desk on the far side of the room. A large red salamander yawned and rolled over among the logs in the fireplace. They'd had one of the elegant flaming lizards to warm their house in Boston, though Emma had kept her distance because it bit.

Overall, the whole room felt very classy and fashionable, except for a handmade cross-stitch sampler on the wall that proclaimed, *A child may spark magic, but only those with worth may kindle*. Reading it made Emma feel like she had an itch in her brain. She'd always heard the saying as *Only those who are worthy may kindle*, but perhaps it made sense this way too.

Papa pulled an official-looking paper with a golden seal from his pocket along with a folded check. "A bit of business before I forget. Here's her kindling permit from the Registry. The fees are paid and here's the check for her first month of tuition. I included the premium we discussed for her late enrollment."

Miss Posterity took the papers and examined the official golden seal on Emma's permit. "Wonderful. Everything's in order then." Was it Emma's imagination or did her smile grow as bright as the foyer chandelier when she read the amount on the check?

"I apologize for having to charge that much, Mr. Harris," Miss Posterity said as she tucked Emma's permit and the check into a wooden box on her desk. "We don't normally allow students to enter as twelve-year-olds, but when I received your letter, I decided to make an exception. It gives the school great prestige to have a student from such an illustrious family."

Emma made a mental note to look up *illustrious* as the headmistress crossed the room and sat in one of the velvet armchairs. Papa took a seat on the sofa across from her and Emma followed his lead. There would soon be miles instead of inches between them and she wanted to stay close for as long as possible.

He draped a protective arm behind her. "I meant to enroll her last year, but I lost track of time. In my head she's still a little girl and I forget sometimes how quickly she's growing up." He sighed wistfully. "Perhaps it's better that she's starting now anyway. Her magic's only progressed from sparking to flickering recently."

Emma bit her lip. It was embarrassing when it was put like that.

"Barely flickering at twelve?" Miss Posterity's eyebrows rose in surprise, but she recovered quickly. "Would you like tea?"

"No, thank you—" Emma started to say just as Papa said, "Tea would be lovely, thank you."

It took all of Emma's manners not to sigh. Grown-ups seemed to love having long conversations over beverages. She wanted to see the school. Papa had told her they had a fine library and she could face meeting new people if there would be new books.

As Miss Posterity spoke, she pointed at a silver bell hanging by the door and it jingled. "Emma will have some catching up to do. Most of our girls have been working with flickering magic for several months already. Term begins tomorrow and runs through the kindling this December. In addition to kindling lessons, our students have a full range of coursework to prepare them for life in magical society." She ticked off a list of classes on her fingers. "Magical History and Society, Everyday Enchantments, Adornment and Embellishments Level Two, and Magic Control and Comportment. The art instructor visits on Fridays and teaches sketching and drawing using magical materials, of course, and the dancing instructor visits three times a week to help the girls master the grace of movement required for kindling, as well as the latest society dances."

Emma's head spun. That sounded like a lot. She'd rather hoped learning magic would involve more reading.

Papa patted Emma on the knee. "Don't worry about her being behind, Miss P. She's already a wiz at colors."

Emma wanted to crawl under the sofa. Anyone who lived in such a black-and-white place was unlikely to be impressed by basic color magic.

"How quaint," the headmistress cooed. "As you know, Mr. Harris, the Kindling Winds begin to blow every December and our twelve-year-olds must be prepared to kindle when they do. Every word, every movement, every tool must be perfectly in order to kindle magic." She squared her shoulders. "We use the best equipment. Our kindling flints have been in the family for generations. Solid gold and diamond encrusted."

Papa gave a low whistle of approval. "Just like at Dalton's when I was a boy."

Miss Posterity preened. "Under my tutelage, I'm sure Emma will be as brilliant at magic as her father in no time."

Emma gulped. Here were even more expectations she'd have to fulfill.

"Which reminds me, Mr. Harris, I had one teensy question while you're here." Miss Posterity smoothed her skirt. “In your letter you mentioned a very generous and substantial donation to the school. I wondered if we might expect that soon?”

Papa cleared his throat. “I’m waiting on the return from my largest project ever. I’ll be designing a whole neighborhood in San Francisco. Harris Hill, they’re going to call it.” His eyes shone with pride. “I’ve invested a great deal of my own money in it, and it’s going to be a smashing success. You’ll have the donation by the time of Emma’s kindling.”

He grinned at Emma and she grinned right back. Papa always said that money and magic opened doors. When he couldn’t find a door, he simply built one himself. She wanted to be just like him.

“San Francisco? But your letters were postmarked from Boston, weren’t they?” Miss Posterity asked.

“I personally oversee my magitecture firm’s projects, so it keeps us moving frequently. Boston, Chicago, Savannah. The best magical cities, you know.”

“How very glamorous,” Miss Posterity said, leaning forward.

While Papa explained the magic required to operate the Transcontinental Railroad and his upcoming journey, the door to the room opened and a servant girl entered. In her black dress and white apron, she looked as serious as the school, except for the lock of red hair that slipped from under her cap and dangled in front of her freckled cheek.

Emma waited for the girl to speak but she remained silent as she set the tea tray down on the table. She'd never seen a servant her own age before. Servants were always old and called her "the Little Miss." If one had to be a servant, she reasoned, it must be very nice to be in such a lovely house and to be around other young girls.

Papa accepted the first cup of tea the girl poured and rested the saucer on his knee.

"I want Emma to be happy here, Miss P. She must have whatever she asks for, though I doubt she'll ask for much. That is, except for books. Those she hoards like a troll."

"Papa!" Emma whispered. She felt a flash of irritation that he kept saying embarrassing things but shoved the feeling down. A proper lady was always sweet and poised, and never showed when she felt cross.

"There's no shame in loving books, sweetheart." Papa pulled a business card from his jacket pocket and passed it across the table to the headmistress. "Cost is no object when it comes to my daughter's happiness. Send the bills to my bank every month and I'll see that they're paid."

The headmistress took the card while Emma glanced at the servant girl. Neither Papa nor Miss Posterity was paying her any mind, but she could tell the girl was listening. It felt rude to pretend she wasn't in the room.

"Thank you," Emma said as the girl poured a second cup. "What is your name?"

The girl's eyes widened at being addressed directly and she gripped the cup tighter. Steam rose out of the top like from a train engine.

Emma gasped. The servant girl's magic was flickering—and it was strong.

"That will be all," Miss Posterity snapped. Sharp lines of anger creased her forehead.

The steam stopped. The servant girl set the teacup down on the table and fled the room. Emma didn't know what to say or do. She felt like she'd witnessed something private and shocking.

She took a big gulp of tea and burned her tongue.

Miss Posterity took a deep breath after the door closed. "I apologize that you had to see that. If it happens again, I'll see that she's replaced."

"She looks old enough that her magic will snuff this year. It's the kindest thing for a servant, really. The world's a safer place for everyone when only the worthy have magic." Papa waved his hand over his cup again and the gem in his pocket watch flashed with magic as the tea cooled.

Emma nodded but inside she shivered at the mention

of snuffing. It gave her a morbid thrill to imagine what it would feel like to see her magic wink out in a puff of smoke. She glanced at the cross-stitch again. *Only those with worth may kindle.* Emma was sure Papa was right about it being kinder for the servant girl. He was always right, but the power of that flickering tugged at her thoughts. Her own magic was nowhere near that strong yet.

"To Emma. And her kindling." Papa raised his teacup in a toast.

Miss Posterity clinked her cup to his. "To new students and patrons."

Emma raised her cup to toast with Papa's. She tried to send up a swirl of steam to impress him. Only a feeble mist rose.

TWO

Papa's Parting Gift

Emma

After tea, Emma got her tour of the school.

"Excellent, the parlor is in the back today. It's at its best when it overlooks the rose garden," Miss Posterity said, opening a door to reveal a huge room with two crystal chandeliers and a grand piano. The bay window showed a snow-covered back garden filled with the January skeletons of rosebushes. "The parlor is where we teach dancing and hold the Kindling Ceremony. This room's always in this spot on kindling days."

By this point in the tour, Emma had pieced together that the inside of the building was much larger than the outside. As such, the rooms shuffled about and sometimes went away entirely. Anchored rooms were like chess pieces that had been glued to the board while the other pieces moved around them, changing their location whenever they felt like it—though the headmistress did explain that they usually shifted overnight when they were empty or their occupants were sleeping. "They can be a bit shy, you know," she said, as if that clarified everything.

"How charming. You said your grandmother was the one who did the anchoring enchantment?" Papa asked as he studied the baseboards with interest.

"Yes." Miss Posterity frowned. "It was part of a short-lived fashion around the time she built this school. Rather inconvenient trying to find an unanchored bathroom in the middle of the night. But Grandmother was a determined woman and made the enchantment permanent."

As if to illustrate Miss Posterity's point, they couldn't find the library. There was a dusty broom closet in what she said was its usual spot on the west side of the house. "It's been finicky lately," Miss Posterity said with a dainty shrug.

A horrible thought occurred to Emma. "Is that where the other students are?"

Miss Posterity laughed. "*Great gems*, no. They're on their daily lunchtime walk in Central Park with our other teacher." She turned to Papa. "Miss Clementine is my younger cousin and will be a fine teacher if she continues to follow my example. She teaches the eleven-year-olds. I will be personally overseeing Emma's kindling class."

Papa put a hand on Emma's shoulder and squeezed it tight. "Thank you, Miss P. I can tell Emma will be well cared for here. Your school quite lives up to its reputation."

"Thank you, sir. Nothing's more important than a good reputation." Miss Posterity spun toward the door in a swirl of skirts. "But I've saved the best for last. Let me show you Emma's room."

She led them upstairs to a white door identical to the other six on the second floor. Inside was a single bedroom already set up with Emma's belongings. Light streamed through large windows on the rounded walls of the turret. A painting of white roses hung over a big bed with a lace-covered duvet. On the floor, a dove-gray carpet looked soft enough to curl up on with one of her beloved books, which had already been arranged in neat rows in the bookcase. The room even came equipped with her own ever-burning salamander. Flames flickered along its back as it snoozed among the logs with a pleased smile on its red face.

Then her eyes landed on Olive, her stuffed toy cat, propped against a pillow, and her stomach clenched. She was afraid the other girls would think it babyish that she still slept with a stuffed animal and had meant to keep

Olive hidden in her trunk. She quickly tucked the cat behind the pillow.

Papa was too busy inspecting the ceiling beams to notice. "The room is smaller than what she's used to, but this will do."

"Thank you, Mr. Harris." Miss Posterity bowed her head. "With that, I'll give you some privacy to say your farewells."

After the door closed behind her, Papa held out his arms and Emma dove into his familiar, comforting embrace. She clung to him like the world had begun to spin too fast and this hug was the only thing keeping her from flying off.

At last, he pulled back to look at her.

"I'm going to miss you, Papa," she said, her voice little more than a squeak.

"Oh, me too, Em." For a moment, his face puckered like he might cry but then the glow of an idea lit up his eyes. "I've got a present for you. A little something to remember me by."

He sat down on the edge of the bed and pulled a velvet jewelry box from his pocket.

She didn't need anything to remember him by. Sometimes she thought she knew Papa better than she knew herself. Still, her breath caught when he opened the jewelry box and she saw the gold-and-ruby ring winking inside.

"The stone was your mother's from her kindling days. I thought it'd be a little piece of both of us." He held it out to her. "Go on then, try it on."

She slid the ring onto her finger and her magic warmed as it came into contact with the glistening ruby. The gem had been Mama's—of course it was perfect too.

"Thank you," she whispered. She looked at Papa, but he was staring at the ruby with a faraway look in his eyes.

She knew that look and the cracks of sadness that appeared whenever someone brought up Mama. Fortunately, Emma had plenty of practice in smoothing them over with good cheer. She grinned brightly enough to prop up both of their smiles and leaned her head against his shoulder.

"It is a lovely school, isn't it?"

He wrapped an arm around her and hugged her tightly to his side. "The loveliest." As he held her, the corners of his mouth righted themselves and the smile she loved and counted on returned. Who would prop up Papa's cheer when he was far away from her?

"Will you write to me, Papa?"

"You know I'm not one for letters, darling. I'll send you pretty things whenever I see them, though." He kissed the top of her head. "You'll be so busy with your new friends and preparing for kindling in December that you'll barely even notice I'm gone."

Emma doubted that very much. She twisted her new ring on her finger.

"Do you not like the ring?" he asked, eyes wide with concern.

"It's not that—" she started, but he hurried to reassure her.

"I can get you something else." He frowned at his pocket watch. "Blast, I have to catch the train. Tell you what, I'll make you a promise. When you kindle, I'll grant you a wish. Anything in the world you want, your papa will get it for you. How does that sound?"

Emma's heart fluttered. She pictured the beautiful house she'd drawn in her sketchbook, a three-story townhouse with roses growing out front. The wish glinted as brightly in her mind as the ruby on her finger.

"I'll try to think of something," she said, a smile spreading across her face.

"I am going to miss you, Em. Ever so much." He gave her a kiss on her forehead. Then he glanced at his pocket watch again. "Is there anything else you need before I go?"

You, she thought but didn't say. He expected her to stay and do well.

"I'll be all right, Papa." Golden sparks flickered at her fingertips. She smiled like she'd done it on purpose.

Papa chuckled. "Oh, my girl. That fire within you will illuminate the whole world one day."

A bell rang downstairs, signaling the driver's return with the car. After that, everything happened quickly. A few hugs later, Papa left, calling out, "Make friends, and not just with books, darling! You'll get your magic yet!"

Then she stood alone in her new bedroom. She pressed a hand to the cold glass of the window. Papa waved out the back of the golden car until they turned onto Fifth Avenue and were gone.

"Goodbye, Papa," she whispered to the glass. Her heart felt like it would shatter into a million pieces. "I promise I'll make you proud."

THREE

The New Girl

Izzy

Izzy paused on the creaky back staircase to enjoy the silence of the house. She liked it best when it was quiet like this, when the headmistress had retreated to her private rooms and the pupils were out on their afternoon stroll. Then she could pretend this was her house, and she was the great lady who ran it.

Today it was harder than usual to pretend because the backs of her legs still stung from the switch. She hadn't meant to flicker in front of the new girl and her father, but Miss Posterity hadn't believed Izzy's protests that it was an accident. Lavishing praise on the new girl one minute and sneering while she switched Izzy's legs the next, the headmistress was as two-faced as the coins she loved so much.

At least Miss Posterity hadn't found the crystal in Izzy's apron pocket. Taking that from the schoolroom a few weeks ago certainly hadn't been an accident. Izzy patted her pocket affectionately and magic tingled in her veins. She'd risk the switch to keep that. It was a necessary part of her plan.

Downstairs, the front door opened and the excited chatter of the returning pupils echoed in the foyer. Izzy sighed as her moment of peace ended. Now there would be muddy footprints to mop, and she still had the luncheon pots to scrub and the serving dishes to polish before dinner tonight.

The weight of the day ahead rested heavily on her small shoulders as she picked up her basket and trudged to the second floor. At the end of the hall, the door to the new girl's room was closed. For a moment, she debated leaving the basket outside the door and fleeing downstairs. She didn't want to see the new girl again. It had been rude the way the girl had stared at her, like she was some kind of Coney Island curiosity. Worse, she'd spoken to her, right there in front of Miss Posterity. Izzy worked hard to avoid the headmistress's attention. The pupils' taunting was enough. *Busy Izzy, fetch this. Busy Izzy, clean that.*

But if Miss Posterity was already cross with her, she

couldn't risk disobeying a direct order. She raised a hand and knocked.

"Excuse me, miss?"

There was a pause, and then the girl's voice rang out, muffled by the door and stiff with sorrow. "If you please, I'd like to be alone for a while."

Izzy squared her shoulders. She had work to do and didn't have time for spoiled girls and their sadness. At least this girl's father was alive and would come back for her one day.

"I've got your new uniform, miss. You'll be needing it."

The door clicked open and the girl peeked out. She was hugging a large leather-bound book with gold-filigree-edged pages. "Oh, I'm glad it's only you. Please come in."

Only you. What was that supposed to mean? Izzy shuffled into the room, trying to keep her head down. She'd deliver the dress and get out as fast as she could. But the girl shut the door behind her and retreated to stare out the window. The magic-lit streetlamps flickered to life below, illuminating her golden curls. The new girl didn't even notice. Didn't she realize what a wonder it was to live in a part of town where there were magical streetlamps? They were loads better than the always-broken gas lamps Izzy had grown up with down-town.

The girl sighed heavily and glanced at a well-worn, stuffed black cat on the bed. Like everything else in this room, it was an extravagance to Izzy. She'd grown up in a three-room apartment smaller than this. Every object in that apartment had been scraped and saved for and meant to serve all four of them. Even the faded cloth doll she and her sister shared had once been Mam's, and Da would sometimes use it as a chin pad when he played his fiddle.

A set of marble dominoes on the shelf caught her eye. On the side of the box, an engraved name: *Emma*.

The other girls had been whispering that name for days with excitement, especially after the deliveries of the fine things for this room began arriving after the winter holiday. Izzy herself had hung up the ostrich-feather hats and silk dresses in every color. The salamander in the fire had bitten her hand when she'd had to coax it out of the crate. It was an awful lot of work, but Miss Posterity delighted in telling everyone that her newest pupil was of the highest social caliber and would have the best room.

Yesterday, Izzy had been scrubbing the floor in here when her least favorite of the pupils, Beatrice Scorn, and her silly friend Lucy Van Vleet had peered in. She'd hoped they wouldn't notice her. They'd stared jealously at the porcelain tea set with pink roses and the array of silk gloves on the bed that Izzy still had to put away. After a few moments, Beatrice had flipped her shiny chocolate-brown hair over her shoulder and announced that the new girl must be a horrible spoiled brat. Then, because Beatrice was a horrible spoiled brat herself, she'd used her magic to freeze Izzy's wash water into a bucket of soapy ice before flouncing from the room.

"Um, so, where would you like me to put your dress?" Izzy looked for a place to set it down so she could escape.

Emma turned around and hugged her book tighter as she studied the room. She pointed at a hook next to an ornately carved mirror. "Over there, please." She watched as Izzy hung the charcoal-gray dress and placed the basket with her uniform ankle boots and tights next to it. "I'm really here," Emma said reverently. "I'm going to be a Diamond Girl. One of the best."

Izzy didn't know much about the other kindling schools in New York, but she rarely thought of the so-called Diamond Girls as being the best at anything except making messes. Miss Posterity's was certainly one of the oldest kindling schools and Izzy had noticed that people often mistook *old* for *important*. When Cook had sampled too much of the sherry, she told Izzy stories about how things used to be under Miss Posterity's mother—back when there were multiple servants, a coach and driver, and a headmistress who cared about education and didn't spend the school's money on social climbing. But she wasn't about to mention any of that in front of Emma.

"Do you need anything else, miss?" Izzy hoped she'd say no.

Emma looked around the room. "What do I do now? Where do I go?"

Despite the difference in their circumstances, Izzy had been new here once and remembered how lost she'd felt. "Dinner's at five thirty in the dining room and I wouldn't be late if I were you. Miss Posterity's a stickler for the rules."

"Thank you for being kind to me." Emma set down her book and perched on the edge of the bed. "It must be nice to have a job where you get to help people all day." Her lip trembled. "I never knew my mother, but Papa says she always tried to help the less fortunate, so I try to help people too. Kindness is its own type of magic, don't you think?"

In Izzy's experience, nothing was as good as magic. Helping the ungrateful girls at this school was her job and she hated her job. But she couldn't leave. Not without a good reference to help her get another job or without the money to escape. One couldn't buy train fare west with *kindness*. She resisted the urge to rub the well-worn letter from Omaha in her skirt pocket.

"Do you have everything you need?" she prodded again.

Emma opened the book and set it on her lap. Izzy was appalled to see that it was full of tiny words without a single picture. "What's your name?"

Izzy shifted, not sure where this was going. "Isabelle O'Donnell. But they call me Izzy here." *Busy Izzy*, she didn't add.

Emma tilted her head to the side. "Which do you prefer?"

Izzy paused. Isabelle was what her mother had called her before she picked up a bottle and stopped calling her anything at all. But she preferred not to think about that.

She shrugged like it didn't matter. "Izzy's easier to holler when you need something, I suppose?"

Emma peered at her. "I wanted to ask you about your flickering, Izzy. How did you manage it? I didn't think servants knew how to do magic."

Oh stones. She hadn't expected this. Izzy backed toward the door. Her mind went straight to the stolen crystal in her pocket. She needed it to practice her magic, but if anyone found out she had it, she'd get worse than the switch. "I didn't mean nothing by it, miss. It was an accident." Her fingers found the reassurance of the doorknob.

"Wait!" Emma called. "I'm sorry. I shouldn't have said anything. You're probably looking forward to your magic snuffing, aren't you? My papa says it's easiest if servants' magic snuffs quickly." She smiled shyly.

Izzy's cheeks burned with anger and shame. She wanted to say that Emma's papa was a fool if he thought that, but she couldn't. Instead, she bit her tongue and turned the doorknob. "If you'll excuse me, miss, I have chores to do."

Though she hadn't been dismissed, she bolted from the room. Only when she was down the stairs and back in the familiar surroundings of the kitchen did she realize her hands were clenched in fists. She shoved open the kitchen door. How could Emma possibly think it would be a kindness for her magic to snuff? For once in her life, she agreed with Beatrice Scorn. The new girl was a brat.

The kitchen cat looked up from where he was curled on the floor next to the stove. He tilted his head and narrowed his yellow eyes like he could see what she was thinking.

"What?" she snapped. "You would dislike her too if you'd heard what she said. Helping people all day. *Stones*, what nonsense. She's the worst of the worst."

The cat flicked his tail in disagreement and stretched. As he stalked away, Izzy's shoulders slumped. She liked the cat and hadn't meant to yell at him. He had a sympathetic way about him and they were united by their shared place on the receiving end of Cook's temper.

She rolled up her sleeves and headed for the scullery. Fine. Izzy didn't need the cat. She was used to being on her own. If she could focus on getting her magic, then she'd be out of this city and out of this life as a servant, and she'd never have to *help* Emma Harris or her kind again.

FOUR

The Blandings

Emma

Emma stood in the middle of the chessboard-tiled hallway, holding a box of pastries for her new classmates and debating which door to try. She had gotten distracted by her books and it was past five thirty. She was going to be horribly late to dinner if she couldn't find the dining room soon.

She vaguely remembered seeing it during the tour but was terrified to guess. What if a bathroom had taken its place and she walked in on someone on the toilet?

If only she'd had a chance to ask Izzy before she'd so rudely fled the room. Emma hadn't meant to upset her by talking about snuffing. She'd said the truth, even if the truth made her stomach twinge.

Emma took a step back and something sharp poked

her between the shoulder blades. She almost dropped the elegant pastry box she was carrying in surprise. Turning, she found herself face-to-face with a marble bust of a stern, older woman. The inscription on the base read: *Prudence Posterity, Founder. 1818–1882.* Though the statue didn't move, Emma felt like its eyes were following her as she inched back toward the stairs.

She looked at the grandfather clock again. Papa would be getting on the train to San Francisco soon. He expected her to do well here, and so she would. That meant being brave enough to find the dining room.

Shifting the pastry box into one hand, she took a deep breath and opened the door in front of her. Inside was a cozy reading room that she guessed was the pupils' lounge. It had three plump couches and several piles of books on every end table.

Movement in her peripheral vision made her jump.

"I'm sorry to disturb you," she said before she realized it was only a sleek black cat. He was lying on the velvet-cushioned window seat, reading a leather-bound book.

Wait. That couldn't be right. She blinked and the cat blinked his yellow eyes right back at her.

"What—what are you doing?" Emma asked, but of course the cat didn't answer. Cats couldn't talk and they couldn't read either. *Great gems*, she was a nervous mess. Still, it was always best to be polite to strange cats. "Sorry to disturb you," she said.

The cat lost interest and stretched out across the open book for a nap.

Emma turned back to the hall right as a girl with bouncy, chocolate-brown curls reached the bottom of the stairs. Her gaze traveled from Emma's feet up to the top of her head, not missing an inch.

"You must be the new girl," she said when she'd finished her inspection.

Emma smiled her friendliest smile, though she longed to dash back into the reading room and hide. *Make friends, and not just with books!* She bobbed a curtsy and introduced herself.

"I'm Beatrice Scorn," the girl replied. She eyed the pastry box in Emma's hands with suspicion. "What's in there?"

Emma opened the top of the box, revealing a dozen square teacakes, frosted in white fondant. On top of each one, a tiny pink candy rose had been magicked to perfection. "I brought everyone petits fours from Foxglove's."

It had been Papa's idea to bring a gift as a means of introduction and, seeing how Beatrice's eyes widened at the name of the most fashionable bakery in Manhattan, Emma knew it had been a good one.

"Miss Posterity says your father is famous. Is it true?"

"Yes," Emma said as pride in Papa overcame her nervousness. "He designs houses and important buildings all over. Do you know the Pearl Tower in Chicago? Some people think it's actually made of pearl because it's so shiny, but it's marble that he magicked to—"

"Have you met any other famous people?" Beatrice cut her off. She twirled one of her curls around her finger.

"Sure," Emma replied. Papa was always introducing her to people at parties. She didn't mention that she preferred to find a quiet corner and read.

Beatrice's eyes lit up. "I'd like to meet someone famous one day. My father's a partner at the Glum, Downing, and Scorn legal firm, you know, so he's practically famous. Everyone says he's the best in the business at magicking paperwork." Quite unexpectedly, Beatrice linked her arm with Emma's. "Come on. You can sit next to me."

She marched them down the hall, talking a mile a minute. "Lucy usually sits next to me, but she's my friend so she'll move if I tell her to. You have a dozen cakes and there are nine of us in the kindling-year class—well, ten now with you. They'll want you to give them to some of the eleven-year-olds, but obviously, you should give one of the extras to me since we're friends now. If I were you, I'd give the other to Rosie. She's the brightest in the class and her father's a state senator up in Albany, you know."

Emma could barely keep up, but her heart beat faster at the word *friends*. She hadn't even been here an hour and she'd made a friend! Papa would be proud. She nodded at everything Beatrice said and agreed that she and Rosie should have the extra cakes.

Beatrice opened a door in the middle of the hallway. "Usually it's right—yes. Here we are."

The electric light sconces cast shadows on quatrefoil-printed black-and-white wallpaper. Miss Posterity sat at one end of a long, rectangular dining table in the center of the room. A tall woman with orange hair sat at the other end. She must be Miss Clementine, the cousin and other teacher that Miss Posterity had mentioned. Between them, eighteen girls wearing the school uniform looked up in surprise.

Miss Posterity stood up. "You're late, girls."

Emma started to apologize but Beatrice squeezed her arm, which was still entwined with hers.

"I'm sorry, Miss Posterity. I was helping my new friend. She got a bit lost."

Beatrice had already been late when they ran into each other, but Emma wasn't about to point that out and get her friend in trouble.

Miss Posterity beamed at them. "I should have known. You're always so thoughtful and kind, Beatrice."

She paused and frowned at a girl with stringy black hair seated to her left. "Frances Slight, that noise you made sounded very much like a snort. May I remind you that I allow pupils and not pigs at my table?"

"Sorry, Miss Posterity," Frances mumbled. The girl next to her hid a giggle behind her hand.

Miss Posterity gestured to the seat to her right. To Emma's relief, there was an empty chair right next to it, so she could also sit next to Beatrice. They sat down directly across from Frances, who developed a sudden interest in the ceiling.

"What's that you have there?" Miss Posterity asked, noting the pastry box for the first time.

"They're petits fours," Emma replied, feeling shy now that she had to speak. "I brought them to share."

"They're from Foxglove's," Beatrice added.

A murmur of appreciation spread up and down the table. Emma silently thanked Papa again for his brilliant idea.

"How lovely," said Miss Posterity. "I'll ring for Cook and have her plate them for us after dinner."

Emma did a quick count. "I'm so sorry, I don't think I've brought enough."

"It's no bother. Cook made cherry pie tonight. The eleven-year-olds can have that."

The girls seated closest to Miss Clementine groaned. Emma wondered why anyone could be so unhappy at the prospect of cherry pie.

When they were seated, Miss Posterity swept her hand toward Emma. "Everyone, I'd like you to meet our new pupil." She launched into a lengthy introduction using words such as *heiress* and *great esteem*. Emma thought it was a terrific story, but the main character in it sounded elegant and nothing at all like her.

She didn't know where to look, so she stared at her plate and puzzled over the odd silverware arrangement. There were a knife and spoon to the right of the plate like she was used to, but on the left a clear crystal the length of her index finger sat next to the fork. She wondered what it might be used for.

After what felt like an eternity of embarrassment, Miss Posterity finished her introduction. "I trust you will welcome Emma warmly. Remember, being around our betters, betters us in turn."

Behind her on the wall, a framed cross-stitch that had previously read *Keep your friends close and your gems closer*, went blank. A moment later, *Being around our betters, betters us in turn*, appeared in loopy gray embroidery. Emma was still staring at it when Miss Posterity went to give the cook instructions for the petits fours.

"Miss Clementine, you're in charge," she called over her shoulder.

The younger teacher's eyes widened in alarm at the prospect.

"Finally, we can talk," Beatrice said, when Miss Posterity was gone. "Let me introduce you to my friends. No one else here matters, really."

The giggler wearing gold-framed glasses next to Frances turned out to be the aforementioned Rosie. Next to her, identical twins, Hannah and Anna, leaned their chins in their hands and stared at Emma with matched expressions of curiosity. Lucy was a petite girl whose lips were set in a permanent pout. Beyond her, Beatrice also pointed out Clara, Catherine, and Caroline, who all had brown hair and friendly smiles, but weren't part of Beatrice's group.

During Beatrice's introductions, Izzy entered. She circled the table, ladling out food that was barely recognizable. There were slices of roast chicken, yes, but also some kind of mushy green vegetable and white ovals that might have been potatoes.

At last, when the plates were full, Miss Posterity returned to the room and announced that dinner could begin.

Emma picked up her fork. The other girls picked up their crystals.

She looked around, trying to figure out what to do. Miss Posterity had unfolded a letter to read and wasn't paying any attention to the girls.

Across the table, Frances caught her eye. She gestured with her crystal at her plate like she was going to stab it straight through. Emma had no idea what she was trying to tell her.

"That's Frances Slight," Beatrice whispered. "It's too bad magic doesn't work on people because she could certainly use some improvement. She's one of the Slights, but I bet you didn't guess it."

Emma had no idea what this was supposed to mean. "One of the Slights?"

Misinterpreting her question as disbelief, Beatrice flipped her hair over her shoulder. "I know, right? She has to sit next to Miss Posterity at meals because she needs help with even basic enchantments. We know Miss Posterity keeps her on because having a Slight gives the school prestige, but my father says her parents are progressives and suffragettes." She whispered the last bit like they were contagious diseases.

Frances must have heard what Beatrice said because she looked away, her cheeks reddening. Emma was too embarrassed to ask for any more details. Miss Posterity had said having *her* here gave the school prestige. What would Beatrice say if she knew Emma was barely flickering? To avoid saying anything, she scooped up a giant forkful of the mushy green vegetable and shoved it into her mouth.

As the fork passed her lips, Beatrice gasped, "Don't!"

Green mush oozed over her tongue and Emma understood her horror. It had a texture like half-melted ice cream but tasted like broccoli, sour milk, and garden soil blended together. She forced herself to swallow and grabbed for her water glass.

"What was that?" She gagged.

"A Blanding," Rosie said, adjusting her golden glasses. The other girls nodded with great sympathy.

"What's a Blanding?"

"That's what they call the food here. They make it bad intentionally." Beatrice daintily lifted her fork in one hand and her crystal in the other. "You have to use the crystal to magic it into something edible."

"Use the crystal to—"

Emma glanced around in wonder, where she now saw things piled on plates that certainly weren't on the platters. Rosie was eating a slice of potpie and the twins were attempting to copy her. Farther down the table, white blobs became fluffy rolls of bread and seasoned baked potatoes. A mushy gray sludge she hadn't been able to identify became rich brown gravy, jam, or butter, depending on the plate. It seemed the only limits were the eater's imagination and ability to do magic. Her heart fluttered in wonder and she smiled. This was exactly what a magical school ought to be.

"There are rules," Beatrice continued as she buttered her potatoes. "Obviously magic doesn't let you make something out of nothing and Miss Posterity won't allow you to make your dinner into a dessert. Oh, and no portion expanding until we have more experience. Lucy once tried to turn a bread roll into a whole loaf and it exploded."

"Bits got stuck on the chandelier," Lucy bragged.

Bearing that in mind, Emma held up her crystal and debated what she would make. Beatrice's scalloped potatoes looked pretty good.

Miss Posterity looked up from her letter. "Girls, I have wonderful news. Our patron, the Mayor of New York, may be paying us a visit in a few weeks. I expect you to be on your best behavior if and when he does."

Across the table, Frances had managed to turn her pile of green mush into peas. During Miss Posterity's announcement, the peas turned back into mush and a great big blob of it fell off her fork and landed in her lap.

"Honestly, Frances. What would your father say?" Miss Posterity scolded over the laughter that ensued.

"I doubt he'd even notice me," Frances muttered. No one else seemed to hear.

Emma lowered her crystal. She felt sorry for Frances, but what if everyone saw her try to transfigure her Blandings and fail? Would they laugh at her too?

Her stomach rumbled at the scent of the delicious food around her, food she now doubted she could make. She'd never transfigured food before. Papa had always taken care of everything—he'd even salted her dinner when it needed it. She wished she'd thought to try it herself before now. It was too scary to try with her new classmates watching.

"How thoughtless of me, Emma. You must be exhausted after the day you've had. Let me help you." Miss Posterity's ring flashed with magic. The lumpy gray and white piles on Emma's plate turned into roast chicken and steaming mashed potatoes with a pat of butter as big as Miss Posterity's diamond.

"Thank you." Emma hoped her relief wasn't too evident.

"Anything for you, dear." Miss Posterity stabbed her fork into her chicken and smiled.

"Lucky," Beatrice breathed as her scalloped potatoes puckered with lumps. She waved her crystal over them and they flattened out again.

By the time they brought out the petits fours for dessert, Emma was full and happy. Rosie and Lucy were competing over who would sit next to her at lunch tomorrow and Beatrice had convinced her to host tea for her new friends over the weekend. It was everything she could have hoped for in a first day.

Emma promised herself that tomorrow she would try her first bit of magic. Papa was right, she'd catch up in no time. If she missed an enchantment here and there it wouldn't be the end of the world—she had her whole life ahead of her to do magic. Besides, it couldn't be that hard, could it?

Frances's peas bounced off her fork and spilled across the table. The room echoed with the girls' laughter as the peas turned back into mush, staining the tablecloth.

FIVE

Toothpicks and Teaspoons

Izzy

Izzy leaned against the classroom door, straining her ears to hear. Inside, Miss Posterity was teaching an Everyday Enchantments lesson.

"Think of magic as a light within you and refract it through the crystal." Miss Posterity's heels clicked on the floor and Izzy could imagine her walking between the rows of desks. "You must concentrate in order to transfigure your toothpicks into teaspoons. Yes, like that, Caroline, but try to keep the spoon's handle level. Easy, Beatrice. Don't force it. Let the magic flow through the crystal."

Izzy snorted. *Toothpicks into teaspoons?* It was both ridiculous and ridiculously unfair. Magic could improve everything, especially the lives of the people who wielded it. The problem was that magic could only improve what already existed and Izzy had nothing. Beyond that, there were limits of reasonability when it came to size and scale. She couldn't take a thimble from the sewing basket and make a mansion. A thimble could make, at best, a nice hat and, without kindled magic to make the enchantment permanent, she'd have a pinched head a few minutes after she put it on.

Besides, Izzy didn't need hats or toothpicks or teaspoons—she needed to get her magic and go. Her hand strayed to the well-read letter in her pocket. She traced the indents in the paper where her sister had pressed too hard on the pencil as she described the train journey west to Omaha.

Izzy was so busy imagining her own future ride on that train that she didn't realize class had ended. The students spilled out into the hallway, abuzz with excitement and comparing notes from the day's lesson and the kindling lesson that had preceded it. It was already three weeks into the term and they were growing more knowledgeable and superior by the day. The girls didn't even glance at Izzy. She pressed her back against the wall and nudged her bucket of cleaning supplies out of the way with her foot.

Lucy's forehead was blackened and her eyebrows considerably smaller than they had been at breakfast. Eyebrow scorching was a frequent accident in kindling lessons. Lucy tried to magic them back as she walked but, as magic had no effect on people, nothing happened. Beatrice walked next to her, lecturing her friend about what she should have done to avoid scorching in the first place. Izzy leaned in, trying to catch as much as she could.

Izzy had never been to school and everything she knew about magic she'd picked up this way. She'd learned reading, writing, and arithmetic at the crowded kitchen table of Mrs. Moran in the tenement building next door. Magic was a forbidden subject and she'd been sent to stand in the corner if she so much as sparked. Her knowledge of magic consisted of a jumble of overheard conversations and class notes she'd found while cleaning in the year she'd worked here.

Today, everyone was whispering about "the words." Izzy wished she knew what that meant.

There was some confusion in the hallway because the parlor and dining room had switched places since breakfast. When everyone had finally gone in to tea, Izzy entered the classroom to clean up. Every day, she scanned the floor between the students' iron desks, hoping to find a dropped note that she could add to her small stash of kindling instructions. She still wasn't sure how she was going to learn to kindle in the next eleven months through these tiny glimmers of information, but she knew that she had to. If her magic snuffed, it would ruin everything she had planned—but if she succeeded, she'd have to get out of town fast, before Miss Posterity or anyone from the Registry found out about her magic. The financial reward for reporting illegal magic to the Registry was too tempting for anyone to turn down. Especially someone as money-loving as Miss Posterity.

The classroom was still warm from magic practice and filled with the lingering scent of burnt eyebrows. It was freezing outside, so she couldn't even open the windows. Izzy wrinkled her nose but forgot everything else when she noticed the blackboard was still full of Miss Posterity's loopy writing. There was a diagram showing arrows coming out of a hand, passing through a crystal, and pointing at what she assumed was a toothpick. It reminded her of the way some boys in her old neighborhood used to fry ants on the sidewalk with a magnifying glass. She hadn't liked those boys, but she wanted to know more about this diagram and what it meant. Presumably the arrows were magic?

Below the diagram, there were half-erased words in another language:

Lumen quod intus lucet qui nos verey simus ostendet.

Izzy scrunched up the rag in her hand, wishing she could copy everything down. Only then did she hear the scratch of a pencil against paper behind her. Izzy froze.

Someone sighed. "*Quod, quud.* That's not right." Another sigh, heavier this time, and the sound of paper being ripped from a notebook and crumpled up.

The scratch of the pencil stopped. "Would you mind being a little quieter, please? I'm trying to finish up my notes," a second voice said.

"Sorry. I forgot you could hear me," the first voice mumbled. "It helps me to say it out loud."

"My papa says the same thing. The letters get jumbled up when he tries to read or write them."

The first girl let out something that sounded like both a gasp and a sob. "But—but that's exactly what it's like for me. Do people say your papa is stupid too?"

The second girl laughed. "Of course not. He's brilliant. He doesn't like reading or writing much himself, but he loves it when I read out loud to him. It's easier for him to learn things by heart than by head."

Curious, Izzy turned so slowly they didn't even see her. It was that Emma Harris girl, looking shiny and happy in her school uniform. Her hair hung in gold ringlets, topped with a white ribbon. In the row behind her, Frances Slight was gaping at her like she'd witnessed a miracle.

"Here, let me try reading it to you," Emma offered. "Don't look at the words, just listen."

She looked up at the board and was startled to see Izzy there. Embarrassed to be caught eavesdropping, Izzy swiped her rag at a desktop.

"Hello," Emma said, a slight hesitation in her voice. They hadn't really spoken since that awkward first day. Not since she'd said Izzy was probably looking forward to her magic snuffing.

"Hello, miss. Don't mind me." Izzy dipped her head politely and pretended to be absorbed in wiping down the desks. Why was Emma helping Frances Slight of all people? Seeing Emma's kindness to the girl made her like Emma a little, and she didn't want to like her.

Izzy snuck a glance at the board, repeating the strange sentence in her head. It kept slipping from her memory, like she was trying to hold on to a wet bar of soap.

"What are you doing?"

Izzy turned. Emma watched her with one delicate eyebrow raised. *Stones*, now she'd tell Miss Posterity. She knew the Harris girl was bad news.

"Um—um," Izzy stammered. "Just wondering whether I can clean the board, miss."

Emma grinned. "I'll help you." She practically skipped to the front of the room, hair bouncing on her shoulders. Then she picked up the eraser and, with a flick of her wrist, destroyed Izzy's hope for the day.

Emma hurried off to join her friends at tea and

Frances followed after, leaving Izzy alone in her disappointment.

Sparks gleamed at her fingertips as Izzy resumed wiping down the desks. She'd dealt with plenty of rich people before, but Emma's determination to *help* rubbed Izzy the wrong way. The Gemstone Society for Orphan Welfare had also claimed to be *helping* when they sent Izzy to work at this miserable job and put her little sister, Maeve, on a train to be adopted by a family out west. Izzy stared at the empty blackboard. What had it said? What language was that and what did it mean? The blank blackboard offered no clues, but Izzy wouldn't let another rich person's determination to *help* keep her from getting her magic and finding Maeve.

Over the following days, Izzy avoided Emma, but watched her from afar. She noted each dirty dress and stocking Emma left lying on the floor for someone else to pick up, and she resented each morsel of uneaten food that came back on her porcelain plate.

She was scrubbing at such a plate a week later when Miss Posterity waltzed into the kitchen in a better mood than Izzy had ever seen her in before.

"Send Izzy to the butcher's with an order for roast beef for dinner tonight."

Cook paused kneading the bread dough. "But you said beef was too expensive, miss."

Izzy's mouth watered at the mention of roast beef. She tried to wash a little more quietly so she could hear.

"Emma Harris said she misses roast beef. I've been to the bank and her father's first check would have her eating roast beef every night." The headmistress clapped her hands together with girlish glee. "I swear that man never let his spoiled daughter raise a finger. She's woefully behind, but I give her easy assignments so she won't know as long as we get her kindled. If I keep her happy, the checks will keep coming and they'll get bigger every month!" Miss Posterity grabbed a handful of flour and flung it in the air like confetti. "Must dash. I'm off to a luncheon."

Izzy groaned, partly because she'd have to clean up that flour, but mostly at the mention of Emma. Her conscience whispered that Emma was being lied to and she should feel sorry for her. At times like this, her conscience sounded a lot like Maeve. The boys on the sidewalk had been twice her size but Maeve had scolded them until they left the ants alone.

"You heard her. Get your coat and get going." Cook resumed pummeling the dough.

Izzy told her conscience to be quiet. Why should she feel sorry for a girl who got everything she wanted? Emma would have her roast beef tonight and Izzy would be the one to fetch it for her.

She wouldn't survive a day in my life, Izzy thought as she put on her coat. She wished something would happen to Emma, something that would make things fair. Emma was everything that Izzy wasn't—rich, pampered, prized—and assured of kindling. Their lives would never have anything in common.

Or so she thought.

SIX

Letters to Papa

Emma

Emma glanced out the classroom window at where a steady March rain soaked the rosebushes in the garden. She wondered what it was like in San Francisco and what Papa was doing right now. Then she set her pen back to the crisp white stationery she'd hidden in her notebook and resumed writing her letter.

At the front of the room, Miss Posterity was regaling the class with a story. It involved a recent shopping trip to a fancy department store downtown, during which the headmistress was fairly certain she had spotted the daughter of the richest man in America, John D. Rockefeller, trying on hats. It was the second time she'd told this story; the encore brought on by a request from several members of the class who preferred learning about industrialists' hat preferences over their business practices.

Lucy raised her hand. "Miss, please tell us again about the time you had lunch at the Vanderbilts' mansion. What was it you ate? Cucumber sandwiches?" She leaned her chin in her hand and stared at Miss Posterity with adoration.

"Well, because you asked." Miss Posterity perched on the edge of her desk and launched into the story of lunch at the railroad magnate's house. She'd attended as one of many headmistresses of elite kindling schools, but she usually skipped this fact. This particular outing was a favorite among the students, and Emma had already heard this recitation three times in the six weeks she'd been at the school.

Their Magical History and Society classes often veered into discussions of Miss Posterity's brushes with New York's magical elite at restaurants and parties. Unlike Emma, who actually liked studying history, Beatrice said learning about rich and famous magical society figures was what made it her favorite class. This week, however, Emma had been so busy she was glad of the chance to write to Papa—hence the stationery hidden in her notebook.

Every Friday, she sent Papa a letter detailing her exciting new life. She told him how Miss Posterity had praised her for magicking grapes into a string of pearls during an Adornment and Embellishments lesson—skimming over the fact that they'd lasted less than twenty seconds. She detailed how the dancing teacher had praised her foot-work and how every Sunday afternoon, Beatrice, Lucy, and the twins came to her room for a private tea where they ate petits fours and cookies from Foxglove's bakery.

Emma wondered who read her letters out loud to Papa and what his life was like in San Francisco. His replies to her didn't provide much detail. Each was a short note saying he missed her, pinned to a lovely present. Yesterday, a box of beautiful white silk hair ribbons had arrived and she'd distributed one to each of her new friends. She glanced around the room and her heart fluttered with joy to see Beatrice, Lucy, Hannah, and Anna were each wearing their hair tied with the ribbons. Life at Miss Posterity's was turning out so much better than she'd ever anticipated.

By the time Emma had finished her letter thanking Papa for his present, Miss Posterity had finished her stories about socializing with Rockefellers and Vanderbilts and had moved on to how the families had made their money during the industrial revolution—today's actual class topic.

As was her habit while lecturing, Miss Posterity strolled between the columns of desks. Emma jumped and turned the page in her notebook to hide her letter to Papa, but she felt Miss Posterity's eyes on her as the teacher approached.

"The industrialists greatly improved the infrastructure of our country. Their inventiveness and hard work created new forms of magic to be used in major projects, from steel to make the new skyscrapers downtown to the railroads that allow us to travel great distances. All the way to San Francisco, even." Miss Posterity paused next to Emma's desk and eyed her notebook. "I hope you're telling him that you're making good progress and that you're very happy here?"

Emma's shoulders tightened. "Yes, because I am," she said in a rush, wincing at how ineloquent she sounded.

To her surprise, Miss Posterity smiled. "Carry on, then." She continued up the aisle and glanced at the clock on her desk. "*Great gems*, look at the time. We have to move on to today's Magical Control and Comportment practice. Tonight, I want everyone to read the section on industrial development in your history texts, pages fifty-six through sixty-eight."

Emma shifted in her seat. The prospect of reading twelve pages of her history book in front of the fire tonight helped steady her nerves, but Magical Control and Comportment classes dealt with complex magic and Emma often found herself struggling during them.

"Today we will begin our study of manifesting flame in advance of the kindling. When the Kindling Winds blow, you must have experience igniting your magic in a controlled way in order to kindle," Miss Posterity said as she approached the blackboard. "Frances, will you fetch the fire buckets filled with sand from the storage cabinet, please? Everyone else, put your papers and notebooks away. Don't leave anything flammable out. If it catches, magical fire can spread even after the initial enchantment fades. We must be careful."

Emma swallowed as she moved her notebook to the shelf below her seat. She tried to exchange a glance with Beatrice. Instead, her friend cast a sly look at Frances, who was opening the cabinet at the back of the room. Emma had a bad feeling about what was going to happen. Beatrice rarely passed up an opportunity to embarrass Frances.

Beatrice raised her hand. "Miss Posterity, I have a question before we move on from history, please?" She waited for the teacher to nod and then continued with a smug look on her face. "Isn't it true that the Kindling Winds sometimes arrive early? How does that work, exactly?"

What? Prickles of fear ran down Emma's spine. It was a fact of life that the Kindling Winds blew every

December and either snuffed or kindled the magic of twelve-year-olds. It had never occurred to Emma that things might be different.

"Yes," Miss Posterity said after what was either a thoughtful or a dramatic pause. "Though it's extremely rare and dangerous when it does occur. It hasn't happened in my lifetime, but my understanding is that if the Kindling Winds blow twice in a year, one occurrence will be in December as usual, but the other could start at any time."

There was a loud crash and Emma spun around to see Frances's feet covered in sand, two empty pails next to her.

"Honestly, Frances," Miss Posterity snapped. "Remind me never to ask you to do anything. Now, clean that up or call Izzy to do it."

"Sorry," Frances mumbled over her classmates' snickers. She knelt and started sweeping sand back into the buckets with her hands.

"Did you see the look on her face?" Beatrice whispered to Emma. She pressed her lips together and her shoulders bobbed with laughter.

Emma tried to make her own face as neutral as possible. She felt bad for Frances, but she was too worried about what she'd just heard to think about anything else.

Frances wasn't the only one who had been caught off guard by Beatrice's question.

Indeed, a moment later, Rosie's hand flew into the air. Her eyes were wary behind her gold glasses. "Does that mean the Winds could start blowing right now?"

"Theoretically yes, but it's highly unlikely." Miss Posterity's expression softened. "Don't worry though, girls. Early Winds are practically the stuff of legend these days—why, there hasn't been one since just after the Civil War. You will all be fine. Besides, I will be here to guide you through your kindling. Don't give it another thought." She clapped her hands. "Now, on to manifesting flames."

Miss Posterity instructed the class to stand while she wrote step-by-step instructions on the blackboard. Manifesting an actual flame was an entirely different process from producing childish sparkings and required a great deal more control. They were supposed to hold their crystals and channel the magic into the air to produce a spark in the center of their palms. It looked simple written out in chalk, but proved much harder in practice.

Emma raised her right palm while gripping the crystal tightly with her left. She focused her magic through the crystal, just like she'd done with the pearls, and tried to imagine it sparking the air aflame. It was almost like slipping a letter into a mailbox. She felt the magic going into the air, but then her grip on it relaxed and it fluttered away.

She tried again. "Come on," she whispered to her magic. Her palm remained stubbornly spark free, though Emma thought her skin looked a little drier in the spot she'd been focusing on.

"Don't be discouraged, girls. Manifesting for the first time can take weeks of practice." Miss Posterity strode up and down the row, monitoring their progress or lack thereof. She stopped to adjust Lucy's grip on her crystal. "By the time you kindle, it should be second nature. Trust me, you'll have plenty of other things on your mind that day."

Emma swallowed. She was still nervous about the whole *engulfed in flames* part of kindling, but she trusted Miss Posterity to get her through it. The thought eased the last bit of worry about early Winds from her mind. Yes, Miss Posterity knew everything about magic, and if she said there was no need to worry about early Winds, Emma wouldn't worry.

She tried again, this time easing her magic into the air instead of pushing it. A bead of sweat dripped down her temple as she focused until she thought her eyes would cross from the effort. The space above her palm shimmered as if from heat and, suddenly, a pinprick of a red ember glowed. It wasn't a full flame and it lasted only a split second, but Emma's heart raced at the sight of it. She'd made that ember!

She glanced around the room. Beatrice caught her eye and smiled before turning her attention back to her palm. As she readied herself to try again, Emma drafted a postscript to her letter to tell Papa about this lesson. Soon she would manifest a full flame, she was sure of it. She only needed to practice.

By the time Miss Posterity excused them to lunch, Emma's face was flushed from making three more embers appear. No one had managed to manifest an actual flame, but Emma felt invigorated by her progress. Doing magic was the best feeling in the world and she wanted to do it forever and ever.

SEVEN
On Fifth Avenue

Izzy

The late-afternoon April sunshine warmed Izzy's shoulders as she hurried along the shops on Fifth Avenue.

It was one of those glorious New York days, where possibilities felt as infinite as the blue sky above. The breeze whispered promises of flowers and green leaves, but the summer humidity had yet to arrive. Walking along Central Park lent a splendor to the day that she'd never experienced growing up in the cramped tenements downtown. There, laundry lines and chimney smoke had always crowded out the sky. She shoved the thought of her old neighborhood out of her mind. South of the park, the new Plaza hotel rose high in the sky like a scaffolding-clad wall between this glittering world and her old life.

Fashionable ladies in long skirts and lacy blouses and

men in bowler hats filled the sidewalk. If she ignored the grocery basket bumping against her side and didn't look down at her uniform, Izzy could pretend she was as grand as they were. She imagined she too was wearing a broad-brimmed bonnet decorated with peonies instead of a white maid's cap. Her vegetable basket would be full of a gorgeous bunch of flowers that she would arrange in a crystal vase in her front window for the world to admire.

Cook called her make-believes "grand notions" and smacked her with a wooden spoon whenever she caught Izzy with that dreamy look in her eyes. But dreams were free and they were the only way she could afford the life she wanted.

Then her gaze landed on the window display of the haberdasher across the street. There was the very bonnet she'd been imagining. She stopped so abruptly that a gentleman behind her muttered a curse, but Izzy was too enthralled to care.

It was a wide-brimmed straw bonnet with pink peonies. Never mind that the pink would clash with her hair, she loved it anyway. The sign next to it advertised that it had real magical flowers that bloomed fresh from buds every half hour. Izzy stared at it longingly, but she knew she couldn't waste her money on frivolities. She needed to save every penny of her meager wages for train fare, and food and lodgings for her journey. The scrimping and saving would be worth it when she finally made it to Omaha and was back with her sister, the only person left in the world who loved her.

The door to the shop opened and a girl in a periwinkle silk dress exited. Of course, it was Emma Harris wearing a brand-new bonnet with freshly blooming pink peonies. It didn't clash with her hair at all.

Steam hissed from Izzy's fingertips. She quickly shoved her hand in her pocket and clutched her crystal. A part of her wanted to be just like Emma, and at the same time, another part wanted to hate everything about her.

Beatrice and the twins followed Emma out of the store, laughing and wearing new hats as well. Miss Clementine hurried behind them in her usual old-fashioned hat and carrying several shopping bags. Izzy turned and pretended to be very interested in a billboard advertising a magical stain-removing laundry soap, hoping they wouldn't spot her.

She'd seen the result of these shopping trips before. Emma was always giving out expensive gifts to the other girls, usually something good to eat, magicked games, or beautiful trimmings for their hair or dresses. Those gifts made for a lot of extra sewing and picking up for Izzy.

Izzy knew she should finish her errand. She had to get

these vegetables to Cook or she might get her ears boxed again. But when Emma and her party strolled in the opposite direction, she turned around and followed them.

Emma pressed her hands against the glass to peer into a jeweler's window, not realizing some poor shop boy or girl was going to have to clean those prints off later. Well-dressed passersby smiled at the sight of such a happy, well-cared-for child. Even the sunshine seemed to follow Emma as she continued down the street, lighting up her hair like she had been gilded with gold.

It was disgusting, really.

Izzy was about to head back to the school when she noticed a ragged little beggar girl ahead on the corner. The younger girl's cheeks were sunken with hunger and it made her eyes look large, like a rabbit's. She wore a blue frayed cloth over her black hair and clutched a mildewing wicker basket in one arm. With her other hand, she held out a defeated-looking rose, begging someone to buy a flower.

Izzy hugged her grocery basket tighter. The sight of such misery brought uncomfortable memories of growing up downtown in the slum neighborhood known as the Tarnish. Though poverty and misery were omnipresent down there, they weren't welcome up on Gem Row. This girl would be told to "move along" by the police soon.

Izzy paused, waiting for Emma to pass by the pathetic

creature without a glance or, even better, with a shiver of horror. Then she could feel justified in disliking her.

"Flower, miss?" the girl asked, keeping her eyes down like Emma was too bright and sunny to look directly at. "They's a penny each."

To Izzy's surprise, Emma dug into her silk coin purse.

"I'll take one." She held out a nickel. Beside her, Beatrice looked as confused as Izzy felt.

The flower girl looked at the silver coin with dismay. "I don't got any change."

"I don't either," Emma said. "Please take it."

"Emma, what are you doing?" Beatrice whispered. "You don't know where that flower's been." Her look of disgust said it wasn't the flower she was talking about.

The flower girl's gaunt cheeks flushed. "I growed them in pots myself. Selling them keeps my brother and me out of the workhouse." She shuddered.

Behind the light pole where she'd paused to hide, Izzy shuddered too. She'd seen some of her old neighbors condemned to the workhouses when they couldn't pay their bills. They came back months or years later, broken husks of the people they used to be. That was, if they came back at all. They took kids too and worked them until their magic was drained and snuffed out by thirteen. The poor girl was right to be afraid of a place like that.

"They're lovely roses," Emma reassured her. Several petals dropped onto the sidewalk.

"Do you want more for your friends?" The flower girl held out a rose to Beatrice.

"No thanks," Beatrice said, stepping back. The twins also shook their heads.

Emma's smile drooped even more than the flowers. "One is plenty, thank you."

The flower girl pocketed her nickel and dashed away before Emma could change her mind. Izzy felt off-balance, not quite sure what had just happened. Why did Emma keep doing kind things? Didn't she know Izzy had made up her mind to dislike her?

Miss Clementine, however, seemed to understand something Izzy didn't. She rested a gentle hand on Emma's shoulder. "I don't think we need to tell Miss Posterity about this."

"Yes, right," Emma agreed. She looked over her shoulder in the direction the flower girl had gone. "I think that sad little face shall haunt me for all my days."

Emma tucked the wilted rose into the sash of her dress. For a moment, Izzy was stunned. Then, with a wink of magic, Emma turned the rose gold, and Izzy decided it was fine to dislike her again.

Now she really had to go. Cook was going to box her ears for being late.

She was about to leave for real this time when a newsboy dashed around the corner, hoisting a paper above his head.

"Extra! Extra! Earthquake levels San Francisco early this morning! City in ruins! Thousands dead!"

EIGHT

Shaken to the Foundation

Emma

There was no news from Papa that night, nor the whole next day.

Emma couldn't sleep and she barely ate. Miss Posterity excused her from lessons, so Emma spent the day in her room, holding Olive tightly. The earthquake had struck on the morning of April 18 and was so strong that the seismographs clear across the country in Washington, D.C., registered the vibrations. Western Union had only managed to get a few telegraphs out of the city on the first day, but by the next morning, all the newspapers reported that San Francisco was in ruins. The city had been rocked first by the massive earthquake and its aftershocks, and then gutted by fires that erupted from the crumbling buildings. Water supply lines had been destroyed in the initial quake, so there was nothing people could do but let the fires burn. In the end, over 28,000 buildings were destroyed. More than half the city's population lost their homes. One paper put the number of dead at five hundred, while others were claiming as high as three thousand. After Emma saw that, she stopped reading the papers.

Emma spent the whole day after the earthquake lying on her bed, surrounded by her books. Books were easier than real life. If someone was in danger in a book, you could always flip back a few pages and there they'd be again, safe and sound. She knew Papa would be fine, he *had* to be fine, but she felt so powerless.

Still, she longed to do *something*. Papa loved being busy. The morning he'd started work on the Pearl Tower, he'd danced into her room and thrown back the covers. "How can you sleep when there are things to build?" he'd exclaimed with his usual joy. Papa would expect her to keep working, not to mope around. So the next morning she dressed and went downstairs.

Rain lashed against the windows of the classroom as Emma took her seat in the front row. The rest of the school was still at breakfast and the rows of iron desks were empty. That morning, the classroom was in what Emma had come to call its "usual spot," overlooking the back rose garden. The black-and-white room was dark without the usual morning sunlight streaming through the windows and the electric bulbs hummed in their sconces.

Beatrice, Lucy, and the twins came in from breakfast. They gasped when they saw Emma and rushed to her side.

"What are you doing downstairs?" Anna asked.

"Did Miss Posterity make you come back to class?" Hannah added.

"No. I want to be here." Emma smiled at the matching looks of puzzlement on their faces. This had been the right choice. She felt better already, surrounded by her friends.

"Poor Emma." Beatrice patted Emma's back. "You look so pale and worried. Should we see if Miss Posterity will let us go to Foxglove's this afternoon to cheer you up?"

"But it's raining," Lucy protested.

Beatrice crossed her arms. "I'm thinking of Emma's happiness."

"That's sweet of you, but I'd rather stay here in case Papa sends a telegram," Emma said.

The door swung open and several pupils rushed in, glancing over their shoulders. "Look out, Miss Posterity's in a mood," Rosie warned as she darted in seconds before the headmistress.

Miss Posterity swept into the room in a swirl of skirts. There were creases in her forehead that Emma had never seen before and the hint of a scowl about her lips.

"Pop quiz today, girls. Notebooks away and crystals

out." She started when she saw Emma. "I didn't expect to see you, dear. Does this mean you've had news of your father?"

"No, but I know he'd hate for me to miss class again, especially on his account," Emma said.

The headmistress took a deep breath like she was summoning patience. "Quite right, dear. We mustn't let other people's problems interfere with our own self-improvement."

Emma wasn't sure she agreed with this statement, but it had such a ring to it that she would bet a cross-stitch had changed somewhere in the house.

"Back to the matter at hand." Miss Posterity's diamond winked with magic and the words *Pop Quiz* appeared on the board behind her. Emma glanced at the door, regretting her timing in returning to class. They hadn't had a pop quiz in the time Emma had been at the school and she felt unprepared for whatever it entailed.

Beatrice raised her hand. "We're so worried about Mr. Harris. It doesn't seem right that we have to take a quiz." Heads nodded up and down the aisle. Emma smiled at her friend in thanks for her support.

Miss Posterity pressed her lips together. "Very well, Emma may be exempted today, but by this point I hope to see fully manifested and controlled flames from the rest of you. Don't forget the pop."

Beatrice frowned. Clearly that wasn't the answer she'd hoped for.

Emma leaned back in her seat, feeling a little uncomfortable. She could practically hear Papa's voice saying, *We Harrises stand out!* and she didn't think that being singled out like this was what he had in mind. Still, a tiny part of her was relieved. Despite practicing, she'd only managed to produce embers and sparks and had yet to manifest a full flame. She wasn't sure if she could do it today when she was so worried about Papa.

"Rosie, you first," Miss Posterity said.

Rosie stood up next to her desk. Gripping her crystal in her left hand, she held out her right palm. She scrunched up her nose in concentration and a pinprick of flame appeared in her outstretched palm with a soft *pop*.

"Excellent form, but louder on the *pop* next time," Miss Posterity corrected. "Clara, next."

One by one, each of Emma's classmates stood up when her name was called and produced a flickering flame in her palm. Each girl performed the magic with a loud *pop*. So that's why they called it a *pop* quiz.

When Frances's turn came, the poor girl scrunched up her face and a tiny golden firework exploded in her palm. She yelped and slapped her hand against her skirt.

"If you don't learn to concentrate, you'll never kindle,

Frances," Miss Posterity lectured. Frances hid her face in her blackened palms.

Emma watched with a growing feeling that she had to try. Perhaps if she was able to manifest today of all days it would be a sign that Papa was fine.

Emma raised her hand. "Miss? I'd like to try. For my papa."

Miss Posterity's smile didn't reach her eyes. "Very well, then. Go ahead."

A hush fell over the room as Emma stood. She tried not to show that her hands were shaking. Inside, her heart burned with worry for Papa. She scraped at that fire and felt warmth blossom in her palm. At the last second, she remembered to add the *pop*.

Emma looked down to see a tiny flame in her palm. It tickled her skin with warmth. She was still staring at it with pride when someone knocked on the classroom door.

Miss Posterity opened it, revealing a frantic Miss Clementine on the other side. The hem of her skirt was muddy and her shoulders were spotted with rain.

"I'm so sorry to interrupt, but it's worse than we feared," Miss Clementine said in a rushed whisper. She thrust a damp newspaper at Miss Posterity.

Whatever news was in the paper drained the color from Miss Posterity's face. "Has March's bill been paid?" she asked quietly.

Miss Clementine slowly shook her head.

"Excuse us for a moment, girls." Was it Emma's imagination, or did Miss Posterity's eyes stray to where she was standing next to her desk? Then the headmistress stepped into the hallway, pulling Miss Clementine after her, and shut the door behind them.

Emma slid into her seat, hoping she'd been wrong.

Beatrice leaned toward her. "What do you think is going on?"

Emma shook her head, not daring to answer. *Whatever happens when that door opens, I will face it with grace and poise*, she told herself, but the words felt hollow. She willed the door to open and, at the same time, hoped it never would.

But of course it did.

"Emma." Miss Posterity poked her head into the classroom. "Would you come out here for a moment, please?" Wisps of her white-blond hair had come loose from her usually flawless bun.

Emma walked toward the door, aware that every eye in the room was on her back.

The sounds of the piano and the eleven-year-olds' dance lesson drifted down the hall from the parlor. It felt at odds with the dark gloom of the hallway as Miss Posterity shut the classroom door behind them.

"We have some very bad news, dear," Miss Clementine began. "I'm sorry to tell you, but—"

"I don't believe in sugarcoating things, Clem." Miss Posterity crossed her arms. "Your father is dead. He was killed in the earthquake two days ago."

"What?" Emma felt like her ears weren't working properly. "That's not possible."

"See for yourself." Miss Posterity handed the newspaper to her.

Emma took it in shaking hands and her heart thumped. Papa's photograph smiled back in black-and-white newsprint. She touched her fingers to the face she'd missed for months. Then she saw what was printed below the photograph in text an inch tall:

FAMOUS MAGITECT DEAD IN SAN FRANCISCO QUAKE

She felt like she was falling, though she didn't move. The article said that Papa had been checking on one of his buildings when powerful aftershocks hit. The building collapsed on top of him. Several construction workers had escaped and reported he was still inside, crushed by the very walls he'd built. Beyond that, the entire neighborhood of the future Harris Hill had been flattened to ruins. Papa's investment had crumbled to dust, his once vast fortune gone. The last line of the article said he was survived by his daughter, currently attending Miss Posterity's Academy in New York City.

"My papa is dead?" She spoke the words like they were in a foreign language. There was a horrible ringing in her ears and she kept blinking, hoping the words on the page would change.

"Yes, and according to the paper, he's left you penniless on my hands." Miss Posterity began pacing up and down the hall. "What are we going to do with her, Clem? You said last month's bill wasn't paid, so that's two months of tuition she owes. Plus she's spent hundreds of dollars on frivolous gifts and sweets that will never be reimbursed and must now come out of my pocket! You know the state of the school's financials. That donation her father promised was supposed to fix everything and now we'll never see a cent of it!"

"Let's take this one step at a time." Miss Clementine wrung her hands. "She's lost her father—"

"And I have lost my patron!" Miss Posterity moaned.

Emma could barely listen. Her heart was still pounding, *Papa, Papa, Papa* so loud it threatened to drown out anything else. He couldn't be dead. It wasn't possible.

"Poor little dear," Miss Clementine fretted. "And your poor father too, may he rest in peace."

"What's going on?" Beatrice pushed open the door,

revealing the rest of the class huddled in the doorway. They stared at Emma with horror and pity and she knew that they'd heard everything. They knew her papa was—*no*. She couldn't bring herself to think it.

"Back to your seats, girls. Miss Posterity will be with you in a moment." Miss Clementine closed the door. She turned to Miss Posterity, who was moaning and rubbing her temples. "Why don't I take Emma upstairs? She'll need a black dress to wear now that she's in mourning."

Miss Posterity waved them off without even looking. "Yes, and leave her there until I decide what to do with her."

"Come, dear." Miss Clementine put a hand on Emma's back and ushered her up the stairs. Emma's knees felt strange and her balance was shaky.

"I'm so sorry about your father, dear," Miss Clementine said gently. "We'll contact your relations for you. They'll set things right with the bills and whatnot."

"Relations? I don't think I have any." Emma's mind reeled. Mama was dead, her grandparents were dead, and she hadn't any aunts or uncles. She'd never needed anyone except Papa before. Sure, he had plenty of friends, but she couldn't think of a single one who would help her—not that she even knew how to get in contact with any of them.

"Oh, this gets worse and worse," Miss Clementine muttered as she opened the door to Emma's room.

Inside, her books and games looked gray and lifeless, like ghosts of the joy they'd once brought her. The vibrant colors of her dresses felt garish and too bright. Since there wasn't a black one to be had, Miss Clementine selected a purple wool dress and removed the frilly collar with magic. The teacher's rose quartz ring winked again, and the purple color ran down the fabric in rivulets, leaving only black behind.

Emma watched, feeling like the color had drained out of everything. When people died in stories, their loved ones sobbed and flailed about in agony, but she couldn't summon any tears. Instead, she felt hollow and numb. This couldn't really be happening, could it?

"I have to go downstairs and see to the younger girls' lessons. Will you be all right, dear?" Miss Clementine asked, when she'd finished with the dress.

"Yes, thank you," Emma replied automatically, but in truth she felt like she would never be all right again.

When the teacher was gone, she grabbed Olive and clutched her tightly. "Papa is dead," she told the stuffed cat.

She repeated it over and over, not believing it at first. But as the rain outside continued to fall, the words sank in and flooded her heart with grief.

NINE

The Workhouse

Emma

Emma didn't remember coming over to the window seat. Her forehead was cold and she had no idea how long she'd been pressing it against the glass. Olive lay in her lap, her fuzzy ears damp with tears.

She wished she could talk to Papa, to tell him how her heart was breaking. He would know exactly how to comfort her, she was sure. It hit her like a fresh blow that she would never hear his beloved voice ever again. She hugged Olive tighter and stared out the window at the bleak, gray, Papa-less world.

It was twilight now and the rain had slowed to a drizzle. Below on the street, businessmen scurried home under their umbrellas. Movement on the sidewalk in front of the school caught her eye. A boy was kneeling in front of the iron bars, reaching his arms through to the front lawn. He didn't have an umbrella and his well-worn coat was spotted with rain. Just beyond his fingertips sat a little brown sparrow with its wing stuck out at a funny angle. The boy spoke to it and the sparrow hopped into his outstretched hands. He cradled the bird to his chest, stood up, and started walking. Emma watched until they turned the corner and were lost from sight.

Emma shifted on the window seat. She wished someone would swoop in and protect her like that. She felt a sudden longing to be surrounded by her friends. With a pang, she realized it must be dinnertime and she was ravenous. The thought of her friends and a warm meal sent a jolt of energy through her.

She changed into the black dress and left her room without a backward glance. If she'd known she'd never see anything in that room again, she might have packed a suitcase. She might have kissed Olive's little head goodbye or taken the cat with her. But as it was, she didn't.

The black wool of her dress scratched against her arms as she pushed open the door to the dining room. Inside, everyone's Blandings had already changed into that night's meals and the air was warm and comfortable with magic.

As she got closer to the table, the back of her neck prickled. She had the distinct impression she'd interrupted something. The other pupils stared at their plates as they ate and not one of them looked at her. Behind Miss Posterity, the cross-stitch read, *Charity doesn't pay*.

That was when Emma realized her chair was gone.

"What's going on?" Her voice shook.

"I was explaining the change in your circumstances to the rest of the school," Miss Posterity said, lifting a forkful of roast turkey to her mouth. "Why don't you go back into the hall and I'll come speak with you in a moment?"

"Might I please have something to eat first?"

Forks clinked against plates as the students paused to listen. As their concentration wavered, the food in front of them shifted back into unrecognizable mush.

"Very well. If you insist, we'll have this conversation here." Miss Posterity dabbed at her mouth with her napkin. "Tell her, Miss Clementine."

Miss Clementine wrung her hands and her voice wobbled as every head in the room turned to look at her. She spoke slowly like she was choosing her words with care. "We've heard from your father's bank and lawyers, dear, and while it's clear he meant to provide for you in his will—"

Miss Posterity cut her off. "He gambled away his fortune on that ridiculous project of his. Harris Hollow."

"Harris Hill," Emma said automatically.

Miss Posterity waved away the correction like it was a pesky gnat. "It's of no matter now. Neither it nor your money exists. Now, I recognize that it's been a hard day, but I run a school, not a charity. This table is for students. I cannot afford to feed those who cannot pay." She picked up her fork to resume eating.

Emma shifted. "But I'm hungry."

At the other end of the table, Miss Clementine put her napkin on the table. "Oh, Petunia, the poor girl's had the worst day of her life. If it's such a big deal for you to feed her, let her wash some dishes or something after."

Emma wondered whom she was addressing, and then realized Miss Posterity's first name must be Petunia. The informal appeal only strengthened the headmistress's resolve.

"I am not heartless, but I am a businesswoman. I cannot spend a penny more. Emma will be leaving our school tonight. I've secured a place for her at a workhouse where she can work off her debts."

Emma froze. She remembered the look of dread on the flower girl's face when she mentioned the workhouse. Had that really been only a couple of days ago? It felt like an entire lifetime. She'd seen a workhouse once. Papa had told her not to look as they'd driven past it, but she'd seen the skeletal faces staring back at her with dull, exhausted eyes. A workhouse was a place without magic and without hope. She couldn't go there. She just couldn't.

"Please," she pleaded. "I can pay you back."

"With what money?" Miss Posterity raised an eyebrow. "Remember, your fortune is gone."

Her mind raced. She'd never had to think about money before. It had always been there when she needed it. What did one do to earn it?

"I can wash dishes," she offered, remembering what Miss Clementine had suggested. She pictured herself dusting the bookcases in the library with one hand while reading a book with the other. "I can help around the school. I'll work off my debts here. Only please let me stay." Her voice broke at the end.

In the silence that followed, Emma noticed two yellow eyes staring at her from the shadow next to the china cabinet. Everyone else was too busy watching Miss Posterity to see the cat slink under the table. Emma didn't have any time to consider it and she forgot his presence a moment later as the conversation continued.

Miss Clementine cleared her throat. "Cook has been asking for another set of hands. We've been short since you fired the last maid."

"Do not tell me how to run my school, cousin," Miss Posterity snapped, but then she paused, considering this. "We wouldn't have to pay her, of course. She'd be working off her debts." The clock in the hall began to chime the hour. Miss Posterity waited until it was done before she spoke. "Fine," she said, the word resonating like a gong. "She can stay."

Relief flooded through Emma's veins. She wouldn't be sent to the workhouse.

"I'll fetch another chair," Miss Clementine offered, but Miss Posterity shook her head.

"She can eat in her room. Come."

Miss Posterity took her out into the hall and left her waiting there. Inside, forks clinked against plates while dinner resumed. Emma had never felt so lonely or out of place in her life. She'd been so sure that her friends would comfort her, but none of them had even looked at her. Her stomach turned. Any appetite she'd had was gone now. She wanted to get back to the comfort of her room.

Miss Posterity returned a moment later with a lamp and a bundle wrapped with a napkin. "Upstairs now. I'll take you myself."

She led her not to the white-carpeted front stairs, but up a rickety staircase at the back of the school, hidden behind a door that Emma had always assumed was a closet. There were no wall sconces to light her way or carpet to soften her steps on this creaking stairwell.

When they passed the second floor, Emma paused. "I thought we were going to my room."

Miss Posterity kept climbing. "Your *new* room. Your things belong to me now. They will be sold, but do not expect that it will be enough to repay your debts. You will start your chores at first light tomorrow."

"But what about class?"

"I don't think you understand your circumstances." Miss Posterity drew herself up. Had she grown taller? Emma suddenly felt tiny beside her. "You are no longer a pupil at my school. You are no longer the equal of the other girls and you will not speak to them, except to do their bidding. If you cannot follow the rules or if you cost me one cent more, I will send you to the workhouse without hesitation."

For the second time that day, Emma felt shaken to her very foundation. No longer a pupil? This wasn't what she'd imagined when she offered to help. She'd thought somehow she could do both. How would she learn? How would she kindle and earn the wish Papa had promised her?

Then she thought of Papa, buried beneath a building and, for the first time, fully understood. There would be no wish. There would be no dream home for them to share because there would be no more Papa. Her knees threatened to buckle and she stumbled. Miss Posterity didn't even notice.

The back staircase led past the bedrooms on the second and third floors, all the way up to the attic. The higher they went, the more the stairs squeaked. At the top, a wooden door with peeling gray paint hung askew on its hinges.

Miss Posterity opened the door and shoved the napkin-wrapped bundle at her. "Here's some bread for your dinner. You will sleep here. In the morning, you will report to Cook in the kitchen."

The attic was cold and creepy. Emma shivered, wishing she'd brought her robe. And Olive. She didn't care if having a stuffed cat made her look babyish now, all she wanted was a tiny scrap of comfort. Instead, she tried not to crumble under the stern gaze of Miss Posterity.

"What are you waiting for? An embossed invitation?" Miss Posterity swept her arm toward the attic impatiently.

Emma hesitated. She twisted her ruby ring around and around on her finger.

That was a mistake.

"Give me that." Miss Posterity grabbed for her hand.

"Please don't take it," Emma begged. "My papa gave it to me. He wanted me to kindle with it."

"Kindle?" Miss Posterity barked an angry laugh.

"I'll be withdrawing your application with the Registry tomorrow. There will be no kindling for you. You're like your father's promises to me—worthless."

Emma was so shocked that she forgot to fight. Miss Posterity yanked the ring off. It scraped over her knuckle, leaving a trickle of scarlet blood in place of the ruby. Emma yelped and clutched her finger.

Miss Posterity didn't even flinch. She pocketed the ring and took the lamp back downstairs, leaving Emma alone in the dark.

"Papa," Emma whispered to the bare walls, clutching her bleeding finger. "Come back. Please come back."

But the dark was unyielding. Emma reached for her magic to spark a light but found nothing there. That was gone too.

TEN
The Attic

Izzy

Izzy dragged her tired feet up the back stairwell to her attic bedroom. Her hands were red and raw from the dishwater and, despite her scrubbing, there was still black boot polish stuck under her fingernails. The stairs creaked and the kerosene lamp she used to light the way flickered. Every part of her ached. She couldn't wait to fall into bed and sleep.

Though tiny and neglected, the attic was Izzy's sanctuary from the rest of the school. It was too hot in the summer and too cold in the winter, but she liked being alone in the round room at the top of the turret.

The shadow of the pile of broken and discarded furniture on the far side of the room greeted her. She set the lamp down on her three-legged dresser and unpinned her cap. It was too dark to see her reflection in the cracked mirror over the dresser, but she knew how she looked: worn out, dirt stained, and freckled.

Someone sniffled in the darkness behind her. Izzy froze. A chill ran down her spine. Was it a ghost? Her da had told her stories of ghosts and the guardian spirits that were supposed to haunt old houses, but she'd never encountered one before. The sniffle came again and Izzy wrinkled her forehead in confusion. Did ghosts cry?

She turned around very, very slowly and raised the lamp high.

Someone was in her bed.

A tangle of golden curls lay on *her* pillow, with *her* patchwork quilt pulled up to cover the intruder's face. It was one of the girls from downstairs, come to invade her space and play some cruel joke on her. Thank goodness she'd hidden her stolen magic notes in a dresser in the furniture pile, where no one would think to look.

Izzy marched over and pulled the cover down. "Do you think you're funny?"

Emma's eyes were red from crying and fresh tears shimmered on her cheeks.

"Leave me alone." Emma rolled onto her back and tried to pull the quilt up over her face. The black-and-gray patchwork shook with her sobs. "Everything's in ruins."

An annoying wave of guilt rose up in Izzy. She'd overheard Cook and Miss Clementine talking about "poor Mr. Harris" and could guess what had happened. She bit back the retort she'd been about to fire off. "I'm sorry about your father."

Her voice wobbled as she thought about her own da. He'd had a bright red beard the same shade as Izzy's hair and when she'd crawl onto his lap and when she'd nestle under it in his lap, Mam said it was impossible to tell where one of them ended and the other began. After work, he'd play his fiddle and tell them stories about Ireland, which he still called home even though he'd left it to come to New York when he was eight. If she could keep him talking past bedtime, the stories always turned to tales of magic. Both her parents' magic had snuffed, but Da had visions of a better life for his girls than being a drudge or factory worker. When Izzy started sparking when she was eight, he was the one who told her to kindle, no matter what it took. Then there was an accident at the construction site. After that, there was no more Da, no more fiddle, and no more stories.

Izzy's hand shook as she rested it on Emma's shoulder.

"Thank you, Izzy," Emma whispered.

They sat that way for a long moment. In her mind, Izzy was back in a dirty tenement room, sitting in this same position over her little sister. *It's just the two of us now. I promise I'll protect you*, she had whispered, and Maeve had smiled up at her with complete and misplaced trust.

Emma sniffled, and Izzy drew her hand back. What was she doing? She stood up and backed away from the bed. Emma was not Maeve. She came from a different world and their situations were not the same.

"You're very kind, and I appreciate that you came to check on me," Emma said, settling in. "Now, if you wouldn't mind, I'd like to be alone again."

"Well, that's a bit of a problem because *you're* in *my* room."

Emma sat up. "But Miss Posterity said this was to be my new room."

"What?" Izzy stared at her, certain she'd misheard.

But she hadn't. Emma fidgeted with a frayed bit of the patchwork quilt while she told Izzy about the newspaper article and her lost fortune. "So now I'm going to help and earn my keep."

The missing pieces of information from the conversation in the kitchen snapped into place in Izzy's mind. *Poor* Mr. Harris. *No, no, no*, this wasn't happening.

"I miss my old room." Emma looked around the attic. "This is a dreary place but I don't mind sharing."

Just like she didn't mind "helping." Izzy sighed. "If you miss it so much, why don't you go down to your old room for the night and we'll sort this out tomorrow?"

"I can't. Miss Posterity said I wasn't to touch anything in it ever again. She wasn't very kind." Emma looked positively confused about this last point.

"Of course not. She's a stingy old phony."

Emma sat up straight like she was about to leap to the headmistress's defense. Then her shoulders slumped and her lower lip wobbled. "I couldn't even get Olive. I've never slept without her before." She hugged her knees to her chest.

"Who's Olive?" Izzy blinked. She was far too tired for this.

"She's my stuffed cat. Papa gave her to me." Emma turned her face away and her voice hitched. "I think I can bear it that the things he gave me are gone, but I don't know how to bear the fact that I will never, ever see him again."

Izzy felt it again, that uncomfortable feeling that Emma might not be that different from her. She wanted to be done with this conversation. It was making her think about Da and she absolutely, positively did not want to cry in front of Emma Harris.

She crossed her arms. "Well, I guess the first step is learning to sleep without your Olive. Now, turn around. I need to change."

As quick as she could, Izzy got into her dingy, secondhand nightgown and slid into bed next to Emma.

Fortunately, the bed was big enough that they didn't have to touch. Emma had the pillow, which wasn't fair, but Izzy didn't complain. The lumpy pillow was a small comfort and Emma had had enough taken from her today.

"What are you doing?" Emma asked.

"This is my bed and I'm going to sleep." Izzy rolled over so that her back was to Emma.

"Why do you always have such an attitude?" Emma asked. For the first time, there was an edge to her voice.

Izzy ignored the question. She extinguished the lamp and the room plunged into darkness. A moment later, her eyes adjusted and she could see the stars out the window. She rested her head on her arm and tried to sleep, but Emma's sad whimpers made her eyes pop open.

"Oh, for stones' sake." Izzy got up and grabbed her apron. She rolled it up and shoved it in Emma's direction.

"What's this?" Emma sniffled.

"Think of it as Olive the Second. And I have an attitude 'cause I need one. Now, can we please get some sleep?"

Emma took the apron silently and Izzy got back into bed. Soon Emma's breath grew quiet and even, but Izzy lay awake, painfully aware of the other girl lying inches away from her.

This was going to ruin everything she'd planned.

ELEVEN

Life Downstairs

Emma

Emma woke at first light, as Miss Posterity had said she must. The attic was cold and the threadbare quilt did little to help. It would be so pleasant to go back to sleep; to slip into the oblivion that meant she didn't have to think about Papa's death. She felt worn out and parched, and wished she could ring for a servant to bring her a glass of water and a warm pastry.

But she was the servant now, and the threat of being sent to the workhouse was enough to drive her from the bed earlier than she had ever risen before in her life.

Izzy was still snoring when Emma stood and stretched. Emma felt bad for not realizing that this was her room in the attic, but there hadn't been any personal belongings to indicate that someone else lived there. She glanced back at Izzy and felt a stab of guilt when she realized she'd used the only pillow without a thought.

"Eh?" Izzy mumbled. Her eyes opened and focused on Emma. "Oh. I hoped this was a bad dream."

"Me too," Emma admitted. At least they could agree on something.

On the stairs, Emma discovered a folded servant's black dress and apron in her size. She shivered and dressed in a hurry. Emma was used to her fashionable puffed sleeves, and the straight arms of the dress felt stiff and restrictive. This was what servants were expected to wear, though, so wear it she would.

"Did you know your mirror is broken?" Emma asked as she peered through the spiderweb of cracks to pin on her cap.

"Really? Well, I'll pop over to the store and pick up a new one this afternoon." Izzy rolled her eyes. "Come on. We'd better get started."

Izzy really did have an attitude problem, but Emma refrained from pointing this out again as she followed her down the back stairs to the kitchen. The house was quiet and everyone else was still asleep. As they passed the second floor, the pain and the loss of yesterday hit her like a locomotive. If Papa were still alive, she'd be snug in her room right now. In an hour or so, she would wake, dress, and go downstairs for breakfast and class, like any normal day.

But she would never have a normal day again. At least until this *new* normal became *the* normal.

The kitchen was down a half flight of stairs from the main house. She was surprised to see a door to the outside, underneath where the back garden should be. When she asked, Izzy told her Miss Posterity's mother had considered the alley behind the house an "eyesore" and had magicked the windows in the rear of the school to show a beautiful rose garden instead. Now Emma realized why they'd only ever been allowed out in the front garden at recess—the back garden didn't exist.

The kitchen itself was a brick room with exposed wooden beams. Emma had expected bundles of herbs to hang from them like they did in the illustrations in her books, but of course this was the home of the Blandings and there were no herbs or spices in sight. There were no elegant ever-burning salamanders either, only a big-bellied iron stove, an icebox steadily dripping in one corner, several cupboards, and a big wooden table. Four tin buckets—two of sand and two of water—sat by the stove in case of fire.

There were two little rooms barely larger than closets attached to the kitchen. One was the scullery, taken up mostly by a sink and drying pots and pans. The other was what Izzy called the servants' hall. This room had a table and chairs and a wall hung with small brass bells. To Emma's amazement, several in the second row rang, and as they did, they morphed into tiny figurines of what the ringer needed. One bell became a washbasin, and another, a broom. How many times had she rung for tea and never even thought about how Cook or Izzy had known exactly what she needed? Too many to count.

"Come on, I'll see to the bells in a minute." Izzy led her back into the kitchen.

"I'm starving," Emma said, and sighed happily at the sight of several loaves of bread on the block table in the center of the room.

"Too bad." Izzy shoved three logs into the belly of the stove. "We've got a lot of work to do before we eat. Now, you better listen to me, 'cause I'm gonna show you everything once. I don't have time to help you."

Izzy pointed and the logs in the stove burst into flame. Emma nearly fell over. How was that possible when the girls upstairs were struggling to make a single flicker? Within seconds, the magic had faded, but the fire had already caught on the wood and continued to burn. Izzy swung the door of the stove closed with a *clank*.

The kitchen door banged open and Cook bustled into the kitchen in a swirl of early-morning spring air. It was fitting that Cook spent most of her time in this underground kitchen. With a tiny pointed nose, squinty red-rimmed eyes, and rounded cheeks, she looked vaguely like a mole.

"Izzy, why's the kettle not on yet?"

"Nearly done." Izzy hurried across the kitchen, struggling with a giant copper kettle, which she hoisted onto the stove.

"Did you show her how to boil the eggs?"

"Getting to it." Izzy kept her head down as she scurried to the icebox and pulled out a tray of brown eggs.

"You do that. I'll send her up to the dining room to set the table. Least she's familiar with how that should look."

Emma had never seen such a flurry of activity, not even at the countless train stations she'd passed through. Cook gave Emma a two-second instruction, tutting over her "soft, magic hands," and then packed her up to the dining hall to set the table for breakfast.

Emma took the half flight of stairs up to the main level. When she opened the door at the top of the staircase, she wondered how she'd never noticed the servants' stairs before. She got her answer when the door melted into the wall behind her. When she reached for the handle again, the doorframe appeared.

The cross-stitches she passed read, *Only those with*

worth may kindle. She wondered at what point Miss Posterity had said that last night. There wasn't a doubt in her mind that the headmistress had been talking about her. Izzy hadn't seemed surprised to hear about Miss Posterity's unkindness, but it still stung. Emma feared it might be one more thing she'd have to get used to.

She found the dining room and retrieved the heavy silverware case that Cook had sent up in the dumbwaiter. Emma had never laid out silverware herself before and it was harder than she would have guessed to make the forks, knives, spoons, and crystals line up. She kept her mind on what she was doing. It was easier not to think, and easier not to feel.

She had just set down the final spoon when voices from the hall drew her attention.

"Well, I heard Miss Posterity closed up her bedroom and unanchored it."

"All those beautiful things gone. What a waste."

Emma spun around in time to see Beatrice and Lucy enter the dining room. They stopped in their tracks when they saw her, staring not at her face, but at her servant's uniform.

"I'm so glad to see you!" Emma exclaimed. The day immediately felt brighter. "You'd never believe—"

"We know. Miss Posterity announced it to the school last night," Beatrice said coolly.

"You're not supposed to talk to us anymore," Lucy reminded her.

Emma had forgotten. "But—but you're my friends," she stammered.

"Friends?" Beatrice flipped her hair over her shoulder. "I'm sorry about your father, I really am, but you have to understand that we can't be friends now." Her lip curled with distaste as she eyed Emma's apron. "My father would be mortified if I were friends with a servant."

This was an unkindness and they all knew it. Anger flared up from deep within Emma and red sparks shot from her fingertips.

Beatrice raised an eyebrow. "If you do that again, I'll have to tell Miss Posterity."

Tears stung Emma's eyes as she fled the room. She didn't even look where she was going until she found herself in the parlor.

While they'd been living on an estate that Papa was renovating in Savannah, a tropical storm had blown through. It had left a path of destruction through the city and debris scattered in its wake. Emma felt like an even bigger storm had blown through her life in the past day, leaving everything in pieces around her.

She reached for the comfort of her magic but, the same as last night, it was like hitting a wall. Her chest tightened. Maybe she really was worthless. Maybe magic had already given up on her. Emma sat down on the piano bench, trying to stave off despair. She wanted to curl into a ball. She wanted Papa. How could she possibly handle this on her own?

Grace and poise: the answer came to her. Her muscles relaxed. Mama had never faced anything like this, but Emma could still follow her example. She would keep her temper and do whatever was expected of her to avoid the workhouse. Papa might be gone, but she could still do what she thought would make him proud.

She straightened her apron using her reflection in the window. That was better already. It was time to go back to the kitchen.

"There you are. What took you so long?" Cook demanded when Emma came down the stairs. She was at the main table where she was stirring a large mixing bowl with a wooden spoon.

"I—" Emma's voice faltered. Fortunately, she was spared from answering by a knock at the back door.

"Well, don't stand there. Go and answer it." Cook jerked her head toward the knocking. "It'll be the paperboy. Let's hope he ain't brought more bad news."

Emma knew that was impossible. The worst had already come.

When she opened the door she was surprised to find

a face she recognized: The boy who had rescued the bird. He tipped his flat cap and held out a folded *Kindled Courier*. "Morning paper, miss," he said with a hint of an Italian accent.

She took the paper. "What happened to your bird?"

He grinned, revealing a gap between his front teeth. "Saw that, did you? I took her home and set her wing. Should be better in a few weeks."

"Why did you help her?"

He shrugged. "Because she needs help. What does it matter to you?"

Emma's face flushed. "I didn't mean to sound impertinent."

"Impertinent? What does that mean?" He shifted the newspaper bag slung over his shoulder. "That's a big word for a kitchen girl."

Was he making fun of her? She was still feeling touchy after the incident with Beatrice and didn't think she could handle being made fun of right now.

"Impertinent means asking questions you shouldn't."

He laughed and then realized she was serious. He held up his hands. "Sorry, I didn't mean to offend you, miss." He touched the edge of his cap again. His hair underneath it was black and shiny. "Are you new? I would remember a girl who uses such impressive words."

Emma bit her lip. He sounded sincere and she felt bad for snapping at him.

"It's my first day," she admitted. *Downstairs*, she added silently.

"I shouldn't ask any more questions. I don't want to be impertinent." He winked at her. "Have a good first day, new girl."

He waved and headed down the alley. Emma wasn't quite sure what had just happened.

"What's taking so long?" Cook hollered behind her.

Emma shut the back door. She had enough troubles right now without worrying over strange boys and birds.

She braced herself to face her former classmates again.

TWELVE

A Shattering Realization

Izzy

Making Emma a servant was the worst idea that Izzy had ever heard. By the second day it was clear that the girl couldn't even boil water without instruction. Now Emma had made breakfast late for the third day in a row and Miss Posterity was cross.

Izzy glanced behind her as they went up the stairs with the breakfast dishes. She carried a full tray laden down with bowls of fruit and a platter of sausages. Emma's arms shook as she carried a single large bowl of porridge.

"You sure you've got that?" Izzy asked. "You can stay in the kitchen if you want. I'm used to doing this by myself."

"I can do it." Emma grimaced. "Face them with grace and poise," she whispered softly.

Sure, whatever that meant. She'd heard Emma coaching

herself like that for the past two days, but it didn't seem to improve her skills. Cook had kept her in the kitchen during mealtimes until this morning. Emma seemed to think it was out of kindness, but truthfully, it'd taken her that long to master carrying a platter and serving from it at the same time.

Izzy thought it wasn't fair that they'd dumped Emma's training on her without any warning. She couldn't spare time to help Emma—not with the clock ticking down to December.

The tension in the dining room was so thick that Izzy could have cut it with a knife and spread it on toast. When she'd first arrived at Miss Posterity's, she'd been astounded at the sheer size of the dining room. She'd never known people could have a whole room just for eating. Growing up, the scents of the other immigrant families' steaming dumplings, frying schnitzel, and stewing tomato sauce had wafted through the thin tenement walls at dinnertime to create a feast for the nose. Here, the kitchen always smelled vaguely of boiled potatoes—the scent of unmagicked Blandings.

"Finally," Miss Posterity huffed when she saw them. "Hurry up now. The girls have their lessons to get to."

Izzy's nose itched with the oily scent of the sausages as she rounded the table, placing them on the students' plates.

As Emma went around the table, scooping out porridge, the pupils did their best not to look at her. Not one of them offered her anything, not even a smile or kind word. For a moment, Frances Slight appeared tempted to speak, but Miss Posterity looked at her. Frances's jaw snapped shut and she stared at her plate. Izzy was surprised by how sorry for Emma she felt.

As soon as she was done circling the table, Emma fled the room, clutching the bowl of porridge to her chest like it was a porcelain Olive the Third.

Izzy sighed. She'd have to explain to Emma that they needed to be dismissed by Miss Posterity or Miss Clementine before they could leave the room. She paused by the door, holding the empty tray.

The girls around the table picked up their crystals. Some added brown sugar, raisins, and whatever their hearts desired to their porridge while others—the wiser ones in Izzy's opinion—magicked their porridge into breakfast cereal. It was so easy for them. They'd been coached and coddled and encouraged to do magic. Emma didn't fit in downstairs, she was too much one of them—

One of them. Izzy almost smacked her forehead at the obviousness of it, but couldn't because she was still holding the tray. Emma had been groomed for magic her whole life—she knew loads more than Izzy ever could about kindling, but she knew nothing about being a servant. They could help each other. Emma was the key she'd been looking for.

Miss Posterity dismissed her, and Izzy practically flew through the door.

Her cheeks felt funny. She touched them, only to realize she was smiling. When was the last time that had happened?

But the smile was fleeting. When she entered the kitchen, she found Emma kneeling in front of the shattered porridge bowl. Cook stood above her, red-faced and mid-rant.

"It ain't fair the mistress saddled me with you. I'm busy enough as it is. She should turn you out and be done with it, I say."

"I'm sorry. It slipped." Porridge oozed through Emma's fingers as she tried to scrape up the broken pieces.

Izzy's hungry stomach flipped in fear. It didn't matter that Cook was saying exactly what she herself had thought ten minutes ago. Now that she had realized how they could help each other, Izzy couldn't let them turn Emma out. There was only one option.

"I'll help her," Izzy announced. "Emma, stop. I'll get a rag."

Cook grumbled. Complaining was her favorite pastime and she hated to be interrupted by someone making sense. "I suppose you'll need me to go to the market, then." She made it sound like another complaint, but on a beautiful day like today, Izzy doubted she minded. Indeed, she didn't even wait for a reply before she grabbed the market basket and headed for the door.

When she was gone, Izzy showed Emma how to scoop up the bits of shattered porcelain using a rag. "Don't use your fingers. You'll cut yourself picking it up that way."

"Thank you." Emma watched as Izzy dumped the first batch into the rubbish bin. "I didn't mean to drop it."

"'Course you didn't. No one ever means to break a bowl," Izzy reassured her with what she hoped was a friendly smile. "We can wash up together in the scullery."

Emma crossed her arms. "Why are you being so nice to me all of a sudden?"

Oh stones. Was she being that obvious? Izzy headed toward the scullery so Emma couldn't see her face. "You have porridge on your sleeves. Come on."

She left Emma at the sink in the scullery so she could wash her hands, and then she went to get the mop. By the time she'd finished cleaning up the rest of the porridge, the tromp of soft leather boots overhead signaled the students had left the dining room for the classroom.

With more patience than she'd known she possessed, Izzy helped Emma collect the dirty dishes and silverware using the dumbwaiter. She made sure Emma never picked up more plates than she could carry. A broken bowl was one thing, but place settings were expensive, and that wouldn't be forgiven as easily. If there was a chance that Emma would help her learn magic, Izzy would do everything she could to help keep her here.

There was a rhythm to the school's upkeep, and over the following weeks, Izzy taught it to Emma like a dance. There was laundry and linen changing on Mondays, baking on Tuesdays and Thursdays, dusting and silver polishing on Wednesdays. The main floor needed to be mopped three times a week, and general tidying, cooking, and cleaning up had to be done every day. Every other Sunday the girls received a few hours off after lunch, but they still had to be back in time to prep for dinner.

Emma hadn't cried in front of Izzy after that first night, but when they retreated to the attic at the end of the day, she quickly got in bed and faced the wall. Sometimes Izzy woke in the middle of the night and her back would tense as she heard the sniffling behind her. She didn't know if talking about magic would make Emma feel better or worse, so she waited a full two weeks until she found a moment that felt right to broach the subject.

"Are we almost done for the night?" Emma asked when they were elbows deep in soapy water after dinner. Dark circles had formed under her eyes from lack of sleep, and Izzy had noticed the blisters on her fingers.

In the hot dishwater, her hands were as red as the boiled crabs they sold at the market.

"Done? I wish," Izzy muttered. "We've got to finish this and get the bread out of the oven."

Emma hadn't said much when they were working besides a few polite thank-yous and questions about the tasks at hand. Not one word about her father, and not one complaint either, so Izzy was surprised when she opened up.

"A wish." Emma laughed, but it was a sad sound. "I'd almost forgotten. Papa promised me a wish when I kindled. He said he'd get me anything in the world that I wanted. Now my only wish is that he would come back." She splashed a cup into the water with more force than was necessary. "It doesn't matter now though, does it? Nothing matters."

Izzy swallowed. It had been hard for Izzy when the Gemstone Society for Orphan Welfare found her this position as a scullery girl. She'd cleaned and scrubbed at home, but never to the degree required here, and she had had to learn how to be polite and serve a proper table. But at least she understood her place in the world of the school. Emma was trapped somewhere in between.

Izzy set the cup she'd been washing on the drying rack and took another. "It's been a lot of change for you all at once."

Emma bit her lip and for a moment Izzy thought she

might start crying. She wished she would. Tears and anger were normal, but this forced calm that Emma kept imposing on herself was odd. But as usual, Emma collected herself. She took another dirty bowl from the stack and dunked it into the sink. Her movements bore the unconscious grace of someone who had taken many dance lessons in her life.

"I was very wrong when I thought it would be nice to be a servant," she said quietly as she scraped a blob of Blandings off the porcelain. "You must think me a horrible brat."

Izzy burst out laughing and Emma reeled back like she'd slapped her. "Sorry," Izzy mumbled. She wasn't sure what to say. Finally, she settled on: "You're not as bad as Beatrice Scorn."

At this, a sad, thoughtful look crossed Emma's face. "I hope I'm not."

"Trust me. You're not."

They smiled and then awkwardly went back to scrubbing. Izzy tried to find something else to say. This was the chance she'd been waiting for, but how could she bring up magic?

"So," Izzy said, stumbling over the words. "Do you miss being in class?"

She winced. She hadn't meant to ask a question to which the answer was obvious.

Emma made a noise that sounded like *mhm* and scrubbed at a stubborn bit of food. She was scrubbing at a rate of about one dish for every three Izzy washed, but it wouldn't help to point that out.

She had to try again. "May I show you something? I think it'll cheer you up a bit."

Emma tucked a limp golden curl behind her ear, leaving a trail of soapsuds down her cheek. "You're welcome to try, but I don't think anything could cheer me up right now."

It wasn't exactly an encouragement, but Izzy couldn't back down now. She stuck her hand into her apron pocket and gripped her stolen crystal. Then she pointed at the murky water and her back stiffened in concentration.

The gray wash water turned perfectly clear. Fluffy bunches of pure white soapsuds floated across the top like swans on a summer pond. It gave her an idea and she pulled on more magic until the bubbles formed swans with long graceful necks. Izzy smiled. It was the best she'd ever done.

Emma watched the soap swans with an expression of pure delight. "They're like toys in a shop."

Izzy's heart gave a happy flutter at the praise. "I heard you're good with colors. Do you think you could make the water blue?"

Emma grinned. "Easily."

Izzy held out her crystal and Emma gripped the other

end of it without hesitation. She stared at the water, a smile of intense concentration on her face.

Nothing happened. Emma's eyes darted back and forth like she was searching for something. She gasped and let go of the crystal.

"What's wrong?" Izzy asked. Her concentration broke and the soap swans popped like the bubbles they truly were.

"I thought it would come back, but it's gone." Emma wrapped her arms around her stomach.

"Are you all right?" Izzy asked with genuine concern. "You look like you ate a bad Blanding."

Emma leaned forward and closed her eyes. For a moment, Izzy thought she was going to be sick. Then she realized Emma was muttering *grace and poise* over and over under her breath, but it didn't appear to be helping.

This was not going well. She had to fix this.

"Let me cheer you up again. I can make soap clouds too." Izzy pulled out her crystal, trying to salvage the situation.

"What was I thinking?" Emma opened her eyes but covered her ears. Her hands looked redder against her golden curls. "Please, put that away and stop talking. I can't get in trouble and risk my place here." That sad, lost look came over her eyes again. "Papa, my magic—everything's gone forever, isn't it?"

Izzy understood. After all, she'd been the one who had stayed awake, staring at the front door of their apartment and waiting for the father she couldn't accept was dead.

"You have to move forward. It's the only way. We could still get our magic."

Emma stared at the floor and shook her head. "Servants are supposed to snuff out their magic. Even Papa said so. We're worthless."

"That's not true." Izzy leaned toward her, ignoring the signs that she should stop. "Why should money be what makes someone worthy of magic? There's different kinds of worthy, right? Maybe how badly you need magic should make you worthy of it. I could get you a crystal too. We could practice together."

"Stop. Just stop." Emma turned away. "I'm going to check on the bread."

She didn't return to the scullery.

Izzy finished the dishes, muttering every curse word she knew under her breath. She had definitely made things worse. The horrible feeling of failure jabbed at her like a sharp stone in her shoe.

She went to bed that night feeling farther from magic than ever before.

THIRTEEN
An Errand

Emma

Her magic was gone.

Emma had been so enchanted by Izzy's swans, she'd forgotten the hard, empty place where her magic should be. Since her first sparking, it had always been there. It had never occurred to her that it might not be. Just like Papa. She could get used to the chores and the constant hunger in her belly, Cook's foul temper, and the lack of sleep, but she couldn't get used to missing Papa and her magic. It left her unbalanced, like walking with only one shoe.

Still, she had to keep up a strict appearance of being fine. All her grace and poise would shatter if she allowed even the tiniest crack. That would cause trouble and causing trouble would send her straight to the workhouse.

So Emma pretended to be fine. She kept her head down and tried not to think about what she'd lost. Whenever she felt sad, there was always something to scrub to distract her. The days were long and exhausting, but the predictable pattern of chores made the weeks fly by. The April showers outside had given way to May flowers, and before she knew it, she had been a servant at Miss Posterity's for a month.

She slapped the mop down on the front hall tiles and scrubbed at the muddy footprints Beatrice and Lucy had tracked in. They seemed to delight in making more work for her. Or maybe they'd always been that rude and she'd just never noticed it before.

She wanted to talk to Izzy about it, but the other servant girl had been cool and distant in the two weeks since the incident with the soap swans. They communicated as necessary to do their chores during the day and at night they barely shared a nod before rolling over to face opposite walls.

Izzy had suggested she wanted them to kindle together, but that would feel like stealing. The boot polish stuck under her fingernails and soot from the fireplace in Emma's hair were constant reminders that she was no longer worthy of kindling and that her magic would snuff in December.

Without magic and the wish from her papa to look

forward to, life as a servant stretched out endlessly before her. It looked very bleak indeed. Muscles she hadn't known she possessed ached. Blisters burned on her hands and feet. She longed to lose herself in the comfort of a book, but there wasn't any time. At night, her arms missed Olive's reassuring softness. She was so lonely and sad, she wanted to fall asleep and forget her troubles but her mind raced with lists of unfinished chores and worries about the debt she still owed Miss Posterity.

When the checkerboard tiles of the front hall shone, Emma trudged back to the scullery with the mopping bucket. Miss Posterity was waiting for her in the kitchen with a brown-paper-wrapped parcel on the counter next to her.

"There you are. I have an errand that needs to be run."

Emma drew back. "Perhaps Izzy should do it?"

Izzy relished every chance to go outside, so Emma had successfully avoided doing errands until now. What would people say when they saw her dressed as a servant?

"Izzy's busy with the linens." Cook glanced over from where she was rolling out biscuit dough on the big wooden table.

Miss Posterity clicked her tongue. "Hurry up, girl. I haven't got all day." She held out a slip of paper with an address. Emma reached for it, but Miss Posterity pulled it back. "You will go straight there, drop these items off, and come back. If I hear any complaints, I will box your ears."

Emma flinched. She wasn't sure what boxing her ears meant, but Izzy lived in fear of it.

"Yes, miss." She bobbed her head in agreement.

With that, Miss Posterity handed Emma the paper and left the kitchen.

Emma's heart lifted when she read the instructions. She was to drop off the parcel with Mrs. Darning at the dressmaker's shop. Mrs. Darning made the best magically alterable dress bases in the neighborhood, as well as ready-to-wear dresses for the unkindled. She had been kind to Emma and had given her tea and cookies the handful of times she'd visited the shop during her time as a pupil. Emma's stomach rumbled, anticipating the cookies she was sure to receive in sympathy when Mrs. Darning saw her.

She clutched the paper like a treasured relic of her old life. As she fetched her maid's cap from the peg by the door, she instinctively reached for the comfort of her magic. It was like scraping the bottom of a fireplace that had recently gone out. Warm but fading fast. A feeling she'd have to get used to soon when her magic snuffed for good.

She tucked the parcel under her arm and stepped

out the back door of the school for the first time. It was so very different from the front entrance. A rat dashed between the rubbish bins in the back alley. Puddles from last night's rain pockmarked the street and she had to pick her way around them.

Her shoulders didn't relax until she turned the corner onto Fifth Avenue and stepped into the afternoon sunshine. While she'd been shut inside the black-and-white school, the world had awakened from its winter slumber. Green leaves sparkled like emeralds on the trees in Central Park.

Fifth Avenue was busy, full of rumbling motorcars, polished horse-drawn carriages, and delivery wagons. Pedestrians crowded the broad sidewalks and no one got out of her way. She'd never been allowed out without a chaperone before and the city seemed a larger and more chaotic place on her own. Had the buildings always been so tall or had she gotten smaller?

On the corner across from the Sixty-First Street entrance to the park, a woman stood on an upside-down apple crate. Her thick black hair was arranged in a functional bun and she wore a blouse and skirt that were several seasons out of fashion. The woman spoke passionately in accented English and waved her hands for emphasis. A scrubbed but still scruffy boy stood next to the crate, offering folded flyers to passersby. Gentlemen pulled down their bowler hats and walked faster like they were in a great hurry, while ladies looked away as if from something shameful or upsetting. No one took a flyer.

"Three years ago our city installed a plaque beneath the Statue of Liberty in our harbor, proclaiming, 'Give me your tired, your poor, / Your huddled masses yearning to breathe free.'" The speaker lifted her right arm in imitation of Lady Liberty. "She says she lifts her lamp by the golden door and yet they deny us at every opportunity. Magic should be free for everyone."

Emma's cheeks warmed and she ducked her head against the boy's offer of a flyer. The speaker's words made her uncomfortable, but she didn't know why. She wanted to stop and listen, and perhaps understand, but the promise of seeing Mrs. Darning and the waiting tea and sympathy for her plight pushed her forward. She gripped her parcel tighter and hurried onward.

Fifteen minutes later, she pushed open the wooden door of the dressmaker's shop and inhaled the familiar scent of the laces and silks for sale.

Gray-haired Mrs. Darning and one of the shop assistants were helping another customer in the back, who was undecided on how much lace she wanted on her dress. The customer's necklace kept flashing with magic as the lace piled up on her shoulders like snow.

Emma waited for someone to notice her. Behind the

counter, bolts of fabric in vibrant shades of cobalt, emerald, and magenta caught her eye. She drank them in, realizing how thirsty she'd been for color in the black-and-white halls of Miss Posterity's. A bolt of canary-yellow silk lay on the counter. She stroked it, relishing the soft swish of it between her fingertips.

"Don't touch that. You'll get it dirty." Mrs. Darning spotted her and made a shooing gesture with her hand. "Did your mistress send you with an order?"

Emma's confidence capsized. Mrs. Darning didn't even recognize her. Numb with the knowledge that there would be no tea, no cookies, and no sympathy, Emma handed over the paper.

"Miss Posterity sent me to drop these off."

"Ah, the returns." Mrs. Darning sighed and opened the parcel. "Some of my best work, these were. They've got so much magic up at that school, they could have altered them there if that rich little girl wasn't happy with them. People with magic can be such snobs, can't they?"

Emma felt like she'd been punched in the gut. The rose, cornflower, and periwinkle silks in front of her were *her* dresses, or at least they had been. Mrs. Darning thought she was the snob who wanted to return these lovely dresses.

"I'll add the money to the Posterity account," Mrs. Darning said. For the first time, she looked at Emma like she truly saw her. Emma swallowed hard, hoping to be recognized, but Mrs. Darning clicked her tongue in disapproval. "That dress is much too large for you. They should find you one that fits." Then she turned and busied herself behind the counter.

Emma hugged her arms around her torso, slipped out of the shop, and turned toward the school in defeat. She dodged ladies with parasols and a crowd of small boys in knickers playing marbles outside the grocer's, but she barely saw them. For the first time, she didn't look at the shimmering and twirling magical displays in the shop windows and didn't even glance at the bookshop. Mrs. Darning hadn't recognized her. Perhaps she'd never really seen Emma before, she'd only seen her money. With the money gone, Emma felt insubstantial, like a ghost floating down the street.

Ahead, a doting young father with a bowler hat and mustache bent to give his young daughter a self-spinning top. The girl smiled at him and he gave her a kiss on the top of her head. Emma brushed past them, tears marring her vision.

Maybe she was a ghost. She felt like a part of her had died with Papa. Her old friends wouldn't look at her. Even her magic had abandoned her. She swiped at her tears with the back of her hand, feeling worthless and alone.

She didn't look where she was going.

"Watch out!" a boy shouted behind her.

Brakes screeched a threat and she looked up to find the front grille of a gleaming motorcar heading straight toward her.

In the final seconds, she knew this was it. She wasn't a ghost. She wasn't insubstantial and the car wouldn't pass right through her. Emma closed her eyes and braced for the impact.

FOURTEEN

A New Kind of Worth

Emma

Hands grabbed her by the arm and tugged her backward. The driver shouted a curse, but Emma was already falling—not into the street, but onto the safety of the curb. Her right knee scraped against the pavement and stung. The car sped onward.

A boy's scuffed black boots stepped into her field of vision. "Are you mad? Do you want to die?"

Her heart pounded and her limbs ached with the most wonderful sense of being alive. For the first time since Papa's death, she felt the distant tingle of magic. Still out of reach, but there. Beautifully, desperately, life-affirmingly *there*.

She looked up at her rescuer and was surprised to

recognize his newspaper bag, flat-top cap, and gap-toothed smile.

"Thank you," she managed when she found her voice. "You saved my life."

"You bet I did. Everything all right? You sure were in a hurry." He offered her a hand up. The calluses on his hand rubbed her palm. It reminded her of the careful way he'd cradled the sparrow. That was a safer subject than what was wrong.

"How's the bird? Did you fix her wing?"

His face brightened in a smile. "She's much better. Her wing's healing nicely, but she's still not flying." He looked down and made a *tsk* sound. "But you're bleeding. Best get that cleaned up."

She looked at her stinging knee. She'd torn a hole in her black stockings and a scarlet thumbprint of blood shone through.

"Will you be in trouble?" he asked. "My older sister is a housemaid up the hill and they take every tiny tear or breakage out of her wages."

"I—I don't know," Emma stammered. She wasn't receiving any wages, but she remembered the threat of having her ears boxed. Or maybe Miss Posterity would add this to the list of debts she had to repay. "Probably."

"My ma could fix 'em for you real quick. She's home, only a few blocks away."

Emma frowned at her knee. Her adrenaline rush from the near-accident was starting to fade and she felt wrung out. "But I don't have any money to pay her."

"*Psh*. You don't have to pay. You're my friend."

Emma brushed off her skirt. "Friend? That's presumptuous. We haven't been properly introduced."

"See, there you go again." He scratched his forehead. "Presumptuous? Properly introduced? Did you work at a fancy hotel or something before that school?"

Emma crossed her arms. "I'm just saying, how can we be friends if I don't even know your name?"

"Good point." He bent at the waist in an overly deep bow. "Very well, my lady. I'm—"

A burst of laughter cut him off. Emma realized they had an audience of two other gangly newsies. The tall, darker one elbowed the shorter one. "Look! Spaghetti's got a girlfriend."

Emma's companion growled and threw a fake punch in the other boys' direction. "Go away and leave her alone. She's too good to even look at your ugly mugs."

"Spaghetti's girl! Spaghetti's girl," the newsies chorused as they ran off, laughing and making kissing noises. Emma blushed furiously.

"Sorry about that," the boy said after the other two

newsies were out of sight. "We're bored because the headline's lousy." He dug a copy of *The Kindled Courier* out of his newspaper bag and showed her the headline: "Mayor Considers Education Budget Increase Despite City Council Concerns." There was a picture of a serious man sporting an equally serious mustache. He looked vaguely familiar, but she was sure she'd never seen him before.

"Is your name Spaghetti?" Emma asked. The words *Spaghetti's girl* bounced around in her head.

"It's Sabetti. Tom Sabetti." The boy took off his cap and ran a hand through his shiny black hair. "They call me that 'cause I'm Italian and they're idiots." He chuckled, but Emma couldn't quite tell whether he liked the nickname or not. Boys were strange, though Tom seemed nice enough. "What's your name?" he asked.

"Emma." She stuck out her hand. "How do you do?"

He shook her hand with so much enthusiasm that her head bobbled. "How do you do, Emma?" He glanced down at her leg. "You're still bleeding. Let's get that fixed up."

Tom Sabetti lived in the bottom two floors of a ramshackle four-story building on Third Avenue. It was an eight-minute walk east from Fifth Avenue, but it felt like another world. The bowler hats and parasols vanished and working-class flat caps and aprons took their place. Emma had never ventured this far before. Here, the steel skeleton of the elevated train line shadowed the street and blocked out the sun. Trains rattled deafeningly overhead at regular intervals and in between, Emma heard several languages she couldn't identify. The brick and wood buildings were shabbier without the polish of having an owner with magic.

The front door of the Sabettis' apartment opened into a rectangular room that clearly served as living room, dining room, and kitchen. The ceilings were low like a train cabin and the furniture was shabby and worn. Five mismatched chairs gathered around a dining table at the center of the room. Emma wondered why they didn't magic them to match and then remembered that they couldn't. A large black stove and fireplace were at the back. On the left-hand wall, a rickety staircase led to an unseen upstairs.

"Ma?" Tom dropped his newspaper bag by the front door. "You here?"

He led Emma down the length of the room and pushed open a door at the rear. Emma gasped. They were outside on a patio with a handful of potted plants and a dozen birds. There were several finches, a one-legged pigeon, two sleek crows, a robin with a chipped beak, and a speckled hen with one wing who looked up and fluttered with excitement to see Tom. A few were in handmade wire cages, while most perched on rails along the walls. One of the crows landed on Tom's shoulder and pecked at his ear affectionately.

"What's this, Tomas? Have you brought me another broken bird to be mended?"

Emma had been so distracted by the strange aviary, she hadn't noticed the woman standing in the corner of the patio. Her Italian accent was much thicker, and she was a little rounder and a little cleaner than Tom, but she was clearly his mother. They shared the same thick black hair and their cheeks bunched up in the same way when they smiled.

She was smiling now. A gray mourning dove balanced on her right shoulder as she shut the door to a cage containing a brown sparrow with a splint on its wing. Emma was pleased to see it eating seeds with enthusiasm.

Tom stood straighter in his mother's presence. "This is Emma. She's the one I was telling you about from over at the school. It's partly my fault that she fell and busted her stocking and I told her you could help. I hope you don't mind." His words tumbled out. He was softer at home, more eager to please, with none of the brashness he'd shown on the street.

"How do you do?" Emma curtsied. Maybe she shouldn't have. From the way Mrs. Sabetti's warm brown eyes widened, she could tell she'd done something odd but endearing.

"You were right. She has an intelligent look about her, Tomas."

Tom winced. "I never said it like *that*." The crow nipped at his ear and he held up a finger in warning. "Knock it off, you."

"At least this girl has better manners than the birds you usually bring me." Mrs. Sabetti chuckled and shooed the dove off her shoulder. "Come in, Emma. Let's get you mended."

"Why do you have all these birds?" Emma whispered to Tom.

"Why?" he asked, like having a roomful of birds wasn't a strange thing. "They're here 'cause they needed help, and nobody else was gonna do it. Let's go inside."

The stove was a tenth of the size of the one at Miss Posterity's but there was a freshly iced lemon cake next to it. The crow flew off Tom's shoulder to inspect the cake.

"That's not for you." Mrs. Sabetti waved her hand at the bird. "Someone bring me my sewing kit, *per favore*," she hollered up the rickety-looking stairs. "And someone else fetch water."

Footsteps pounded on the stairs, and two young girls and a boy peered through the railing, all with eyes the same brown as Tom's. Both girls wore their hair in long dark braids and looked to be around nine or ten. Emma remembered that Tom had said he had an older sister who was a servant too. Five children in such a small house? She felt sorry for them. For a moment, her mind drifted to the house she'd dreamed about for her and Papa and it was a struggle to keep the smile on her face.

"Who's that?" the younger girl asked.

"She's another hurt bird that your brother's brought home. What does she look like?" Mrs. Sabetti huffed with impatience. "Maria, fetch the water. Antonia, light the stove for tea. Matteo, I don't know. Do something useful."

The children hurried to do their mother's bidding. Matteo hobbled down the stairs on a crutch, his left foot twisted inward at a forty-five-degree angle from his knee. Emma wondered what had happened to him. It took him twice as long to navigate the stairs as his sisters, and he was winded when he got to the bottom and proudly held out his mother's sewing tin.

"Thank you, dear. And why are you standing around?" Mrs. Sabetti rounded on Tom. His eyes widened with surprise. "Cut her a piece of cake."

"Oh, I couldn't possibly," Emma protested, though her stomach gurgled. As servants, she and Izzy ate only the leftovers from the school's meals. Regular Blandings were bad enough, but choking down the scraps without magic to improve them was horrid. She looked around the meager kitchen with its mostly empty pantry. How could she take anything from them?

They're happy here and better off than you, a nasty voice whispered inside her. *You're worthless.*

"I insist," Mrs. Sabetti said. "It's for a special occasion and now we've got company. We'll each have a slice."

"Before dinner?" The oldest, Antonia, clapped her hands with delight. Mrs. Sabetti nodded, and Antonia set herself to lighting the fire with even more fervor. She flicked sparks out of her fingertips, trying to get the wood to catch.

"Yes. Your father's working the late shift at the factory tonight anyway, so we'll save him a piece. We don't have to tell him we had ours early." She winked at Matteo, who grinned and hobbled over to fetch napkins from the sideboard.

"What's the special occasion?" Emma sat up straighter.

Tom scuffed the toe of his boot against the floor. "It's my birthday," he muttered. "I'm twelve today."

"Happy birthday," Emma told him. He shrugged like it wasn't a big deal.

Every year, her birthday had been a countdown. *One year closer to kindling*, Papa would say as he lifted a glass to her. But for Tom and the others like him, it was one year closer to their magic snuffing. The mood in the kitchen became somber instead of celebratory.

At Mrs. Sabetti's instruction, Emma took off her stocking for mending. Maria, the middle girl, tended to the cut on Emma's knee with gentle hands. Tom set the table without having to be asked. The family flowed like a stream that knew its course well, working together. Before she knew it, her knee had been cleaned and bandaged, her stocking mended and handed back to her, and she was seated at the table between Maria and Matteo. The cake sat in front of them on a plate in all its lemony glory.

She hadn't felt so comfortable and cared for since before Papa left. She smiled, watching Tom pour cups of canned milk for his younger siblings to drink. He sat down on the other side of Matteo and draped an arm across the back of his brother's chair. The Sabettis were lucky to have one another. Now that she really looked, this kitchen was wonderfully cozy.

"I know the cake's probably not as fancy as what you're used to up at that school," Mrs. Sabetti fretted as she sipped coffee out of a chipped cup.

"I'm sure it's so much better." Emma told them about the Blandings and how the students were expected to improve them with magic.

"Horrible rich people. Imagine having enough money

and magic that you could intentionally make food bad." Tom folded his arms and slumped in his chair.

"No slouching." Mrs. Sabetti bopped the back of his head with her palm.

"Ma!" He waved her off, but he sat up straight again. "It's not enough that the rich folks deny the rest of us magic, they have to go and do dumb things like that just because they can. Wasting magic. I'd make better use of it and help people."

"What would you do? Become a doctor?" Matteo tore his gaze from the cake and looked at his brother in hopeful surprise. Emma thought again about his twisted foot.

Tom ruffled his hair. "I don't think I'm smart enough for that. But I don't want to sacrifice my magic in order to get a job as a cog in some industrialist's factory."

"But I thought the industrialists' inventiveness and hard work greatly improved the infrastructure of our country," Emma said, repeating what they'd learned in class.

Tom's mouth twitched with amusement at the word *infrastructure*, but he shook his head. "Yes, but at what cost? They only take workers who've snuffed their magic. The owners say sparkings and magic are too dangerous, but it's really their way to stay in control. So you can't get a job if you don't snuff it—but you can't get a better job if you don't have magic. The system's rigged."

Emma had never thought about it that way before. "But how could it be different?"

Tom looked around the table. "It shouldn't only be the rich families that get to keep their magic. If I kindled, I could get a good job and a better house, with a roof that doesn't leak. Then you all could go to a better school instead of that overcrowded mess they call a classroom."

"And get me a better foot so I could run in the relay races at recess?" Matteo jumped in.

Emma was confused by this as well. "But magic doesn't work on people. Why don't you take him to a doctor? I'm sure a good one could help him."

An uncomfortable silence followed. Matteo stared down at his lap.

For the first time, Tom wouldn't meet her eye. "Magic doesn't help that, but money sure does. Good doctors are expensive, Em. I had to drop out of school and sell papers so we could eat."

She stared at the lemon cake. She'd had no idea.

"I'm sorry." Emma's face flushed with shame. "I didn't mean to sound—" *Like a horrible snob? A privileged brat?* They all fit. The Sabettis were some of the kindest people she had ever met and she'd gone and insulted them.

"It's fine, dear. Be thankful for your good health," Mrs. Sabetti reassured her.

Tom leaned forward. "Someday, I'm not gonna sell papers, I'm gonna write for them. There are these journalists—people are calling them muckrakers because they're stirring things up. Maybe you've heard of them?" he asked, and Emma shook her head. "They write articles exposing how the system's broken and one day, I want to be like them. Only, my articles won't just expose how the system of who gets magic is corrupt—I'll find a way to fix it so that everybody gets a fair share."

"If I had magic, I would help people so everyone could run in the relay races and no one would have to sit and watch." Matteo lifted his eyes to the ceiling like his words were a prayer.

"Maybe someday." Tom squeezed his shoulder.

If Papa knew she was sitting at this table, listening to someone speak about the world and magic this way, he'd drag her back to Fifth Avenue. But he'd have to be alive to do it, and if he were, she would never have been sitting here. She wouldn't even be questioning her own worth.

She also wouldn't be wondering why this conversation made so much sense.

"How would you even do it?" Antonia asked. "They give us the switch in school if we so much as spark accidentally. Nobody knows how to kindle except rich people."

"There's people like us that have done it. I've heard

about a guy downtown who sells the supplies and knows how."

His sister looked skeptical. "Even if you did kindle, someone would report you. We could eat for months on what the Registry's paying for accurate reports of illegal magic these days."

"Well, I'd have to make sure no one finds out."

"How? That's foolish—"

"Tomas, Antonia, please," Mrs. Sabetti shushed them. "No more talk of kindling today. Remember what happened to Paolo."

The Sabettis stared at their laps.

"What happened to Paolo?" Emma asked.

Tom winced. "You know the beggar in the park with the burn marks?"

Emma nodded. She'd given him a few coins from her purse when she was rich.

"That's Paolo. He was our neighbor. A few years ago, he got this crazy notion he could kindle. When the Kindling Winds blew and he ignited, he refused to snuff his hands in a bucket like would have been smart. He had no idea what he was doing, just flinging his arms around in circles and shouting. The fire crew had to put him out with a hose. The Registry court put him in jail for a year and fined him for everything his family was worth. Now he's begging in the park."

Put him out with a hose? Emma's entire body tightened in fear.

"Tomas. Enough. You're scaring everyone." Mrs. Sabetti banged on the table, ending the conversation. "There will be no more talk of kindling. It's too dangerous."

Emma felt sorry for Paolo, who had tried and failed. What would it be like when the time came for her magic to snuff? Would she quietly accept it, or would she fight it too?

Mrs. Sabetti watched her. "Tomas tells me you've been at the school for about a month now? Where were you working before?"

Emma hadn't realized how much she'd been dreading this question. Tom clearly disliked rich people—would he dislike her too if he knew she used to be a pupil? She was terrified that he might, because she liked him and his family quite a lot.

"My father died so I had to go to work, you see," she said, choosing her words more carefully than she used to choose her silk dresses.

Mrs. Sabetti gasped and covered her mouth with her hands. "Oh, child. And the rest of your family?"

"My mother died when I was very young. It's always been Papa and me."

Antonia and Maria shared a look. Tom watched her with such a sad intensity that Emma had to look away.

"I'm so sorry. This must be very hard for you," Mrs. Sabetti said.

Tears stung Emma's eyes and her voice cracked. "I miss him so much." It was the first time she'd admitted it out loud. It was like she'd popped a cork and the grief she'd tried to keep bottled up came gushing out. She dropped her head into her hands and her shoulders shook with sobs.

Mrs. Sabetti's chair scraped the floor and a moment later Emma felt soft arms encircle her. This was the most sympathy she'd received from anyone, and Mrs. Sabetti had been a complete stranger an hour ago.

"He'd be so disappointed if he could see what's become of me," Emma said, her voice thick with tears. "I haven't been able to summon a single spark since he died. What if it's already snuffed and I've lost it forever?"

Through this, Mrs. Sabetti held her. "There, there. That'll be the shock, my dear. For better or worse, no one's magic can snuff before the Winds blow."

At last, Emma took a deep shuddering breath and was able to collect herself.

Mrs. Sabetti pulled back and squeezed her shoulders. She looked around the table. "Such sad faces, but we'll fix that soon. Life always looks brighter after a slice of cake." She dug into her apron pocket and pulled out a man's gold pocket watch. "Tomas, do you want to do the honors?"

Tom took it with gentle hands. This watch was clearly a family treasure. "It was my grandfather's from back in Italy," he said by way of explanation. "I think Antonia should do it since she's flickering now."

Antonia's eyes widened as he passed her the watch. "It's your birthday, silly," she teased, but she took the watch with a grin. Then she plucked a feather from the crow, which squawked at the indignity and flew away to the windowsill.

Antonia twisted the feather in her fingers and it became a smooth stick. Maybe she'd watched her parents or her older brother and sister do this for years, and now she could finally join in. Maybe in the same proud and envious way that Maria and little Matteo were watching her now.

Sparks and light burst from the feather—for now it wasn't a feather, but a sparkler, burning in the shape of a feather. Antonia stuck it on the cake and the five Sabettis and Emma watched as it burned. They looked so content.

Tom's eyes met Emma's over the sparkler. This would

be his last magical birthday. Come the December Winds, they'd both have to snuff out their magic.

It wasn't fair. Anger burned within her, and for the first time in her life, it felt right.

Why were the Sabettis any less worthy of magic than Miss Posterity? They were so kind while Miss Posterity had treated Emma so horribly when her circumstances changed. Emma had been raised to believe that most people didn't want or need magic and that they understood they weren't worthy of it and accepted it. Anyone who looked at the Sabettis could see that they treasured their magic—they *needed* their magic. *Just like Izzy.* The thought leaped unbidden into her head.

Maybe Izzy wasn't being greedy–maybe she loved her magic as much as Emma did and didn't want to lose it either. It wasn't like stealing something—magic was already hers. It had flickered in her fingers and lived in her heart for years.

Papa had been wrong about it being kindest for servants to snuff their magic. There was nothing kind about losing her magic. If he were here and she could show him the Sabettis' kindness and how hard Izzy worked, then surely he would understand. It burned her how much she still wanted his approval, even when she knew he was wrong about this. Emma didn't have Papa's money but she'd find her own worth. She wouldn't resign herself to her place and go down without a fight.

A tingle rose in her hands and she looked down to see blue sparks webbed between her fingers. She opened and closed her hands, relishing her magic's return. It was like coming home again.

She was so happy, she forgot she was running late.

FIFTEEN

Two Arguments and an Agreement

Izzy

Dinner was almost ready and Emma wasn't back yet.

Izzy boiled green beans for that night's Blandings but kept one eye on the back door. What could have happened to the girl? It wasn't that she was worried about Emma, she told herself. Still, her gaze kept returning to the clock.

She started chopping the onions, the pieces coming out large and uneven. It didn't matter; they'd get blended into the Blandings. Nothing she did here mattered except for getting her magic and that was starting to feel impossible. Her eyes watered and she wiped them with the back of her hand. Stupid onions.

Without any fanfare, the back door opened and Emma slipped into the kitchen. Izzy sighed in relief, but then braced herself when she saw the look on Cook's face.

"And where have you been, eh? It doesn't take three hours to get to the dress shop and back. I had to do your chores when you didn't turn up."

That was a lie. Cook had merely complained while Izzy did the work.

Cook tapped her foot next to the stove, hands on her hips. The ladle in her hand dripped gravy onto the stone floor. The kitchen cat eyed the drips from his roost on the stairs, but like Izzy, he knew better than to get involved when Cook was angry.

"Oh, it's the most wonderful story." Emma hung up her cap on her peg by the door. "I fell and I think I understand life so much better now."

Her cheeks were rosy and she looked so much like her rich, happy self that Izzy almost forgot to feel sorry for her. But the feeling didn't last long.

The kitchen door thumped open and Miss Posterity stormed down the stairs. The cat made a strange noise like a grunt and raced under the counter.

"What is taking so long? Do I need to come down here and make dinner myself?" The headmistress fixed the three of them with a glare that made Izzy want to dive under the counter with the cat.

"We're doing the best we can, miss," said Cook. "We were shorthanded on account of this one getting lost—"

"I—I didn't get lost, really. I only lost track of—of time," Emma stammered. "They were so kind, you see." She looked between Cook and Miss Posterity, suddenly seeming to realize this was not going well.

"Who?" Miss Posterity demanded. "Who were you meeting? I told you to come straight back here."

Emma looked at the headmistress and the glow from her eyes faded like she was remembering something. She bit her lip and didn't answer the question. This only made Miss Posterity angrier.

"Cook, fetch the boxes. It appears our new maid needs to be taught a lesson."

Izzy's hands flew to her ears instinctively as the cook opened the farthest cabinet on the right and took out two wooden boxes the size of apples. Izzy couldn't watch. She turned to the stove and stirred the gravy, hoping it would be over soon.

Something soft bonked into her shin. She looked down to find the kitchen cat staring up at her with insistent yellow eyes. What did he want? The gravy?

Izzy stared into the pot, trying and failing to ignore what was happening. Emma didn't so much as whimper when Cook affixed a wooden box over each of her ears. She didn't know enough to be afraid.

But when Miss Posterity pointed at the boxes and her ring flashed with magic, Emma screamed. It was one sorrowful and shocked sound, and then she fell silent. The boxes spun, getting smaller and tighter. Izzy knew how Emma's ears must have been aching, but not even the tiniest whimper escaped her lips. Her lips moved and Izzy recognized that phrase again, *grace and poise*. Izzy wondered what it meant.

Izzy averted her eyes from Emma's rapidly reddening face. It was then that she saw the sapphire-blue sparks crackling between Emma's fingertips. Her mouth went dry at the fierceness of the color. Emma had said she was done with magic, but Izzy had hoped that'd been a lie. Those sparks made it clear that magic hadn't given up on Emma—and neither had Izzy.

The boxes were now the size of thimbles and Emma's face was turning purple from holding in her cries.

"I never saw someone who can hold their tongue during an ear boxing." Cook looked back and forth between the unflinching girl and the pitiless sneer on Miss Posterity's face. "That's probably enough, don't you think?"

Miss Posterity didn't even blink. "She needs to learn her place."

Izzy gripped the edge of the counter. She had to stop this, but how?

The cat bumped his head against her leg again. This time he looked pointedly at the stove. Izzy got the distinct impression he was trying to tell her something. She followed his gaze. *The gravy. Of course.* She gripped the crystal in her pocket and focused her magic on the copper pot on the stove.

Flames whooshed up around the pot and thick black smoke billowed toward the ceiling.

"The gravy's burning!" Izzy shouted.

The boxes stopped spinning.

Cook shrieked when she saw the smoke. She threw one of the fire buckets over it, extinguishing the flames. Izzy turned to Emma, hoping it had been enough of a distraction. She was relieved to see Emma had the boxes in her now-sparkless hands. Her ears were bright pink.

Miss Posterity brushed off her hands. "Let that be a lesson to you. I expect dinner to be on the table within five minutes."

Izzy bobbed her head and hoped no one would notice the flush in her cheeks from the heat of the enchantment. She looked around for the kitchen cat but he had vanished. Had he been trying to help? Or had he wanted gravy?

"Are you all right?" she whispered to Emma after Miss Posterity was upstairs and out of earshot.

"I think Miss Posterity wanted me to see those dresses. That's why she sent me on that errand, not you," Emma replied with narrowed eyes, which Izzy took to mean no.

"Don't stand around gabbing," Cook demanded, and they both jumped. "We've got a dinner to serve." She pointed at Emma with one hand while dumping the ruined gravy in the rubbish bin with the other. "Never be late on me again."

Emma swallowed. "I won't."

Cook's gaze softened as it strayed to Emma's ears. For a moment it looked like she was going to say something kind, but then she harrumphed and turned back to the stove. Emma grabbed a tureen of what was either lumpy mashed potatoes or congealed rice and Izzy took a platter of green goo that no longer resembled beans.

Emma spun around to face her the second they were alone in the front hall. Her ears were still pink and tender. "You were right about there being different kinds of worth. I'm sorry for what I said before. Is the offer to try to kindle together still open?"

Izzy struggled to keep her face neutral. She didn't want to appear too excited and scare her off. "Maybe. What made you change your mind?"

"I met some people today." Emma glanced at the still-closed dining room door and then quickly told her about meeting a boy on the street and following a bird or something. Izzy was too busy trying to contain her glee to follow the details. What mattered was that Emma was going to work with her. Her plan to learn to kindle wasn't ruined.

Emma's eyes drifted to Izzy's apron pocket. "So, any idea where I could get a crystal too?"

"I can arrange it. Give me a few days though."

"Of course." Emma shifted the tureen and her hand strayed to her ear. "Thank you, by the way. I know you saved me back there."

Izzy snorted. "Thank the gravy. But you're welcome."

She followed Emma into the dining hall, barely hiding her grin.

While they washed the dishes after dinner, Emma explained in more formal terms what Izzy already knew. Besides the gems or crystals necessary to wield any magic, kindling itself required three parts—an incantation to start the process, the precise physical movements to awaken magic and pull it from the kindler's hands through the rest of her body, and the solid gold kindling flints that they held during the process to keep the magic from flaring out instead of inward. Emma's notes had been taken away with her other possessions, so they were starting with the knowledge that was in her head and what little Izzy had gleaned. It would be a lot of work, and they agreed they'd best start as soon as possible.

The next night, Izzy slipped out the door of the darkened classroom as the clock in the hall chimed ten. Using the brassy gonging of the clock to cover her footsteps, Izzy crept along clutching a pinkie-size quartz in one hand and a flickering candle in the other. Everyone else had long since retired to bed and the school was quiet.

"Is that it?" Emma stepped out of the shadows.

Izzy scarcely managed to swallow her scream. "Don't do that! I thought you were Miss Posterity." She handed Emma the crystal. "Step one complete."

"Thanks," Emma said, and then frowned. "It's really small."

"It's half a crystal, but it will still work. One was already cracked in the storage cupboard. This way they won't notice anything is missing." Izzy pressed a hand to her still-racing heart. "I thought you'd gone to bed."

"I'm looking for the library. There might be some books about kindling that could help in there, but it's hiding again." She looked up and down the hall. "Any ideas?"

"Let's look."

Emma took the candle and they tiptoed down the hall,

searching for the correct door. They didn't dare turn on the electric lights, so the hall was dark and full of shadows.

Ahead, a face came into view, frowning and stern. Again, Izzy barely suppressed a yelp of fear that they'd been discovered, but it was only the stone bust of Prudence Posterity. There was a thin mustache of dust across her upper lip.

"This thing gives me the creeps," Izzy muttered as they passed it.

"Me too," Emma admitted. "What do you think happened to Mr. Posterity? There must have been one at some point, don't you think?"

"Dunno. Maybe the women gobbled him up like spiders do to their husbands."

They shared a nervous smile. It was a strange thing, being on the same team as Emma. They weren't friends, more like allies.

"So what exactly are we looking for in the library?" Izzy asked.

"The incantation is bound to be in at least one of the books. I can't remember it, but I'll know it when I see it," Emma said as they inched toward the next door. "It starts the whole process and Miss Posterity explained that kindling has to be done absolutely perfectly. In kindling, magic manifests as fire."

"Yeah, I know. I saw the ceremony last year."

"You did?" Emma's nose wrinkled. "You aren't supposed to watch that."

"Well, it's lucky for us that I did. I remember some of it."

Emma opened the door next to the parlor and a broom tumbled out of a cramped, dusty closet. Izzy lunged to catch it before it clattered to the floor. The rush of air blew out the candle and the hall was plunged into darkness.

"Light it again," Izzy said, trying to shove the broom back into the closet as quietly as possible. The room remained dark. "Will you hurry up?"

"I'm trying." Emma gulped. "I've manifested fire once before. It was on the day that—"

Izzy froze. "Wait, what? I'm learning to kindle with a girl who's barely manifested?" The crystal in Izzy's pocked winked with magic as she relit the candle herself. "Maybe I was better off on my own."

Emma crossed her arms. "You don't know the first thing about kindling."

"I do too."

"No, that *is* the first thing about kindling. You can't kindle on your own. It's physically impossible."

"What?" Izzy froze, broom still in hand.

"You have to work with someone else who has been trained. They serve as the grounding in the initial flare-up of magic. Otherwise the magic goes right through you.

I thought that's why you wanted to work together. You didn't know that?"

Stones, how did she not know that? "I was testing you."

"Liar," Emma shot back.

"I'm not the one who—"

"Will you two stop arguing?" a new voice said from the shadows.

It was a man's voice with a strange accent she couldn't place. Izzy looked at Emma and saw her own fear reflected back at her.

"Who said that?" Izzy demanded.

"I did."

They both glanced at the bust of Mrs. Posterity, but she was still stone.

"Show yourself," Izzy demanded, brandishing the broom like a sword.

Something stirred in the shadows. At first it looked huge, filling the hallway. Izzy gulped as Emma raised the candle higher.

The shadows condensed to ankle height and the kitchen cat stepped out. He lifted his whiskers in a self-satisfied way and leveled them both with a yellow-eyed stare.

"I'll show you how to find the library, but you're going to have to work together," the cat said.

SIXTEEN
Figgy Pudding

Izzy

Izzy clapped a hand over her mouth to hold in her scream.

"What?" The cat spun around, looking behind him for the source of her terror. "What's wrong?"

"You!" Emma sputtered. "You're a cat and you're talking."

The cat rolled his eyes. Could cats roll their eyes? Izzy had never considered it.

"I'm not a cat, I'm a house dragon." He said this like it was a reasonable explanation. "I appear as a cat to your human eyes. Let's get out of the hall so we don't have to whisper."

With his tail straight like an exclamation point, he stalked back and forth in front of the broom closet three times, muttering to himself. The air above him shimmered like heat rising from a fire.

"Try it now," he suggested.

Izzy opened the door to reveal a cavernous library, much bigger than was reasonable for a house of this size. The cat trotted inside with Emma right behind. For a second Izzy debated slamming the door shut and running away, but as peculiar as this was, she was curious. So she followed.

Emma clasped her hands to her heart. "Look at the books! Hello, my friends!" She dashed to one side of the room where she began pulling books off the shelves and hugging them.

Izzy didn't see what was so great about the library. Dim electric lamps buzzed low, casting a golden glow over the inviting black leather armchairs on the white Persian carpet. The ceiling was higher than it should have been for a single-story room, and shelves of books covered every available wall. She hated cleaning this room.

"How did you make the room appear?" Emma asked the cat, her eyes alight with joy.

"I could explain it, but then it'd be far less interesting. Right now I want to talk about your magic." The cat hopped onto one of the armchairs and a puff of dust rose around him. "So, you're going to try to kindle, eh? Good for you."

"I'm sorry, can we back up for a moment, please?" Izzy said. "Who or what is a house dragon? Is that a real thing?"

Emma nodded. "House dragons protect old institutions of magic. They're quite rare."

"Let me guess, you read about them in a book," Izzy snipped.

"I saw one or two when I was touring with my papa. Well, I think I did. We didn't get close and they're hard to tell apart from regular cats at a distance, you know."

"*Ahem*. My name is Figgy Pudding." His whiskers trembled with pride. "I am not surprised you haven't heard of us, Isabelle. As magic has shrunk to so few humans using it, our once great numbers have declined." He turned to Emma. "I am sorry about your father. I've been wanting to say that for a while."

Emma swallowed hard, and her eyes grew misty. "Thank you, Mr. Pudding." She curtsied and his feline head bowed.

"It's rare these days for people to remember the proper manners for greeting an ancient and noble being," he said. "You may call me Figgy."

"It's an honor—"

Izzy laughed. "He's not an ancient and noble being. He eats gravy off the floor. I've seen him."

"Gravy is delicious." Figgy licked his lips.

"He's talking, Izzy. He can't be a normal cat."

Izzy had to admit this was a good point, but a thought still burned in her mind. "So all those times I talked to you, you could understand me? Why didn't you protect me when Cook lashed out or Miss Posterity boxed my ears?"

Figgy's whiskers drooped. "For that, I am sorry. A house dragon's protection doesn't work like that, you see. My magic sustains the structural integrity of this house. Dragons are masters of flame. Without me, this old place would go up like a tinderbox." He narrowed his eyes and glanced at the walls. "Plus there are the mice. Such a nuisance."

Izzy could barely keep the laugh out of her question. "Mice? Are you sure you're not a cat?"

"Clearly, you don't understand how mice work." The house dragon's ears flicked. "They're drawn to anything that's been magicked. When they consume magic, their eyes turn red. They nibble the magic right out of things and turn it back into what it was before."

His words awakened a memory that Izzy preferred not to think about. Mam had been out of the house that night when she and Maeve saw the mouse. Maeve had screamed and Izzy turned in time to see a small blur racing toward the wall. Izzy cried for an hour, clutching at the boards and strings that had been Da's fiddle and their family's only magicked possession. After that, Da was truly gone. Until this moment, she'd never understood how one tiny mouse could do so much damage so quickly.

House dragons and magic-nibbling mice. Clearly Izzy had even more about magic to learn than she'd thought.

Figgy jumped down from the chair and studied the bookshelves. "Now, we've got work to do. I only have an observer's knowledge of human kindling but I'm happy to guide you as best I can. I think we should start in the Magical Objects section. Ah, here!" he cried, spying a green volume. "*Schreiber's Symposium on Magic Sensitivity*. A favorite of mine." Emma hurried to grab the book he indicated. "Oh, and DeGennaro! Grab that too."

"I *knew* I saw you reading that day," Emma said triumphantly. She sank into one of the armchairs and opened a book Figgy had picked out.

Izzy studied his feline face, looking for some hint she might have missed in the past year. "Does Miss Posterity know that you're a—a—"

"House dragon," Figgy supplied. "Yes. My family has protected this school for generations. The current Posterity has no manners, she is not like her forebears. She says food for me is a waste of money. That woman underestimates my power and overestimates her own."

He glanced away, muttering what sounded like "Tinderbox! Mice!" and "No respect!" under his breath. Then his manner brightened visibly. "This Posterity's allergic to cats, you see, so we both keep our distance. I like Clem, though. She feeds me chicken under the table."

"So why are you helping *us* then?" Izzy asked.

He looked thoughtful for a moment before he replied, "There are many different routes to magic. People have only forgotten them. We house dragons seek to expand the number of people doing magic again in order to restore us to our full power. It's been a long time since the last litter of house dragon kits and our numbers have grown dangerously small while magic remains constrained by your so-called elite. I figured I'd start my part of the expansion plan with you two. Not for years have I seen such different people working together. You remind me of better times."

"Um, are we still doing this? We can't kindle alone, right?" Emma looked up from her book and shyly met Izzy's eye. "Together?"

Izzy shrugged, but her heartbeat quickened. "Together," she agreed.

It was a fragile agreement, but an agreement nonetheless.

"So it's settled," Figgy announced. "Tell me, what do you want to do when you get your magic? Are you to be captains of industry? Politicians? Perhaps even teachers? Having magic will open every door, you know."

Izzy's jaw snapped shut. She was not prepared to talk about her plan to leave town in front of Emma. She was going to leave this life behind her and didn't want anyone to know where she'd gone.

"I want to be a magitect like my father," Emma announced.

"Excellent choice. Color talent is often the first sign of an artist's magic, you know," he said, and Emma beamed. Figgy turned to Izzy. "And you?"

"I want to be independent. I don't want to have to rely on anyone." The words burst from her before she knew how to stop them.

Figgy regarded her like he saw something in her that she didn't yet. "Take care, Izzy. Even with magic, people still need one another."

His words pierced her heart like a needle through fabric. But for an ancient and noble being, he didn't understand real life. She worked best on her own. Kindling presented a challenge to that.

She flopped down into one of the armchairs. The leather was wonderfully soft. "So we're going to need gemstones, right? Emma, which of your old friends wouldn't notice if a few things went missing from their jewelry box?"

"We are not stealing anything." Emma's voice had an edge to it. Izzy liked it.

"How else are we going to get them? You were droning on about how they're necessary for kindling last night. 'Stones draw the magic out of you. The better the stone, the easier it is to focus your magic,'" Izzy said in her best hoity-toity voice.

"I don't sound like that." Emma crossed her arms.

"Such ridiculousness." Figgy *tsked.* "In my day, people with magic and sense didn't go flinging themselves about during their kindling and they didn't need gems either."

Izzy caught Emma's eye as they both bit back a laugh.

"Are you saying you're older than rocks?" Izzy teased.

Figgy ignored her. "Crystals or gems, you just need to be clear. Focus on the magic if you want to kindle. With fewer people using it, magic has become overconcentrated and harder to control. It's calling to more people and straining to burn free. You'll see," he said.

Izzy inhaled. "That's not very reassuring."

"It's not meant to be." The house dragon curled up on the armchair. "You won't survive kindling without preparation. Especially this year."

Emma gulped. "I guess we'd better get to work."

We. That would take some getting used to.

They settled in with the books that Figgy had indicated. Izzy sighed when she saw there were no pictures, just columns of dense text, some of it in that funny foreign language she'd seen on the blackboard. Or at least, she thought it was the same. Emma would probably know.

She peeked at her new partner. Emma's nose was deep in her book, her mouth quirked to the side in concentration as she turned a page. Sensing Izzy's gaze, she looked up and raised a questioning eyebrow.

Embarrassed to have been caught staring, Izzy jutted her chin at Figgy, who had settled in for a nap. "Some guide, eh?"

Figgy gave a little snore and his sleek black side began to rise and fall in steady slumber.

Emma's shoulders bobbed in silent laughter. She smiled at Izzy, shrugged, and then returned to her reading.

Chuckling to herself, Izzy propped her book open on her lap. "All right, let's find this French incantation."

"It's in Latin," Emma corrected without looking up from her book.

"Whatever works," Izzy mumbled.

She turned the page and began to read.

SEVENTEEN

The Man in the Tweed Coat

Emma

Over the next month, the girls met every night to practice magic and search for the secrets of kindling. Emma pulled from her school lessons to create a basic curriculum they studied at night, and during the day, they practiced enchantments whenever no one was looking—manifesting flames to light the fireplaces in empty rooms or magically wiping the banisters clean and seeing how long they could hold the enchantment before the dust reappeared.

Emma was surprised how much fun doing magic with Izzy turned out to be. Last week, they'd been changing the students' sheets on the third floor when Emma suggested they alter the embroidery patterns; an exercise they'd done in class. Instead, Izzy magicked a wadded-up pillowcase into a snowball and hit Emma in the stomach. The snowball fight that ensued lasted a whole three minutes—longer than Emma had ever held an enchantment before.

Inside the servants' hall, Emma wiped the sweat off her forehead and smiled at the thought of snowballs. It was hot outside for June and hotter still in the room thanks to her magic.

She pinched out the candle flickering on the table in front of her. Emma didn't need it to see the stockings she was mending—the electric lights buzzed behind her in the kitchen—but she was practicing. To give the room a chance to cool, she concentrated on her stitches, trying and failing to make a row as tidy as Mrs. Sabetti could. She'd been back to see Tom and his family twice on her every-other-week Sunday-afternoon break and had enjoyed each visit more than the first.

When the stocking was done, she glanced over her shoulder to make sure she was still alone in the hall. Then she gripped the crystal in her apron pocket and lit the candle again with a soft *pop*.

Her magic was getting stronger and every day felt like a step in the right direction. They still needed the incantation and the right tools for kindling and it wasn't proving easy. Last night, she'd read a particularly dense but fascinating section about the kindling flints. The author kept referring to them as being stones but Miss Posterity had been quite clear in class that they were made of gold. It was very confusing. Emma was about to start on another pair of stockings when the bell for the front door rang. Someone must have bloomed the rose.

The stockings went back into the never-ending pile of sewing she still needed to get to. She straightened her apron and cap and went to get the door. Outside, thunder rumbled a distant threat.

Despite the heat and the dark clouds that lined the sky behind him, the man on the doorstep wore a brown tweed coat. He had gray hair and a ramrod-straight military posture. The gem in his wristwatch winked in the sunlight.

"Excuse me. Is this Miss Posterity's Academy for Practical Magic? I'm looking for the headmistress."

He handed her a calling card that read *Inspector Conduit, Pinkerton Agency.*

Little prickles of uncertainty ran down Emma's spine. What was an inspector doing at the front door? He had bloomed the rose, so he must have magic and be someone important. "If you wait here a moment, sir, I'll go get Miss Posterity."

He tried to look past her into the hall. "Do hurry. I'm a busy man."

She shut the door, thankful to step away. The inspector's voice was as stiff and intimidating as his posture.

Fortunately, Miss Posterity was in the first place she checked: seated at her desk and frowning at the school's account books. She snapped the books shut when Emma poked her head in.

"There's a man here to see you, miss." She handed her the card.

"Show him in," Miss Posterity replied, smoothing her hair. "And bring us some tea."

Emma kept her gaze down as she showed the man in the tweed coat to Miss Posterity's office. When Miss Posterity waved her away, Emma gladly scurried back to the kitchen.

That man must be practically boiling wearing a coat like that. Would he even want hot tea? The coat itself was odd. Most of the men in New York wore gray or black coats, not brown tweed, and definitely not in summer, but she didn't know what it meant.

She set two cups on the tray and poured the steaming water from the kettle into the teapot. Drops of hot water splashed onto her sleeve and she hissed. She wished it was ice water. Nice cold water to cool her off.

Out of the corner of her eye, she thought she saw the water in the teapot flash with magic. Then ice crystals began spiraling down her arm. Emma gasped. It wasn't possible. Her crystal was in her pocket and she hadn't touched it. No sooner had she thought it than the water on her sleeve was warm again. Clearly the heat was affecting her imagination. She shook her head at her own ridiculousness and trudged upstairs with the tea tray.

The door to Miss Posterity's office was still closed but she could hear voices as she approached.

"I'm sorry I don't have a more satisfactory answer for you, Inspector," Miss Posterity said. "The girl is gone."

Emma hesitated, one hand on the door handle. What girl? Who were they talking about?

"My client will be disappointed to hear it. Mr. Horace was so sure she'd be here, but I'll let him know I've turned up a dead end." The chair groaned as he stood up. "Thank you for your time, ma'am."

"It's miss, actually. I'm not married." Miss Posterity let out that fake tinkling laugh she used on clients. The one she'd used on Papa. "Won't you stay for tea?"

"I must be going. I shan't keep my client waiting for my report. If the girl turns up, please contact me immediately, Miss Posterior. I'll want to take her to the station right away."

"It's Poster*ity*, actually." This time there was strain in the headmistress's voice.

"That's what I said, is it not? Good day." The inspector's approaching footsteps clacked on the floor.

Having learned a few tricks from Izzy, Emma backed up and pretended to be approaching as the door opened. The man in tweed brushed past her without a second glance. Her breath caught at the rigid set of his jaw. She wasn't sure why he frightened her, but she'd be glad when he was gone.

As soon as the front door shut behind him, Miss Posterity gestured her inside the office with a finger. "You. Come."

Emma entered, still carrying the tea tray. It felt like everything else in the world had changed, but the room was exactly the same as it had been on her first day at the school. The only difference was the headmistress, pacing up and down the carpet like a caged animal. Even the ever-burning salamander in the fireplace turned around on its log bed, disturbed by the tension in the room.

"Do you still want the tea?" Emma asked.

"Set it down." Miss Posterity gestured at the low table. "It's time I showed you."

She strode around her desk and pulled a stack of white envelopes, tied with a string, from inside the bottom drawer. Some had been torn open, but a handful were still sealed. Emma's gaze rested on the unsealed ones, but Miss Posterity waved her hand dismissively.

"Don't bother. They're the same. Bills, from unpaid debts. It's become clear that your father spent freely and foolishly before he died." She plucked one of the unopened envelopes from the pile and pointed it at Emma. "The inspector's client, whichever one of these he is, must be rich and powerful to afford a Pinkerton agent. He was here looking for you."

"Me? Debts? Papa?" It was like Miss Posterity was speaking another language and Emma's brain had to translate.

"See for yourself. Keep them if you'd like. They're yours, after all."

Miss Posterity pushed the pile of envelopes across the desk and Emma took the one on top. It had her name scrawled across the front in an unfamiliar hand and a postmark from San Francisco. She brushed her finger over the stamp, not wanting to open it and give Miss Posterity the satisfaction of witnessing her distress. This surprise mention of Papa had thrown her carefully ordered emotions into disarray and her anger at her situation threatened to seep through. Trying to keep it at bay, she picked up the stack of envelopes and focused on tucking them into her apron. There were maybe fifteen in total and the letters bulged from her pocket like they longed to escape and wreak havoc in her life.

"What did that man want with me? Is he coming back?'

"He was here to collect you for his client." Miss

Posterity frowned. "From there, I assume they'd deliver you to the workhouse when his employer learned you couldn't pay."

Emma made a choked sound in her throat. She'd thought it bad enough when Miss Posterity threatened to condemn her to the workhouse. These people didn't even know her.

"Don't worry, I'm not about to let that happen. Why should *their* debts take priority over what you owe to *me*?" The headmistress perched on the edge of her desk. "I told him that you were gone. My word is as good as gold and I expect that will be the end of it. You may stay here and continue to work for me."

Miss Posterity was using that fake voice again and desperation clung to every syllable. Emma couldn't trust Miss Posterity's words, but she could trust her greed. To keep up appearances and protect the reputation she treasured, Miss Posterity needed more than one maid, and for as long as she continued working here without wages, Emma was valuable.

"Thank you, miss." Emma glanced uneasily at the letters sticking out of her pocket. "But what if one of them finds out I'm here?"

"Don't tell anyone outside the school your full name." Miss Posterity reached out a hand and Emma flinched. She expected a slap, but instead, the headmistress patted her on the head like a dog. "You can be our little secret." She stood and walked back around the desk. "Now go back to the kitchen. You're getting dirt on my carpet."

Emma headed downstairs in a daze. She kept one hand on the letters. When she blinked her eyes, she saw a tweed pattern.

In the kitchen, Izzy mashed potatoes with a vengeance while Cook shouted orders from in front of the stove. Neither of them looked up as Emma slipped out the rear door and sat on the step. Wind tugged at her cap and the scent of the air warned of the coming storm. She searched the stack, but not one was addressed in Papa's jumbled-together handwriting. The unopened envelope on the top of the pile seemed to taunt her as she stared at her name.

A part of her didn't want to open it. For as long as it remained sealed, she could pretend this wasn't real. She'd learned to live with the fact that Papa had left her penniless, but this new fear brought the acute ache of his loss crashing down upon her again. This was a different kind of sorrow than before; a more complex grief that was part missing him and part frustration at him for being gone in the first place.

The door opened and Izzy stepped out. When she saw Emma's face, she shut the door behind her.

"You all right?"

Emma tried to keep her voice even. "I'm fine."

Izzy sat down next to her on the steps. "No, you're not. Is it about Figgy or practice last night? I didn't mean to turn your shoes into bricks, I really didn't. Are you having second thoughts?"

Emma shook her head. "It's not that." Her insides felt tangled up in hope and dread. "A man came looking for me." She told Izzy what Miss Posterity had told her and showed her the envelopes.

They both stared at the letter on top of the stack as the wind picked up, rustling their skirts. A curl of Izzy's red hair blew across her forehead like a question mark.

"Well, aren't you going to open one?" Izzy asked. "You have to know if she's telling the truth."

"Why would she lie about this?"

Izzy pressed a finger to her chin. "Let's think. Because she's a mean, selfish cow who wants you to keep working for her for free?"

They shared a sly smile at the daring of this statement.

"It's growing on me," Emma said.

Izzy wrinkled her forehead in confusion. "What is?"

"Your attitude. Your sense of humor. All of it," Emma said. "Thanks for being here."

Izzy looked surprised but pleased. "Where else would I be? So are we opening it or not?"

Lightning flashed in the sky above their heads and Emma made up her mind. She tore open the envelope and unfolded the paper inside. As she skimmed the words, her hope that this was a misunderstanding burst like a soap bubble.

To the estate of Mr. George Harris, the salutation read. She scanned the rest with growing unease.

"She wasn't lying. It's a bill." Her voice trembled. "For a considerable sum from before my papa died." She looked up at Izzy. "How could he leave me like this? And these people—they really do want to take me to the workhouse, don't they?"

Izzy didn't answer, which was worse than a yes. A raindrop dotted the page and then another, smearing Papa's name. "What about the rest of the envelopes?"

They tore through half the stack before Emma flung them to the ground in despair. As Miss Posterity had claimed, they were the same: bills, some large and some small, but all addressed to her.

"We'll figure something out." Izzy tugged on her shoulder. "Let's go inside. It's going to pour."

Emma wanted to be soaked, to let the cool rain pour down on this hot anger burning inside her. This was the anger she was afraid to touch because she was afraid if she so much as poked at it, it might consume her. She was furious at the world and furious at Papa for leaving her alone in it. He hadn't prepared her for what a hard and cruel place it could be and now she had to navigate it on her own. It felt like everyone was out to get her and no one wanted to help her.

"I'll have to run away," Emma whispered. "Go somewhere they can't find me." She didn't want to, but it was the obvious answer.

"Please don't. I—I need you." Izzy fidgeted with her apron, not looking at Emma. "Look, after I get my magic, I'm going to leave New York. I know I'll never be able to get a kindling license from the Registry, so I'll have to go. If you stay until December and we kindle when the Winds come, you can go with me. Deal?"

Emma paused, considering it. They'd be like outlaws in a story, but they could have a better life out West. It was a life Papa never would have imagined for her and one she could hardly imagine herself, but it appealed to her more than she would have guessed. If she had Izzy, she wouldn't have to face the world alone.

"I might have to leave before then, but I'll think about it. Thank you."

The sky opened above them like a torn seam, crackling with thunder and drenching them in a sudden downpour. It woke Emma out of her daze. They dashed back into the heat of the kitchen and slicked the water from their faces with their fingers.

When Cook wasn't looking, Emma shoved the stack of envelopes into the stove. They blackened and curled in the flames. She watched until the last letter was completely burned before turning away. It didn't solve the problem, but she felt a lot better.

EIGHTEEN

Unexpected Winds

Emma

Emma was changing linens on the second floor when a strong gust of wind howled past the window. Up and down the street, the flags and bunting set out for tomorrow's Fourth of July celebration whipped in the wind. The glass rattled and sparks shot from Emma's fingertips, singeing the sheets.

"*Stones.*" Izzy's now-familiar curse leaped to her lips.

A door banged open downstairs.

"Clem! Come quickly!" Miss Posterity shouted with alarm. The fear in her voice made the hairs on Emma's arms stand up. "The Winds are early!"

Emma rushed into the hall just as Miss Clementine shrieked and raced down the stairs two at a time.

Another gust buffeted the school and the whole house shook. Then Emma felt it. Magic, yearning to break free. Her fingers crackled with golden sparks. As a child, she'd seen how the Kindling Winds made the sky seem to shimmer. They always carried a sweet scent that was awfully familiar and impossible to identify. But she'd never *felt* the Winds before. They tugged at her now, trying to drag the magic out of her. She tried to shove the magic down, but it pushed back.

It was too soon. She was angry at herself for believing Miss Posterity's assurance that they didn't have to worry about early Winds. Why had she ever believed anything the headmistress had said? Emma didn't have the incantation or know the right movements to kindle. If her magic ignited now, it would surely snuff.

Izzy. She had to find Izzy.

Downstairs, someone screamed. A shiver of terror shot down her spine. Emma didn't think twice. She took off running toward the classroom.

Miss Clementine arrived in the doorway right before her. Her face was deathly pale. "Who is it?"

But the answer was obvious. Most of the girls were backed up, pressed against the blackboard. Rosie stood in the center of the room, eyes wide behind her gold glasses. Smoke wafted from her hands and she whimpered at the sight of it.

"We should separate the other girls," Miss Clementine said.

"No," Miss Posterity countered. "We have to keep them together so we can keep an eye on them. If we send them away and one of them ignites . . ." She didn't finish her sentence, but she didn't need to.

It was a struggle for Emma to control her magic. It rippled like it wanted to break free and burn like wildfire. She gripped the crystal in her pocket and tried to soothe her magic. *Not yet*, she told it.

Miss Posterity spotted Emma lingering in the doorway. "You!" she shouted. "Clear the parlor! We need plenty of space." She turned back to her smoking pupil. "I'll get my gems."

"Why?" Beatrice demanded, her voice shaking. "What's happening?"

"Rosie is going to kindle today," Miss Posterity said in a way that was clear there was no other option.

"Why me?" Rosie looked up at the teacher, her face full of fear. "I'm not ready—I'm not. I don't know the steps fully yet."

Miss Posterity put a hand on her shoulder and then jerked it back like she'd been burned. Perhaps she had. There was steam coming from Rosie's ears. "I'll help you." Her head snapped up and she glared at Emma. "What are you waiting for? The parlor! Now!"

Ignoring decorum, Emma ran to the parlor. Just like Miss Posterity had said on their tour, it was in its best position at the rear of the house for Kindling Day. She remembered the way Papa had smiled at her with pride and her insides twisted. Then she saw the magicked fake rose garden out the back windows and she felt a steely resolve settle over her.

She was about to disobey instructions and go find Izzy when Miss Clementine hurried into the parlor. With a flick of her gem, the teacher reduced the grand piano to dollhouse size and tucked it away on a shelf. Together, they set up chairs in a semicircle, facing the open space at the front of the room.

The tromp of footsteps in the hall announced that the rest of the school was on their way. "Miss Clementine! The flints!" Miss Posterity commanded from the hall.

Miss Clementine glanced at the double doors, and then back at Emma, an unreadable swirl of emotions on her face. "Take care of yourself today, dear. If you're in trouble, come find me. Don't tell the headmistress." She squeezed Emma's shoulder once and then rushed out of the room.

Emma wasn't sure exactly what the offer meant. Surely Miss Clementine didn't mean to help her kindle, but it was such a kind gesture that she had to blink back tears.

Miss Posterity entered and opened the window. The Winds rushed through the room like searching hands, reaching for her. Emma felt her magic rise up to meet it and it took a great deal of concentration to stuff it back down again.

Where was Izzy? Was she alone, burning somewhere? Or was she too trying to fight it?

Rosie entered, smoke rising from her hands, the rest of the class right behind her.

"With my luck, I'm surprised it wasn't me," Frances mumbled morosely, but either nobody else heard her or no one cared.

"Everyone take a seat! Give Rosie space!" Miss Posterity ordered. The room was in such chaos, for a moment Emma hoped no one would notice her.

The headmistress stepped to the front of the room. She waved her hand and a painfully familiar ruby ring sparkled in the sunlight.

Emma almost lost the grip on her magic. She hadn't seen the ring since the terrible night she'd learned Papa died. She'd thought it had been sold with the rest of her belongings. The sight of it on Miss Posterity's bony finger stung like a slap in the face. Her hands clenched into fists at her side. Magic tugged at her, urging her to burn.

The headmistress spotted Emma. "Out. Do not come near this room again until we're finished."

Emma longed to let her magic flare up at Miss Posterity, but she couldn't give in. Not now, not when she and

Izzy had a plan. So she obeyed. She dodged girls vying for chairs and walked as slowly as she could toward the doors. Miss Clementine passed her, hurrying back into the room carrying a wooden box no bigger than a loaf of bread. Emma peered over her shoulder to see her hand it to Miss Posterity. Inside, two golden orbs the size of eggs were nestled in a scarlet velvet lining. Each was encrusted with tiny diamonds in the shape of the letter *P*.

"Take these," Miss Posterity said, handing the orbs to Rosie. "Grip them tightly and don't drop them or the magic will spill out of your fingertips when the kindling begins."

That was the last thing Emma saw before the door closed behind her. Outside in the hall, Emma tried to quell her rising anger at the injustice of her situation by pressing her forehead to the cool wood of the door. She should be in there, learning how to kindle, not out in the hall on her own.

Izzy came hurrying toward her, out of breath and clutching a beat-up notebook.

"Where have you been?" Emma burst out. She couldn't explain how happy it made her not to see flames around Izzy's hands.

"Why? Were you worried about me?" Izzy teased, and then her mouth dropped open. "You were, weren't you?"

"No," Emma said, but she couldn't fight her smile.

"I had to run up to the attic and get my notebook so we can write down what we learn." Izzy held up the notebook, which had clearly had a full cup of tea spilled on it at some point. "Cook's at the market, but she'll be back soon and will come looking for us."

Emma debated telling her about the ruby ring, but just then the chatter on the other side of the door hushed.

"They're starting!" Izzy dropped to her knees and peered through the crack between the doors.

Emma leaned above her. The crack between the doors offered a limited view of the center of the wood-paneled room. Emma could make out Frances Slight's hunched shoulders directly in front of her, but she looked past her, and then she couldn't tear her eyes away.

Rosie stood in the parlor in front of a line of mostly occupied chairs. Miss Posterity had her ring pressed to Rosie's sapphire.

"It's the grounding, like I told you. You can't do it alone," Emma whispered to Izzy, and then she shut her mouth because she knew what came next.

In unison, the kindling student and the teacher chanted the incantation.

"Lumen quod intus lucet qui nos verey simus ostendet."

Recognition fluttered in Emma's heart like wings. That was it! She knew she'd remember it as soon as she heard it. "Give me the notebook." She made a grab for the pencil in Izzy's hand and jotted down the words.

"What does it mean?" Izzy asked.

"'The light that shines from within reveals us for who we truly are,'" Emma recited as the memory came rushing back.

Just then Miss Posterity barked, "Control it!" and they both pressed their eyes back to the crack between the doors.

There was a noise like a loud exhalation and then flames spread from Rosie's fingertips to her shoulders. The initial grounding over, Miss Posterity stepped back and lifted her right arm. Rosie copied the gesture.

The headmistress led Rosie through the steps of the kindling dance. It was slower than a ballet but no less graceful. Rosie pliéd, twirled, and swept her arms. The girls in the audience *oohed* and *aahed*, but Rosie whimpered with every movement.

"Does kindling hurt?" Izzy asked. Her voice sounded tiny and far away.

"I don't know," Emma admitted. She tried to focus on the movements, but her eyes kept going back to the ring on Miss Posterity's finger. Why had she kept it?

Whereas Miss Posterity was elegant and controlled, Rosie was distracted and shaky. The fire crept from her arms, up around her neck, and back down toward her legs. Each movement was choreographed to encourage the magic forward. It moved toward her extremities with agonizing slowness.

Hurry, Emma wanted to shout. Every moment they lingered here was a moment in which they might be caught.

"Move with intention! Pull the magic through you," Miss Posterity shouted. She swept her arm in circles and the ruby ring twinkled over and over in the light.

The girls silhouetted on the chairs in front of Emma leaned their heads together to whisper. Emma tried to peer around them so she could keep her eyes on the ring. She knew she was distracted and should be paying more attention to the moves than to Papa's ring, but the longer the kindling went on, the more her sense of injustice grew.

"This doesn't look like it did last year," Izzy whispered.

A trickle of sweat ran down Rosie's brow, and then, without warning, flames whooshed up above her head in a burst of bright blue.

Emma and Izzy both cried out in surprise, but their shouts were lost among those of the pupils. A few threw up their hands in front of their faces to block the sudden brightness. The white trim on Rosie's uniform began to blacken. She trembled and the flames spread outward, growing brighter and brighter.

Emma could barely stand to look. "Something's gone wrong. This can't be how it's supposed to go."

"Don't stop!" Miss Posterity shouted. "Keep moving!"

That was when Rosie screamed.

Two swirling spirals of flame shot away from Rosie's shoulders. The girls closest to Rosie abandoned their chairs.

Izzy muttered a curse under her breath and leaped away from the door. "This is madness."

Rosie was still screaming when thick black smoke poured out of her mouth and ears.

"The drapes are on fire!" Beatrice shrieked. The other girls backed away from the flames.

Miss Posterity didn't take her eyes off Rosie. "Concentrate and keep moving!"

"I can't!" Rosie moaned, leaning forward and clutching her stomach. The ends of her hair began to char.

"Girls, come with me, please." Miss Clementine shepherded the terrified other girls toward the doors. "Let's give them some space. Everyone into the dining room and we'll ring for a steadying cup of tea."

Emma turned to Izzy with wide eyes. "Look out!"

They dove against the wall as the parlor doors burst open, expelling a herd of frightened pupils.

"Quickly. No talking, please." Miss Clementine put an arm around Lucy's shaking shoulders as they hurried down the hall. The twins walked with their arms around each other and even Beatrice looked dazed.

When they were gone, Emma and Izzy emerged from behind the doors. Smoke wafted through the open doorway and flames licked the wood paneling. Rosie cried out, but whether it was in effort or in fear, Emma couldn't tell.

"Concentrate on the magic and move," Miss Posterity demanded over and over, but Rosie sobbed. She looked so helpless next to the towering form of Miss Posterity.

"We have to help," Emma said.

Izzy's face had gone completely pale behind her freckles. She stared at the inferno that was the parlor. "Where's Figgy? Isn't he supposed to stop this?"

"There's no time!" Emma had an idea. She took off toward the kitchen. "Help me get the fire buckets."

She raced through the hall and down the hidden steps. The kitchen was quiet, a shelter from the storm upstairs. Cook stepped in through the back door, a basket of vegetables on her arm. "It's breezy out there! Done with the linens already?" she asked.

Figgy came tearing around Cook's ankles and ran

to Emma's side. He had a wild look in his yellow eyes. "Something's wrong," he said so only Emma could hear. "I was enjoying the sun on the stoop when she left—I got shut out. I can't stop it."

"It's the kindling!" Emma screamed at both the cat and the cook, forgetting propriety in the heat of the moment. "Bring the buckets."

"*Great stones*," Cook cursed, but she followed with a bucket in each hand as Emma charged down the hall to the parlor as fast as her feet would carry her. Izzy was nowhere in sight, but Emma couldn't focus on that now.

She entered the parlor and gagged at the scent of burning hair. Maybe because Figgy was back in the house, the fire had stopped spreading. Rosie huddled on the wooden parquet floor, bright yellow flames engulfing her body like she was a lump of coal. At first, Emma feared she might be dead, but then she saw her shoulders were heaving with sobs.

Cook went straight for the curtains and threw the first fire bucket at them. The flames hissed out with a puff of smoke. Then she turned and saw Rosie. She raised the fire bucket, but Miss Posterity leaped in front of her.

"Don't!" she shouted. "If you put her out, her magic will snuff. She has to master this."

The headmistress looked half wild. Black soot streaked her white-blond hair and pieces of it had come loose from her bun.

"You're almost through, girl!" Miss Posterity shouted at Rosie. "Strike them and be done!"

Rosie's lower lip trembled, but then a calm look came over her face. She closed her eyes and raised her shaking arms over her head. She smacked the golden objects in her hands together. Every flame in the room flickered and died.

Rosie let out an exhausted little *oof* and collapsed. Her once-white silk stockings were scorched to black and her skin had the angry red sheen of a burn. She curled herself into a ball.

"Cook, send for the doctor." Miss Posterity stood, her shoulders thrown back with relief. "She's managed it."

Ruby-red spots danced across Emma's vision where the flames had been moments before. She knew she should have been terrified when presented with the magnitude of what she and Izzy were attempting to do, but instead she felt determined. Magic sang in her veins, glorious and wonderfully hers, and she knew then that she'd die trying to keep it. She'd lost everything else—she wouldn't lose this.

And she'd get her ring back while she was at it.

NINETEEN

Maeve

Izzy

When the stairs creaked under Emma's step, Izzy pulled up the quilt and pretended to be asleep.

She was too embarrassed to explain why she'd run away this afternoon. Getting her magic had always sounded so easy in her head. Mutter a few words, learn a few steps, and *poof*, she'd be set for life. What she'd seen in the parlor today had terrified her. If that was how hard it could be to kindle with a professional teacher helping, what chance did she and Emma have on their own?

None. None whatsoever.

"I know you're not asleep."

Izzy didn't move. She'd successfully avoided Emma for the rest of the day and wasn't about to start talking now. Emma kicked off her boots with two hollow *thumps*.

Something warm settled across Izzy's ankles and she stiffened. Without intending it, her eyes popped open.

"I let Figgy in," Emma said dryly. "He was waiting by the door when I came up."

The warm thing draped over Izzy's ankles purred. "This is much better than sleeping by the stove."

"He's probably got fleas," Izzy mumbled into her pillow.

"I most certainly do not," Figgy protested, but started to groom himself anyway.

Izzy stared at the wall. "What happened to that girl?"

"Rosie? Miss Clementine took her to the hospital. They're not back yet." Emma tapped her foot. The effect would have been better if she'd left her shoes on. "So are we going to talk about the elephant in the room?"

"It's not an elephant, it's a cat."

"House dragon," Figgy corrected, and resumed grooming.

"I meant how you left, Izzy," Emma huffed. "We needed your help."

"*We*," Izzy scoffed. "You still talk like you're one of them. Do you honestly think they'd help you if the situation was reversed?"

"How can you have an attitude about this?" Emma demanded.

Izzy didn't answer. Her attitude was her shield against the world and if she let it down now, she'd be completely defenseless.

Emma yanked the quilt off her entirely and Izzy shouted in protest.

"Get up. We have to practice while everything's still fresh in our minds."

"Are you crazy?" Izzy grabbed at the quilt. "You saw what happened."

Izzy wanted to keep her magic, but she couldn't risk dying if she wanted to find Maeve. Before this afternoon, she'd wanted to get her magic and make a better life for both of them. Now it felt like an impossible choice. She rolled over and covered her head with the pillow.

"Come on, Iz. We have Figgy to guide us," Emma said in a softer voice. It was hard for Izzy to hear with the pillow over her head but she didn't budge. "I don't know what went wrong this afternoon, but we'll do it right. We have the incantation now. We're on our way. Speaking of which, where'd you put the notebook?"

"It's in the drawer where we keep the crystals." Izzy waved her hand vaguely toward the broken dresser. "Em, today was—" What was the right word? *Awful? Terrifying?*

Something heavy settled on the pillow over her head. "Figgy, get off," Izzy muttered into the mattress.

"I warned you that it would be worse this year. You'll have to focus on the magic and practice hard," the house dragon said.

"Figgy, did you know there would be early Winds?" Emma asked.

"Well, not exactly." Figgy's voice was muffled. "Magic's become even more concentrated than I thought, stoppered up like a corked bottle. Early Winds are always dangerous, but even the few I've seen were never as wild as today's."

Izzy could hear Emma pacing around the room. How she still had energy after the backbreaking work of cleaning up the charred parlor, Izzy had no idea. Finally, her curiosity got the better of her. She peeked out from under the pillow. "What's got you riled up?"

"Nothing," Emma said.

"Liar," Izzy shot back. "Who has the attitude now?"

Emma glared at her. "Fine. Miss Posterity was wearing my ring today. The one my papa gave me."

"What? I thought she'd sold everything." Izzy sat up, sending Figgy tumbling off the pillow. He flicked his ears in displeasure as he climbed back up and curled into a furry circle.

"I thought so too. I don't know why she kept it. Or why she was wearing it. The sight of it on her vile finger." Emma shuddered. "I'm going to get it back. I'll kindle and show her and everyone else that I'm not worthless." The bed frame creaked as she sat down next to Izzy. "Did you see Miss Clementine bring in the golden kindling flints? I wonder where they keep them. Don't suppose we'll be able to get our hands on them?"

Would Izzy be worthless if she couldn't get her magic and couldn't help Maeve? She could feel her shield slipping. She tried to think of something sarcastic to say. Instead she began to shake.

"What if we die?" Her voice cracked. "I want my magic, but—"

"Izzy, what's wrong? You're crying!" Emma's forehead creased. She looked more frightened by this than she had by the kindling that afternoon.

Izzy couldn't answer. She cried harder thinking about Maeve and her dreams that had turned to ash today.

Emma scooted closer and wrapped her arms around Izzy.

Every instinct Izzy had honed over the past two years screamed at her to flail and lash out. It had been so long since anyone had hugged her and she'd forgotten how nice it felt. A new wave of uninvited tears washed over her.

"I can't risk dying," she blubbered. "There's something I have to do."

Emma held her tightly until Izzy's shoulders had

stopped shaking. Then she sat back on her heels. "Is this about your plan to go out West?"

It was hard to remember disliking Emma when she sat watching Izzy with such a patient look. Somehow in the past few weeks she and Emma had become something more than allies. The idea of being friends with Emma pinched like new boots, but maybe, just maybe, it could become comfortable with time. She thought about how Emma had looked so relieved this afternoon when she'd seen her hurrying down the stairs with her notebook. The memory warmed that cold, scared place inside her.

"You can tell me," Emma encouraged. "Let me help you."

To her great surprise, Izzy wanted to. She was so tired of carrying this secret alone. Besides, she wanted Emma to understand.

"I—I can't die because I have to find my sister."

Figgy, who she'd thought was asleep, popped his head up. "What?"

Emma's mouth dropped open. "Sister? But you said you were an orphan!"

Izzy snorted a laugh. "You can still have siblings and be an orphan, silly."

"Right. Sorry." Emma thought for a moment. "She's why you want to go out West, isn't she?"

Figgy put a paw on Izzy's leg. "What happened to her? Why didn't you tell us?"

Izzy's heart warmed at the concern on their faces. "Are you two going to give me a chance to talk or what?"

Their mouths snapped shut in unison. Izzy took a deep breath.

She told them about the tenements in the Tarnish, about how their tiny apartment wasn't much but her family had been happy enough. Mam had been a washwoman in a laundry shop and Da worked in construction.

"Then, when I was eight, there was an accident at work and my da died." Her voice faltered. "Mam started drinking more and more and then she got sick. Right before she died, she made me promise I'd look out for Maeve, that I'd always protect her."

She stopped and took a deep shuddering breath. Here came the worst part. The part where she'd failed Maeve. Emma and Figgy waited patiently until she was able to continue.

"After she died, these policemen came and told us that we were being evicted. The police took Maeve and me to a building on Seventeenth Street. The Gemstone Society for Orphan Welfare." Izzy scrunched her nose up, remembering. It had been two years, but she could still feel the way the sun had burned the back of her neck while they waited on the sidewalk. "Some women came to talk to us. They said they ran a school and that they'd take care of us." She drew her knees up and hugged them. "We shouldn't have trusted them, but they were so nice and proper and they had magic, so we thought they must be good. They took us to a big room where there were lots of other kids waiting. Maeve held my hand until they split up the big kids and the little kids. I was ten and she was eight, so they said we were in different classes. I was so excited. I'd never gone to a real school before, but Maeve didn't want to go. I made her though. I promised her she'd be all right."

"But it wasn't a real school," Emma guessed.

Izzy shook her head and fidgeted with the hem of her nightgown. "By the time I figured it out, they'd put her on a train headed out of town. They said there were people in the country who wanted little kids they could adopt who could grow up and help on the farm." She sat with her legs folded. Her shoulders were hunched forward like she was about to cave in on herself. "I should have looked out for her better."

"You were only ten, Izzy. What were you supposed to do on your own?"

Figgy crawled into her lap and snuggled against her. "I never knew," he said simply as she stroked his head.

"I never told anyone before. I thought if someone

knew I wanted to leave to find Maeve, they would try to stop me."

His steady purr reassured Izzy enough to continue without fidgeting or caving in.

"The Gemstone Society taught me sewing and cleaning and servant stuff there so I could get this job. I've been saving every penny I make for the journey, but after today, I don't know what to do. If I don't have magic or money, what can I offer her? A life as a servant, doing drudge work? But I also can't help her if I'm dead."

Izzy stared at the drafty ceiling with its wooden beams. She had thought she might start crying again after sharing this, but instead she felt like a weight had been lifted from her heart.

"Do you know where she is?" Emma asked.

"She sent me a letter from Omaha, but that was well over a year ago. I don't know if she stayed there or if they took her somewhere else. I have to go look for her myself." Izzy got up and retrieved the well-worn letter from her apron pocket. She held it out to Emma, who took it and read it.

When she looked up from the letter, there was a fierce determination in Emma's eyes. "We're going to get you your better life, Izzy O'Donnell."

"How?" Izzy shifted her feet on the floorboards.

"You offered me a deal and I'll take it—but I'm offering

you my terms first. If we can find a way to kindle and if we knew we could do it right, would you be willing to try?"

Izzy thought it over. She still wanted her magic, but she was scared. "Yes, but we'd have to know for sure what we're doing."

"Figgy, will you help us?"

The house dragon sat up, ears at attention. "Absolutely."

"All right. So we'll get our magic and then I'll go with you to Omaha to find Maeve. Deal?" Emma extended a hand.

"Really? You'd do that for me?" Izzy's heart leaped as Emma nodded. For the first time in what felt like forever, she felt hopeful and light. She hadn't known she could ever feel this way again.

Izzy jumped onto the bed and tackled Emma in a hug. "Deal!" she cried. "Thank you," she said over and over.

Emma laughed. "Look out or you'll squish Figgy!"

"Too late," came a muffled voice from underneath them.

They were laughing so hard they almost missed it. Figgy's head popped up a second before the girls heard it. The top stair outside the attic squeaked.

Someone was at the door.

TWENTY

A Visitor to the Attic

Emma

Emma's heart raced as the stair outside the attic room creaked again. It had to be Miss Posterity. Who else would know they were up here?

Poor Izzy was frozen, staring at the opening door with horror. Of course she was. If Miss Posterity knew they wanted to leave, she was spiteful and desperate enough to do everything in her power to prevent it.

The door creaked fully open. Emma whirled around to face it, expecting doom to walk in.

The intruder held out a kerosene lamp, but the face it illuminated was six inches lower than Emma expected and framed by long black hair.

"Emma? Are you up here?" Frances Slight called into the darkened room.

What was she doing in the attic? Had she come to spy on them? Emma hated to think it, but why else would she be here?

"I'm here," she said, drawing Frances's attention. "Do you need something, Fr—I mean, miss?"

"This place is hard to find." Frances shut the door behind her. She clutched her lamp with one hand and held her dove-gray silk robe closed with the other. Emma tried not to think about how she used to own a robe like it in pale pink.

Frances looked around, taking in the uncovered windows, the exposed rafters with their cobwebs, and the pile of discarded furniture. These things had become normal to Emma, but she thought they must look shabby to Frances.

"The stairs are concealed by magic," Izzy said, pawing at her still-red eyes with her nightgown sleeves. "You can only find it if you have a strong need to get up here."

"Oh, I do!" Frances said, her eyes as wide as saucers. Emma had never seen her so focused before. "Emma, did you hear what happened to Rosie today?"

"I didn't know gossip counted as a strong need," Izzy muttered under her breath.

"I saw it for myself—well, the end bits." Emma caught herself in time. "We came running to help when everyone started screaming. Poor Rosie."

Frances sagged in relief. "So you understand." She sat down on the bed and then scrambled up again. "That's hard as a rock."

This was getting a bit ridiculous. "Frances, what are you doing here?" Emma asked.

"I didn't know where else to go." Frances looked around the attic and her voice wobbled. "You once said your papa was like me, Emma. How did he manage it? Was he stupid in school too? How did he kindle?"

"Oh," Emma said, understanding creeping in. "You're not stupid."

"Miss Posterity says I am. She says I'm going to embarrass my father. He expects me to go on to high school and maybe even university, but I can't even face class tomorrow. I don't want *him* to think I'm stupid." Tears trickled down Frances's cheeks.

Behind Frances's back, Izzy gestured at the door as if to say, *Get her out of here!*

Emma draped an arm around Frances's shoulders and tried to steer her to the stairs. "Don't listen to Miss Posterity. She shouldn't say that about you. My papa always learned best by heart, not by head. You're like that too, I'll bet."

Frances stilled. "I'm so sorry about your papa. It isn't right the way Miss Posterity treats you."

"Thank you." Emma's eyes brimmed with tears. She

hadn't realized how long she'd been hoping to hear someone besides Izzy acknowledge this. "You'd better go back downstairs. She'll be furious if she catches you up here."

"Why even bother?" Frances set her lamp on the broken chair they used as a nightstand and buried her face in her hands. "I'll be burned to a crisp, I know I will. Rosie was the brightest in the class and you saw what happened to her. I'm dreadful at my lessons. Always have been, always will be." She sniffled again. "I'm not worthy of magic."

A few months ago, Emma would have protested that Frances was rich and must have worth, but now she knew that true worth was something deeper than that.

She grabbed her ripped and smudged handkerchief from the dresser. Her crystal lay under it, and instinctively, Emma picked it up and transfigured the handkerchief into a clean white square with sunflowers embroidered around the border. She offered it to Frances.

Frances's tears dried up and she stared at the handkerchief in shock. "How did—I never saw servants do magic before. I didn't know you could."

It was hard to believe she'd once thought the same thing. Now that Emma's eyes were opened, she couldn't ever go back to that way of thinking, but she wondered if she'd ever have woken up in time to Izzy's plight and that of others like her if she hadn't suffered herself. She liked to believe she would have but there was no way to tell now.

"A lot of things have changed for me, but that isn't one of them," she told Frances. "I can still do magic. Well, at least until it snuffs."

Frances dabbed her eyes with the handkerchief. "If you still have magic, Miss Posterity should give your ring back. I heard her telling one of the neighbors that it was an old Posterity heirloom, but we know it was yours."

"Do you know why she keeps it?"

Frances grimaced. "I'd say it's because she's dreadful and mean, but nobody cares what I think." She sat down on the edge of the bed and noticed Figgy for the first time. "Oh, there's a cat up here. Hello."

Figgy swished his tail but kept quiet.

"I think—" Emma started to say, but now that Frances had found someone to listen, it was like a dam had been broken and words she'd held back for years were rushing out.

"Life is so unfair." Frances huffed and tugged her robe tighter. "You're the only one who was decent to me here. Why do people think bratty Beatrice has more worth than you do?" Her shoulders slumped. "I wish there was something I could do to help, but you probably wouldn't want my help anyway."

An idea flickered in her mind. Emma swallowed. "Do you really mean it? You want to help?"

"Oh, yes." The other girl looked at her with watery but earnest eyes.

"Maybe we can help each other." The idea grew brighter. She had promised Izzy they'd find a way to do it correctly. "What if I could help you kindle? What if we could do it together? You can bring your books and notes to us at night and I'll read things out loud to help you learn them by heart."

Izzy jumped to her feet, knocking Figgy from her lap. He licked his paws and glared at them.

"No, this isn't what we agreed," Izzy argued.

"Izzy, don't you see? Frances is exactly what we need and she needs us." Emma turned to Frances. "Izzy and I have already been practicing. We can help you. Look how much I've already learned."

A look came over her face, one she would have recognized if she could have seen it. She looked like her papa when he became enraptured with a new magitectural design.

The attic warmed as she transformed it. She took one of the old bedsheets off the pile of furniture and laid it on the floor. With a wink of her crystal, it became a thick and soft rug. The pile of furniture became three cozy sofas, separated by end tables with lace doilies on top.

The quilt on the bed puffed with down, and Figgy rose three inches as his pillow expanded.

Izzy joined in, adding floral wallpaper to the bare boards and lacy curtains around the windows.

By the time they were done, Emma was sweating and parched. She hadn't meant to do quite this much, but once she'd seen how lovely the room could be, the magitect skills she'd learned from Papa took over and she couldn't stop. She'd never done magic on this scale and it had been harder than she anticipated. Papa would have been so proud of her. The bittersweet thought zapped her last bit of energy and she sat down on the soft bed. Figgy purred happily on his pillow.

Frances and Izzy stared at her, the first with an expression of wonder, the other with guarded optimism.

Emma turned to Frances. "Izzy and I could kindle but we don't know how. You know how but you need help. No one has to know."

"Practicing with you would be almost like having friends." A slow smile spread across Frances's face. "Let's do it."

The house creaked and they all jumped, even the house dragon. After Izzy peeked out the door to make sure there were no more unexpected visitors lurking, they had a hushed conversation in which it was agreed that Frances would meet them in the library after bedtime as often as possible. If someone saw them, Frances could pretend to be studying and Izzy and Emma could pretend to be cleaning. It wasn't a foolproof plan, but it was the best they had.

Finally, when they reasoned that they needed to get some sleep, Frances headed downstairs. As soon as the door shut behind her, the magic wavered and collapsed.

Emma grunted in exhaustion from holding the enchantment so long and flopped onto the hard bed. She turned to Izzy and found her own grin mirrored back at her. Figgy purred on the lone pillow but neither of them minded.

"For a moment, the attic reminded me of your old bedroom." Izzy sighed and pulled up the threadbare quilt. "Frances won't report us, right? They'd throw us in jail if they catch us."

"I'm certain we can trust her." Emma extinguished the lamp. "You heard what she said about Miss Posterity."

"I'm glad we're doing this," Izzy said in the dark. "Maeve would be proud of us."

"We'll find her. I promise."

"Em?" Izzy's voice hitched. "You're not so bad, you know."

She smiled, recognizing this was a compliment.

"Thanks. You're not so bad either. I'm glad we're friends now."

"Me too."

Emma snuggled into bed. Though it had returned to its normal bleak state, the attic felt warmer and cheerier than it had before Frances had come.

TWENTY-ONE
Word on the Street

Izzy

Izzy stifled a yawn behind her hand as she strolled through the Saturday market stalls.

Vendors called out their wares to the shoppers, advertising the plump zucchinis, green beans, and eggplants that lined their stalls. The vegetables were as colorful and pristine as the Gem Row houses for which they were destined.

It'd been eleven days since the early Winds. Rosie had returned from the hospital covered in bandages, only to be whisked home to recuperate by her proud but concerned parents. The mood in the school was quiet, everyone preoccupied with thoughts of her own upcoming kindling.

Izzy and Emma were no exception. Frances had met

them in the library again last night and they'd practiced what Frances had learned of the kindling ceremony dance. Though her body was tired, Izzy felt a wonderful sense of accomplishment. Every step felt like a victory, like they might actually be able to pull this off. They had their crystals, the incantation, and were learning the movements. Their biggest problem would be getting their hands on a set of kindling flints. Miss Posterity would never lend them hers and they had no idea where they could get a set of their own.

Izzy glanced around at the bustling street. Where was Emma? They should be heading back soon. A woman with a broad skirt pushed past her, nearly knocking the basket of vegetables from Izzy's hands. She stepped out of the way and found herself next to a stall selling beautiful summer flowers. Dazzling golden-petaled sunflowers stood in a bucket at knee level. She bent forward to breathe in their sunbaked scent.

"My papa used to say it was hard to be unhappy in a world in which there are sunflowers," Emma said, coming up behind her. She carried the jar of boot polish she'd gone in search of.

Izzy snorted in disagreement.

"I know now." Emma sighed wistfully. She took the basket from Izzy and tucked the boot polish inside. "Papa loved sunflowers. Someone gave him a packet of seeds when we lived in Savannah and he grew them in front of the houses we rented in Charleston and Washington, D.C. I think he would have kept going, but he ran out of seeds."

To Izzy, who had never left New York City, these places were exotic names on a map. "How come you never talk about this? How many homes have you had?"

"They were houses, not homes," Emma corrected. "I've lived in at least sixteen places, though I hardly remember some of them. I'll always remember those sunflowers, though." She touched the yellow petals fondly.

Izzy was still struggling with how to respond when the hair on the back of her neck prickled. Someone was watching them. She glanced around, looking for the source of her discomfort, and spotted a man peering at them from the butcher's stall. His suit was far too clean to be a butcher—in fact, he was wearing a heavy brown tweed coat despite the heat.

"Em, do you know that man watching us from behind the ham?" she whispered.

The blood drained from Emma's face. "That's the inspector. The one who came to the school."

Seeing he'd been spotted, the man stepped toward them. "I recognize you." He pointed at Emma and Izzy. "Do you both work up at Miss Preposterously's school? I need to ask you a few questions. I'm looking for a young lady—"

"We don't know her," Izzy called back as she grabbed Emma and hauled her away through the market.

"Wait!" the man shouted after them.

Emma stumbled over her own feet and the grocery basket banged into Izzy's side.

"Don't run, it'll draw attention," Izzy warned.

They hurried through a stall selling eggs—carefully on account of the eggs—and kept their heads down as they threaded their way toward Fifth Avenue. When they reached the edge of the market, they paused beside a stall selling dried pasta.

Izzy risked a glance over her shoulder but didn't see the man in tweed. "Take off your cap and apron. He's looking for two maids," she said, pulling off her own.

"Is he following us?" Emma worried as she stuffed their uniforms into the vegetable basket.

"Emma!" a voice called behind them.

As Izzy readied herself to flee, Tom stepped out from behind a sign advertising magical tooth-whitening powder. He had a small sack of flour under one arm and his newspaper bag was slung over his shoulder.

Emma pressed a hand to her chest, a flush rising in her cheeks. "What are you doing here?"

"Shopping for Ma." He stopped in front of them. "Are you all right? You look awfully pale."

"We're fine," Izzy insisted. She'd met Emma's friend many times when he delivered papers and he seemed nice enough for a boy, but she didn't want him hanging around now. "We have to go."

Emma clutched the grocery basket tighter. "Sorry, Tom. Nice to see you."

"Let me walk you back up to the school. You look like you've had a fright," Tom offered. "I'll carry that basket for you."

First Frances, now this boy. What was it about Emma that had people falling over themselves to help her? At first Izzy'd thought it was her money but from what Emma had told her, Tom had no idea she'd been rich.

Before Izzy could protest, Emma handed the basket to Tom. "Thank you. I do feel a little light-headed."

Izzy grumbled under her breath, but then realized that walking with Tom aided their disguise. She risked a look over her shoulder and saw the man in tweed in the next row over of stalls. He was facing the other direction and Izzy wasn't about to wait for him to turn around.

"Let's walk through the park," she suggested. Between the crowds and the twisting trails and winding walks, he'd never be able to follow them there.

They crossed the street toward the leafy green canopy.

Parasols dotted the lawn as the residents of Gem Row gathered to enjoy the beautiful day. As they walked, Tom filled the silence with a funny story about his little brother's first sparking a few days ago. Matteo had singed the chicken's tail feathers and she'd laid an egg in surprise, right in the middle of the living room.

Izzy sized Tom up, trying to see what about him made Emma blush. She didn't exactly know how to tell if a boy was cute or not, but she thought that gap between his teeth wasn't doing him any favors. There were different levels of poor, and even though Emma had described Tom as being quite poor, his family was clearly better off than Izzy's had been. His boots didn't have holes in them.

"Shall we walk this way?" Emma suggested, pointing at the broad path that led alongside the pond.

"We shall," Tom and Izzy replied at the same time in hoity-toity voices. They all laughed and, for the first time since they'd seen the man in tweed, Izzy let herself relax. Either he hadn't cared that much about questioning two servant girls or they'd lost him. Emma was safe for now.

They made their way along the path. The air was different in Central Park. While so much of the city was gray and brown, the park felt like breathing blues and greens.

A girl and her younger sister stood at the edge of the

pond, watching the ducks. Maeve loved animals. Or at least she used to, but it'd been two years since Izzy had seen her. Had her sister changed? Izzy swallowed a lump in her throat and turned to find Emma observing her like she guessed what Izzy was thinking. It was surprisingly nice to have someone understand.

Tom followed their gazes and smiled at the ducks. "The birds love this place."

"Did you know Central Park was designed by a famous magitect, Frederick Olmsted?" Emma's face shone in the bright sunshine. "My papa studied . . ." Her voice trailed off. "Never mind."

"Your father what?" Tom encouraged.

Emma shook her head. Tom looked curious, but didn't pry further. Izzy respected him for that.

They turned up the East Drive, parallel to Fifth Avenue. The sidewalk was busy on this sunny afternoon and they dodged mothers pushing prams and children riding the pedal-powered toy cars that were popular at the moment.

As they neared the old arsenal, the energy in the air changed and a noise like the distant rumble of a streetcar filled the air. Quite a few people turned around and hurried back the way they'd come. The closer they got to the arsenal building, the louder the noise got and Izzy realized it was voices—lots of voices. People were hurrying toward the building, most of them dressed in working-class clothes and carrying signs and banners.

Three boys carrying picket signs stopped when they saw them. They had the hunched shoulders of street shoe-polishers and stained fingers to match. Their signs read I AM WORTH IT, MAGIC 4 EVERYBODY, and STOP THE SNUFFING. The word *snuffing* was squeezed against the side of the sign, each letter decreasing in size. Izzy wasn't sure if it was an apt commentary on snuffing or if they'd simply run out of room.

The tallest boy was about their age with eyes the same warm brown as his skin. He waved at Tom. "Spaghetti! Are you coming too?"

"How's it rolling, Dice?" Tom said, slapping palms with him. "What's going on over there?"

"We're standing up for our rights." Dice shifted his sign to his other shoulder. "Some kids downtown got hurt in the early Winds. The city says they shoulda had the snuffing buckets ready, but people aren't gonna settle for that. We want to kindle."

"The system is rigged and we're ready to fix it," the boy with the MAGIC 4 EVERYBODY sign insisted with the hard *r*'s of a Polish accent.

"Word on the street is that the mayor is going to make a speech. They say he's sympathetic to our cause." Dice arched an eyebrow. "You should come with us."

Tom shifted the basket. "I wish I could, but I promised these ladies I'd see them home. Unless they want to come too?"

Izzy would have laughed at being called a lady, but the threat of the rally was enough to squash her humor. She'd seen protests before in the Tarnish, over food and housing, and she'd seen them turn ugly.

"No, thanks," she said before Emma had a chance to respond.

"It might be nice to hear the mayor speak?" Emma suggested.

"Cook's expecting us." Izzy held out her hand for the vegetable basket, but to her surprise, Tom didn't relinquish it.

"Well, you heard the ladies, boys. Give a good shout for me." Tom shrugged.

"You can stay if you want," Emma said as the boys and their signs headed toward the noise of the crowd.

"Nah," Tom said with a dismissive wave. "Someday I'll go to rallies and write about them too, but I'd never hear the end of it from Ma if I went without her permission. Let's go."

They turned right onto the path toward the exit at Sixty-Fourth Street. The crowd there was thinner, mostly mothers and their young children coming or going from the menagerie. The children were too enraptured by their balloons and the mothers too preoccupied with their children to care about two servant girls and a newsie. It felt quieter, with none of the lingering tension of the protest crowds.

"Did you know there was a protest today?" Izzy asked Tom. "You must have read about it in the paper."

Tom shook his head. "There wasn't anything about it in *The Kindled Courier*, at least. They did run an article yesterday about how the summer Winds stirred up conflict around the city. They're expecting more unrest before December."

"Is that why the mayor is speaking? Trying to stop it?" said Izzy, disliking him if it were true.

"Nah," Tom said. "He's a progressive and believes in rights for all people." He scratched his nose. "Still, I wouldn't put it past him to try to prevent riots. People aren't going to take this quietly anymore. Mark my words, the world's changing."

"Magic's calling to more people again. It wants to burn free," Emma said, echoing Figgy's warning. She had a funny, contemplative look in her eyes that Izzy guessed might have something to do with her father and the magitect she'd mentioned earlier.

"*Burn free.* That'd look great on a protest sign," Tom suggested.

Izzy snorted. "You won't catch me at a protest. I'm

not sticking my neck out to help anybody get their magic except Emma and myself this December."

She realized her mistake as soon as the words left her mouth.

Tom stopped short with a stunned expression on his face. Apparently, Emma had not told him about their plan. He looked between them. "You're going to try to kindle."

"Don't say it so loud," Izzy hissed. She was furious with herself for such a terrible slip-up.

"But you're—"

"Shush." Ignoring propriety, she dragged him off the path over to the trees. A nearby young mother gave them a funny look, but then her little boy began to wail and she hurried away.

Izzy stuck a finger in Tom's face. "Don't you dare report us to the Registry. Emma knows where you live."

"Whoa." Tom threw up his hands. "Ease off, Iz. You can trust me." Tom turned to Emma, lowering his voice. "Are you really going through with this?"

"I'm sorry, Tom, but I have to." Emma bit her lip. "I know what your mother said about it being dangerous, and about Paolo, but we have a plan. We're being careful."

Tom took off his cap and ran his hand through his wavy black hair. He stared at the ground for a long moment. A bird sang in the trees above them. Izzy didn't know birds well enough to tell what kind it was, but its song sounded sweet and sad.

At last, Tom spoke again. "If you're going to kindle, I want in too."

"Absolutely not," Izzy replied.

"Come on," Tom pleaded. "I won't report you. I'm sure there's something I can do to help."

"We're fine on our own, thanks."

"Both of you, keep your voices down," Emma insisted. She looked back and forth between them. "Actually, Tom, there is one thing we could use some help with. We need something, a last piece necessary to kindling that we haven't been able to get on our own."

A knot hardened in Izzy's gut as Emma explained their lack of kindling flints.

"You mentioned someone who could get kindling supplies downtown. Do you think he could help us?" Emma asked.

Tom nodded. "I know a guy who knows a guy. I can ask around."

"Emma, you can't seriously be considering this. Involving Frances is bad enough. How are we going to sneak a *boy* into the school to practice?"

"We'll figure it out." Emma looked at Izzy. "But I won't agree to it unless we're unanimous, Izzy."

"I'll find you the flints. I promise. Just let me kindle with you," Tom said.

Izzy could tell Tom was serious because he didn't even smile when Emma said *unanimous*. They really did need help finding the flints. It was too hard for her to leave the school and few people knew New York better than the newsies.

"Fine," she said, and huffed. Their rapidly expanding kindling circle made her uneasy. This was so far away from her plan of kindling by herself, she didn't know what to make of it anymore.

A slow grin spread across Tom's face. "We could change the world if we do this, you know. Kids like us, keeping their magic."

Izzy glared at him. "News flash, newsboy. Every person we bring into this means a risk of exposure—and jail, so let's leave the rest of the world out of it, all right?"

Tom raised his hands in defense. "I won't even tell my ma. Happy?"

The clock above the entrance to the menagerie chimed four.

"We'd better go," Emma said. "I'd prefer not to have my ears boxed again."

Izzy agreed wholeheartedly, so they left the privacy of the trees and hurried back to the bustle of Fifth Avenue.

"So where is this guy downtown?" Izzy asked as they walked.

"Somewhere in the Tarnish. I heard about him from a newsie who sells down there."

Izzy's heart gave an uneasy thump at the name of her old neighborhood. She glanced at where the tops of the skyscrapers in Midtown were visible above the trees in the park. South of them, the Tarnish waited. She'd promised herself she'd never go back there.

Emma shivered. "I heard it's violent in the Tarnish."

"I can protect myself, don't worry," Tom reassured her.

Izzy also knew how to protect herself from the street thugs and hooligans. It was the memories lurking there that frightened her.

"Are you all right, Iz?" Emma asked.

"I'm fine," she said a little too quickly. They reached the corner of Sixty-Fourth and Izzy grabbed the basket from Tom so fast she almost spilled the vegetables. "You'd better go. No one at the school can see you. If they reported us—"

She didn't need to finish the sentence. They all understood the risk they were taking.

They said their goodbyes, and Emma and Izzy headed toward the back-alley entrance to the academy.

"Are you sure you're fine?" Emma asked.

"You trust people too easily." Izzy didn't want to tell

her about the Tarnish and what was really bothering her. "You can't keep doing that—bringing people in. Soon we'll be teaching everyone in Manhattan to kindle."

"I'm sorry," Emma apologized. "I wasn't planning it. But you see the sense in it, don't you?"

Izzy harrumphed. She did, but she wasn't in the mood to admit it.

TWENTY-TWO

The Kindling Club

Emma

Sneaking Tom into the school to practice magic proved even more complicated than they had guessed. It took a full two weeks for them to convince Frances, who went pale and had a tendency to drop things every time someone uttered the word *boy*. Then there was the matter of locating a spot to practice where they wouldn't be discovered and finding a night when they were sure Miss Posterity would be out late. As such, it was mid-August before they convened for their first kindling practice as a group.

The grandfather clock in the front hall chimed ten o'clock as Emma opened the hidden door to the kitchen. Miss Posterity was at a society dinner a few blocks away and wouldn't be back until after midnight. The rest of the school had gone to bed, but every creak and groan the old house made set Emma on edge. Figgy had helped them with their plan but Emma was still nervous.

She started at the sight of someone leaning against the kitchen counter but it was only Frances.

"I told her she wasn't allowed in here," said Figgy.

Frances eyed the house dragon. He'd decided to trust her with the secret of his true nature recently and she was still getting used to it. "But what if someone saw me waiting in the hall?"

"Keep your voices low," Izzy cautioned, coming down the stairs behind them. "If Miss Posterity catches us, we're toast."

"Toast is revolting. Is there any gravy left?" Figgy licked his lips. "I need my energy if I'm going to recall a practice room for you tonight."

"I wish you'd stop being so mysterious," Emma said.

"Yeah. Can't you just tell us how your magic works?" Izzy prodded.

Figgy glared at her. "I told you before, if I explained everything, it would be far less interesting."

Izzy rolled her eyes, but she went to fetch the gravy from the icebox anyway.

Frances looked unconvinced. "So as a dragon, can you breathe fire?"

"Don't be disgusting." Figgy put a paw to his throat. "Do you know what that would do to my vocal cords?"

Emma glanced at the door. It was dark outside the windows, and the night felt full of expectation. "Do you think he changed his mind about kindling?"

"It's possible. I almost change my mind every day," Frances said, and shrugged.

Emma folded and refolded a napkin. It wasn't just the flints. She couldn't explain why it felt so important that Tom get his magic too. She set the napkin aside and paced up and down the length of the kitchen.

Izzy shut the icebox door. "Emma, stop. You're making me dizzy. He'll be here." She set a bowl of gravy down on the floor.

Figgy recoiled. "It's cold."

Izzy put her hands on her hips. Emma would never tell her that she looked like Cook at that moment. "I'm not lighting the stove. Take it or leave it, Figs."

Frances wrapped her silk robe tighter and poked her head into the scullery like a sightseer. "Are we a secret club now? I've always wanted to be in a secret club but it's hard to get invited to things when no one likes you."

"Do you ever listen to yourself?" Izzy shook her head and went into the scullery to wash gravy off her hands.

Frances blinked. "What did I say?"

"Can you two please get along?" Emma sighed and

stopped pacing. Something glinting on the floor caught her eye. A shard of broken glass lay on the floor from where she had dropped a water glass earlier.

As she bent to pick it up, Emma wished she had a mirror so she could make sure there wasn't any dirt on her face before Tom got here. The glass flashed and her dirt-free reflection stared back at her, as clear as in any mirror she'd ever seen. She almost dropped the glass in surprise. A thought niggled at the back of her mind, but she couldn't quite summon it into words. The magic must have happened because she had her crystal in her pocket. It couldn't possibly have been the glass itself.

Three soft knocks sounded at the door, a pause, then two more.

"That's the password." Emma threw the glass in the rubbish bin and hurried toward the door.

Frances's eyes lit up. "We have a secret club password?"

Emma opened the door, careful not to make a sound. Tom's face looked longer and more angular in the moonlight light. He took off his cap. "Evening, Emma. Should I, uh, come in?" He shifted and glanced around the kitchen behind her.

Emma realized she'd been blocking the entrance. She stepped aside and shut the door quietly behind him.

"Tom, this is Frances. She's been teaching us."

Tom held out his hand. "Pleased to meet you." He squinted. "Have we met before?"

Frances shook his hand limply. "Don't think so. I get that a lot."

Emma was puzzled. Why did people think Frances looked familiar? She hadn't thought so when she first saw her. Tom must have seen her while he was selling papers near the school or something.

Izzy emerged from the scullery. "Any news on the flints?"

"Not yet, but soon, I hope. Some people in the Tarnish don't like to be found."

Emma opened her mouth to reassure him that they understood, but Izzy wasn't one for chitchat.

"Then let's get started. We have two hours before Miss Posterity gets back," she said. "Figgy?"

The house dragon had a gravy mustache. He trotted toward the stairs, tail straight in the air. "Shoes off, please. Tonight we will be as quiet as mice."

Tom's eyes went as wide as dinner plates. "Did your cat just talk?"

"He's a house dragon," Emma explained.

"Uh-huh." He looked around the kitchen like he wondered what other delightful surprises might be hidden at the school.

They left their shoes in the broom closet and tiptoed after Figgy into the upstairs hall. He'd assured them he knew the perfect place to practice. Emma wished she'd pressed him for more details when he stopped in front of the bust of Prudence Posterity in the front hall.

"Everyone stand back," Figgy whispered.

Muttering to himself, the house dragon marched back and forth in front of the bust three times. The air shimmered above him like it had that first night when he'd recalled the library. Emma was about to ask what he was doing, when, without warning, the front of the pedestal disappeared. Emma blinked. One second it was marble, the next, an inky blackness.

"Come on," Figgy said. He dashed inside at a full run. Emma waited for the *thunk* when he hit the other side, but it never came. When he spoke again, his voice echoed as if from far away. "It's a little chilly, but your magic will fix that. Hurry up!"

Izzy and Emma exchanged a look. The pedestal was only as high as the kitchen counter and barely wider than their shoulders. It looked like the perfect place for a cat to hide, but there was no way four humans could squeeze into it.

Everyone shifted, not wanting to go first. Emma clenched her hands. She'd brought them together.

"I'm sure it's fine," she said. She crouched forward,

ducking her head to fit under the pedestal, and stepped forward into the blackness.

The floor beneath her stockings was cold, and the room was so dark she could barely see her hand in front of her face. "Figgy?" She reached a hand overhead and found she had more than enough room to stand up straight. Behind her, the small rectangle of light that was the doorway looked farther away than it should have.

"Over here. I found a lamp."

She followed Figgy's voice. Emma knew she was still indoors, but something about the space gave her the strange feeling of being outside under a starless sky.

Her hands found the glass of an old-fashioned oil lamp. She gripped her crystal and lit the wick. A chain reaction followed, as two more lamps sparked to light, illuminating a space twice the length and width of the upstairs hallway. Around the edges of the light, majestic black clouds of what looked like fog or smoke billowed at knee height. On a whim, she reached out to her magic. The whole room shifted to be the bright purple of a plum, the exact shade she'd pictured. Emma grinned. Whatever this place was, it was pure magic.

"Emma?" Izzy called. "Where are you?"

"You can come in. It's safe, I think." Emma's voice echoed, though she wasn't sure how without any visible walls. Her friends entered through the purple fog, one by one. Frances hugged her class notebook to her chest and looked around in wonder.

"Watch," Emma told them. She shifted the smoke to a soothing pale blue.

Frances kicked at the swirling mist and then shrieked and ducked as it spun back at her in a harmless whorl.

"What is this place?" Izzy asked.

"The space between rooms. Where else did you think they went when they're not crowding the first floor?" Figgy replied like it should have been obvious.

"Does Miss Posterity know about this?" Frances asked as Emma's sparking faded and the smoke turned black once more.

Figgy shook his head. "Only a house dragon can access this space. You're safe to practice here."

"This is brilliant, Figgy!" Izzy applauded. They each rushed to thank him.

"You are most welcome." The house dragon bent his front knee in a bow. "Now, get practicing. I'll be over here." He bounded away, black fur disappearing into the swirling black.

The space felt bigger without him. Tom pulled his pocket watch out, passing it from hand to hand. Emma wondered what to do with her own hands. Everything she did seemed to look strange and awkward. Finally, she dug her hands into her apron pockets, gripping the stubby crystal hidden there.

"Um, should we start the lesson?" Frances asked. When everyone murmured his or her agreement, she swallowed nervously. Black smoke swirled around her ankles.

Izzy shifted. "It's only just occurred to me—do you think kindling is different for boys? Do they do the same dance?"

"Dance?" Tom chuckled and stopped abruptly. "Oh, you're serious. It's a dance?"

Frances bit her lip. "Kindling starts in your hands and the dance moves the magic through your entire body. Miss Posterity has never mentioned boys."

"It's the same. Figgy helped me look it up in the library." Emma smiled at Tom with reassurance, but he was distracted and kept fiddling with his watch.

"Might as well get started." As she spoke, Frances's shoulders hunched closer and closer to her ears. Without waiting for a reply, she clutched her gem necklace with one hand and held the other up toward the ceiling. A small flame flickered to life. This had become their nightly starting ritual.

Izzy closed her eyes, concentrating, and held up her palm. Flames burst in her hand like a rose, burning red at the base.

Red like blood. Red like a ruby ring. Emma bit back the anger and pain that always accompanied thoughts of her ring on Miss Posterity's finger.

To her surprise, Tom's palm lit next to her. His fire burned a different shade than Izzy's—more orange than red. Emma felt a surge of pride. He must have been practicing on his own already.

Emma looked at her friends, waiting for her, and she had a vision of them living together in a big magical house somewhere. The unexpected idea filled her with so much joy, a golden flame whooshed into her palm. It tickled.

"Good," Frances said. "Now, um." She paused and shuffled the pages in her notebook. She seemed unusually flustered, even for Frances.

"Tell him how we'd start if this was a real kindling," Emma prompted.

"Right." Frances swallowed. "In the real kindling, the flames would start on their own as soon as the Winds begin to blow. You would take a kindling flint in each hand, and strike them together." Frances demonstrated, knocking her two fists together like she was ringing an invisible gong, then stretched her arms wide.

"Why are these flints so important?" Tom asked.

Frances flipped back in her notebook. "You have to hold on to the flints or the magic could leak out of your hands after it ignites. Then there'd be no magic left to kindle."

Emma swallowed. There were so many ways for magic to snuff and only one right way to kindle.

"So you hold them and the magic stays in you?" Tom asked. "I guess it's similar to how you put stones around a fire to keep it from spreading."

"Um, sure." Frances bit her lip.

Izzy rolled her eyes and looked ready to make a sarcastic comment, so Emma jumped in. "Miss Posterity told the class you put magic in them, but we're not sure how yet."

"We think there might be holes in them somewhere," Frances explained.

Izzy swung her arms around. "Enough talk. Let's move."

Frances fidgeted and blue sparks fizzled at her fingertips. "So, um." She looked to Emma. "Will you read the steps out loud as we go, please?"

Emma nodded and began to read. Frances moved through the steps slowly so Tom could keep up. What Tom lacked in grace, he made up for in enthusiasm. He swept his arms through the air and turned a half second behind the girls. Whenever he caught Emma's eye and smiled, she felt a sense of rightness that he was here.

With each step, Frances's shoulders relaxed away

from her ears. She even stopped and corrected Tom's plié form.

The mist swirled around them as they danced. Their bodies warmed with the heat of the magic and the exertion of dancing the steps over and over. At some point, Figgy came back and watched them.

"So much time wasted on dancing. You should be focusing on the magic."

"We are," Emma insisted. "This is an important part."

For a moment, Figgy looked like he was about to launch into another "in my day" speech, but then he eyed the door. "Miss Posterity will be back soon. Time to go."

Izzy picked him up and gave him a kiss on the top of his head. "Thank you for showing us this place."

The house dragon purred. The spinning of the clouds around them increased.

When they emerged through the pedestal, the house felt still, like the whole world had been holding its breath while they practiced. They crept back to the kitchen to get their shoes while Figgy stood sentry in the hall.

"This was the most magical night of my life," Tom whispered. "We're actually going to do this, aren't we? We're going to kindle."

Emma suddenly felt shy, though she'd been with him

for the past two hours. Her stomach flipped like it was practicing a dance of its own. “We’re going to kindle,” she repeated.

She unlatched the back door for him and he turned to wave at the end of the alley. His smile was as bright as the stars. As she watched him fade into the night, Emma wondered whether she’d made a mistake by promising to leave with Izzy as soon as they had their magic.

TWENTY-THREE

The Man in the Tweed Coat Returns

Izzy

The days grew shorter and the attic grew colder at night. Across the street, the trees in Central Park burst into beautiful red, orange, and gold. Izzy's arms and legs ached from practicing the kindling dance more and more and, as a result, getting less and less sleep. It was well into October and Izzy knew she should be worried because there had been no sign of the kindling flints, yet magic felt closer and closer every day. Last night, Frances had manifested flames in both palms at the same time and the week before, Tom and Emma had both managed to do the kindling dance perfectly without anyone calling out the steps.

One particular afternoon, Izzy paused on the back steps to enjoy the silence. The students were on their daily walk under the fall foliage with Miss Clementine and the house felt still and serene. She supposed a part of her would miss this place when she was gone. Or at the very least, these quiet moments.

"Everything all right?" Emma asked, entering the stairwell from the first floor.

Izzy felt an excited whoosh in her chest. They were going to kindle and Emma was coming with her to find Maeve. This was really happening.

"Never better," Izzy replied, and grinned the whole way down the stairs.

When they reached the kitchen, they found a scene that was anything but quiet. Cook staggered around, knocking pots off the shelves while clutching her hand to her chest and howling in pain. A shiny and painful-looking burn was already starting to blister on her palm.

"What are you gaping at?" she snapped.

Emma blinked away her surprise. "Your hand! What happened?"

To Izzy's surprise, tears glistened on Cook's cheeks. "I burned it on the stove making the tea." She swung her free hand at the offending appliance. "It's my own fault. I was thinking about everything I've got to get done today and wasn't looking at what I was doing."

Not sure how to handle the situation, Izzy picked up the kettle and one of the pots that had been knocked to the floor by Cook's blunderings. She set them on the counter and went to get a rag to clean up the spilled water.

"There, there," Emma said. "It looks painful. Have you run cold water on it?"

"No time. The mistress will be back any minute from her fancy garden party luncheon and she'll want tea when she arrives. I've been here for fifteen years but she wouldn't hesitate to sack me if I displease her."

"I'm sure—never mind." Emma paused, reconsidering whatever false reassurance she'd been about to utter.

With a shock, Izzy turned and saw that Emma was consoling Cook, patting her on her good arm. Her own instincts told her to keep far away from Cook when she was upset.

"Come with me. You can't do anything until we get that cleaned up." Emma led Cook into the scullery, and a moment later, the faucet squeaked on. Cook sighed with relief, and then, shockingly, began to cry.

"I don't know why you're being nice to me." She hiccupped. "I don't mean to be cross with you two. No one understands what it's like to have to make horrible food and for such low wages, year in and year out. I wanted to be a real chef in a fancy restaurant, not be here serving up Blandings. But the restaurants don't hire chefs without magic, y'know." She blew her nose loudly in her handkerchief.

Izzy was stunned. She'd never thought of Cook as having dreams. With a shock, Izzy realized that if she didn't kindle, she might end up bitter and magicless too one day. It was strange feeling empathy for Cook.

Emma appeared at the scullery door. "She's not going to be able to do anything with that hand today. We'll have to cover for her so Miss Posterity doesn't know she's injured."

"What and do the cooking plus our work?" Izzy's hands flew to her hips.

"Yes. It's the right thing to do," Emma said simply. "Will you get us some bandages, please? She says they're upstairs in the headmistress's office."

Izzy hesitated. Every reflex shouted at her to not get involved, but she could still hear Cook's whimpers.

Muttering under her breath about her own foolish sympathies, Izzy hurried upstairs. She knocked once at the headmistress's office and waited. Then she remembered Miss Posterity was away at one of her many social engagements. Trying not to disturb anything, she crossed the room and opened the medicine chest.

She pulled out the bandages and as she did so, a tiny golden key slid out from beneath them and clinked across the floor. She picked up the key and her eye caught on Miss Posterity's desk. There was a keyhole in one of the drawers.

Curious as to what Miss Posterity would keep locked up, Izzy tiptoed over and slipped the key into the drawer. Inside, she found a pearl necklace and several sets of diamond earrings. There was no sign of Emma's ruby ring, but this was clearly where Miss Posterity kept her jewelry. This could have been useful if Emma wasn't such a goody-goody about not stealing anything when they left.

She pushed the drawer back in and locked it. On the top of the desk, Miss Posterity's ledger of the school accounts lay open. Izzy's stomach twisted. They'd been so wrapped up in practicing, they hadn't discussed Emma's bills in weeks. In fact, she'd almost forgotten about them. She wondered how often Emma thought about them. Probably a lot.

Izzy was sliding the key back into its hiding spot in the medicine cabinet when the front doorbell rang. *Stones*, who could be calling at this hour? She was tempted to ignore it, but anyone who could bloom the rose was too important to be kept waiting.

The house felt still and empty, and her footsteps sounded loud on the tiled floor. She put on her most polite expression and opened the door.

Izzy's knees went weak when she found herself eye-level with the lapels of a tweed coat. The man who'd been chasing them in the market looked older and more weathered up close, but the stern look on his face was the same.

"Can I help you?" Her voice shook. How much trouble would she get in if she slammed the door right now?

"I'm Inspector Conduit. Tell Miss Poultry I must speak with her immediately."

"I'm sorry, but our headmistress Miss *Posterity* is out. Good day to you." Izzy tried to shut the door.

The man stopped it with his hand. "Perhaps you can help me—"

The front gate swung shut with a *clang*, and Miss Posterity strutted up the front path behind him. She wore a large hat with an ostrich feather bursting from the brim like a fountain.

"Hello, sir. What can I do for you?" she called.

Izzy winced. A few more seconds and he would have been gone.

"Ah," said the inspector, turning around. "Just the person I was seeking: Miss Prosperity."

"Posterity," the headmistress corrected, but truth be told, her smile widened at the mistake.

The headmistress glided up the front stairs and Izzy

opened the door for both of them. Inside, Miss Posterity removed her gloves, but the man didn't take off his bowler hat.

"Would you like to come in, Mr.—?" Miss Posterity asked, her face a mask of polite indifference.

"Inspector Conduit, ma'am." The man frowned. "We met this past June?"

"We did? Forgive me, I meet so many people in my line of work."

Izzy knew Miss Posterity was lying, but the inspector merely frowned. Izzy looked back and forth between them like she was watching a game of catch. They both seemed to have forgotten she was there. She wished she wasn't.

The inspector opened a leather notebook and spoke, sometimes reading from the writing inside. "I came to you on the matter of a young lady named Ella"—he consulted his notes—"er, Emma Harris. I've been making inquiries and a Mrs. Meddler of Fifty-Eighth Street claims to have seen a girl matching Miss Harris's description riding a golden bicycle in Central Park last Tuesday." He looked up. "What say you to that, eh?"

While he spoke, Miss Posterity's face turned an amusing and alarming shade of purple.

"A golden bicycle? Don't be preposterous. What exactly are you asking me, sir?"

"Ma'am, it's a simple question. I'd like to take Miss"—he glanced at his notebook again—"Harris down to the station today. So, is she here?"

Izzy held her breath. He was going to take Emma to the police station—and then to the workhouse, because some stupid client in San Francisco sent bills she couldn't pay. She waited for Miss Posterity to reply, dreading the answer.

"No," Miss Posterity said with finality. "I told you before, she's gone and not coming back."

She put her hand on her hip and Izzy nearly gasped when she saw Emma's ruby ring twinkling on the headmistress's finger. The inspector's eyes went right to it. For a moment, Izzy feared that he had recognized it too, but then he smiled.

"That's a lovely ring, ma'am."

Miss Posterity looked at it. "Oh, this old thing? It's been in the family for years."

Izzy's blood began to boil. She longed to yank the golden band right off her finger. She must have made a noise, because the inspector turned his gaze on her. "You look familiar," he said. "Have we met before?"

"N-no," Izzy stuttered. She dropped her gaze to her hands. Cook's bandages were still clutched in her palms. Never in her life had she wanted to get back to the kitchen so badly.

The inspector handed a card with his name and address to Miss Posterity. "I will be continuing my own inquiries. If the girl does return, contact me at Pinkerton headquarters."

Miss Posterity nodded, though clearly she had no intention of doing so. He adjusted his tweed coat and left. When the door closed behind him, Izzy realized her heart was racing like she'd run a great distance.

Miss Posterity harrumphed. "I'll be in my office. Tell Cook to send tea."

As soon as she disappeared from sight, a feline shape detached itself from the shadow under the bust of Mrs. Posterity and stared at Izzy with bright yellow eyes.

"That was a close one," Figgy said.

"I know."

"Cook's still crying downstairs."

"The bandages!" Izzy yelped, and raced toward the kitchen.

Her resolve strengthened as she rushed down the steps. It wasn't safe for Emma to stay here a second longer than necessary. They had to be ready to kindle in December, and to leave immediately after. Tom had better find those flints soon.

TWENTY-FOUR

In the Space Between Rooms

Peony-pink smoke curled around Emma's ankles. She chanted the incantation with the others and they swung their arms in synchronized arcs.

Now that it was November and the December Winds were getting closer every day, it was rare for one of them to miss a practice. But Tom was at a workers' rights rally with his father, so the girls danced facing each other in a triangle. Their faces were red from the exertion and the heat of the magic. A thin trickle of sweat dripped down Frances's forehead. Their magic depended on every step being perfect.

"Everyone get some water," Frances said when they'd reached the end of the sequence. "That's enough practice."

"You're hardly practicing, the way I see it. All this

whirling about. How many times do I have to tell you to focus on the magic? You need to be able to control it." Figgy's tail rapped the ground, sending the smoke swirling.

"We are focusing on the magic, Figgy!" Izzy groaned. "Frances is a good teacher."

"Oh." Frances's already flushed face reddened even more. "Thank you."

Emma headed toward a tray with a pitcher of water, some glasses, and a handful of delicious cookies that Cook had left on the counter with a note that said *For E. & I.* in cramped handwriting. They'd covered for her for five days while her hand healed, and she'd been leaving them little gifts like this ever since. She seemed to know they were up to something but, bless her heart, she hadn't asked for any details.

Izzy made a spreading gesture and the smoke condensed into a sofa. She grabbed a glass of water and collapsed onto it. It'd gotten a lot cozier in here since she'd figured out this trick. The only problem was, if her concentration broke, so did her seat.

"How can you nap when we've got magic to do?" Emma teased.

"We've been working for hours. It's hard to concentrate when I'm tired." Izzy draped an elbow over her eyes.

"It'll be even harder to concentrate when you're on

fire," Frances piped up. The silence that followed underscored the accuracy of this statement.

Emma played with the colored smoke to distract herself from thinking about the flames. Papa had taught her to build sandcastles at the beach in California, and this wasn't so different. Smoke followed the shapes she made in her hands, and if she concentrated, it stayed where she put it.

She molded a front door and shutters around the windows. Like she had in her sketchbook, she added little smoke rosebushes out front and an iron railing to the front steps. She felt a pang of sadness at its loveliness. Why hadn't she shown Papa her design when she'd had the chance? It was hard to believe he'd been gone for over six months now. When she missed him most it helped to think about the good times they'd shared, like building the sandcastles. Ever the magitect, Papa had sculpted his with Corinthian columns. The memory made her smile.

"That's a pretty house, Emma," Izzy said softly.

Her words shattered Emma's focus. The beautiful house disintegrated and for a moment, the smoke took on a distinctive tweed pattern. Izzy had told her about Inspector Conduit's visit. There'd been no sign of him or his distinctive coat since then, but Emma knew now he wasn't giving up. She had to get her magic and get out of there.

Emma brushed her hands off on her apron. "Shall we start again?"

Suddenly, the whole room lurched. Emma spread her arms wide to keep her balance. Izzy grabbed on to the back of her smoke sofa, barely managing to keep her seat. A loud knocking boomed through the air, seeming to come from everywhere at once, but mostly from the door under the bust of Mrs. Prudence Posterity.

"What is that?" Emma's heart raced in her chest. "Are the rooms shifting?"

Figgy leaped to his feet, tail alert and whiskers quivering. "Someone's trying to get in."

"I thought you said Miss Posterity didn't know about this place!" Izzy cried.

"I'm fairly certain she doesn't."

"Fairly certain?"

"We're going to die," Frances said matter-of-factly.

The knocking ceased. A gap of light appeared at the far end of the room and then winked out again.

Someone had opened the door. Footsteps pounded against whatever material the floor was made of.

Emma hardly dared breathe. There was nowhere to hide.

The intruder walked toward them, a dark silhouette wearing . . . knickers?

"Tom? What are you doing here?" Emma felt dizzy with relief.

The smoke parted around him like it sensed his urgency. "Emma!" he shouted as he broke into a run. "I found them! I found kindling flints."

"Where? How?" Emma sputtered at the same time Izzy shouted, "Don't scare us like that!"

"Well, this is a relief," Figgy said, and promptly started giving himself a bath.

"The newsie I'd been trying to get in touch with was at the rally tonight. The one from the Tarnish." Tom's cheeks were flushed and his words came out in great gasps like he'd run the whole way there. "The guy's name is Bilk. He runs a pawnshop that deals in magic on the corner of Corrosion and Mott Streets."

Izzy's smoke sofa dissolved, sending her crashing to the ground with an *oof*.

"I'm fine," she said, before anyone could ask. She took the hand that Emma offered to help her back to her feet and brushed off her skirt.

Emma could guess what had broken her concentration now—though she was surprised Izzy had held it that long. "Do you know the store?"

"Maybe. There are a lot of pawnshops in the Tarnish. But *Corrosion Street*? It's too dangerous for you to go alone." Izzy shuddered and then squared her shoulders. "We need those flints and I know my way around there. I'll go with you."

Emma could see the effort this took her friend. "Then I'm going too," she said, and crossed her arms to ward off any disagreement.

"How much are these flints going to cost?" Izzy asked.

"I don't know, but it's not going to be cheap," Tom conceded. "We could go and scope it out first?"

"No." Izzy shook her head. "If he knows we're interested, he'll raise the price. We pick a day and we go together with as much money as we've got."

"Leave the last part to me," Emma said.

Tom raised an eyebrow, but it was too hard to explain the idea that sparkled in her mind like a gem. Besides, she didn't want to risk disappointing them if she couldn't get her hands on what she needed.

"So when are you going to get them, these kindling stones?" Figgy asked.

"Kindling *flints*, Figgy," Izzy corrected.

Figgy licked his paw, looking thoroughly unimpressed.

Thanksgiving was next week and there was no way that Cook would let them out of her sight while there was a school feast to prepare. They would have to wait until that Sunday when Emma and Izzy had their every-other-week afternoon off. They agreed that Frances would stick out too much in the Tarnish and should stay behind. The rest of them would go together. After much back and forth, they decided that on that Sunday Tom would meet Izzy and Emma at the entrance to the underground subway at Fifty-Ninth Street and Broadway. They'd have to cross the park to get to the Broadway line, but it was less likely they'd be recognized and questioned than if they took the closer Third Avenue elevated line.

Emma's chest tightened as she realized the date they'd chosen: December 2. The Winds could come at any time after that.

This would be their only chance to get the flints.

TWENTY-FIVE

The Tarnish

Izzy

It was all too familiar.

There was no official entrance to the Tarnish. Izzy knew they'd arrived by the narrowing of the streets and a vague feeling of unease that permeated the air as thoroughly as the shouts and piano music pouring forth from the ramshackle storefront taverns and coffeehouses.

Fire escapes ran up the fronts of the brick buildings like rickety skeletons. Izzy didn't know much about architecture, but she would call the style of the tenement buildings "defeated." She hadn't realized how much she'd grown used to the polished black-and-white world of Miss Posterity's. In the Tarnish, everything was brown, from the clothes to the buildings to the piles of potatoes for sale.

Though she knew the way, Izzy felt smaller and more lost with every step. The streets were crowded with rickety pushcarts selling crockery, pots, pans, glasses, secondhand clothes, and withered vegetables. Despite the cold, mothers and fathers, sons and daughters perused the wares, trying to escape the small and airless apartments where they lived. Just like Da and Mam had come from Ireland, the people living in the Tarnish were mostly immigrants from around the world, and the languages and cooking smells shifted from block to block.

The only sign of magic was the magically deiced water buckets that had been placed out by the city in anticipation of the upcoming Winds. Passersby gave the snuffing buckets a wide berth.

Children watched Izzy from the doorways and windows. Their faces were as varied in shape and color as the fabric of a patchwork quilt. What would they think if they knew she'd once been one of them and that she was planning to kindle?

Tom shouted something in Italian, shattering her reverie. He made a fist and two small boys who had been following them ran off to find an easier target. Emma watched them go with pity.

"Don't stare," Izzy cautioned. "You have to act like you belong. We gotta get what we came for and get out."

"You lived like this?" Emma whispered.

Izzy ducked her head. She didn't want to see the pity in Emma's eyes. "Be glad it's winter or it'd smell a lot worse."

She had feared that Emma would stick out in the Tarnish like the golden girl she used to be, but her friend's cheeks had become hollow over the past months, and dark circles ringed her eyes from overwork and lack of sleep. In their oldest dresses and the cast-off coats the school provided, they looked like any other tired, half-starved residents of the tenements. Which was good, because they couldn't afford to get robbed today.

"Come on," Izzy said, and walked faster. Her stomach rumbled, but she ignored it. They'd skipped lunch to get here but it was already two o'clock and they had to be back by four thirty to start dinner.

Her lungs constricted when she spotted the narrow entrance to Corrosion Street. It was one of the dark alleys that Da had always warned them not to venture down. Stiff, frozen bedsheets hung from laundry lines overhead like flags to the misery below. Three mice huddled over something and didn't flee as Izzy and her friends approached.

A hand-lettered sign read BILK'S EMPORIUM: ITEMS FOR SALE AND TRADE in the bottom of a window so dirty they couldn't see inside.

"Like we agreed?" Tom said, and both girls nodded.

Izzy's chest felt tight and she couldn't draw in a full breath. She was more frightened than she'd ever been before. Worse than when Da had died. Worse than when they'd taken Maeve away. At least then she'd had options. If they didn't get the flints today, if they didn't kindle their magic this month when the Winds came, all her possibilities would be gone forever.

A bell over the door tinkled as they entered, but it was the only thing cheerful about the shop. A dusty L-shaped glass display case filled most of the space. It featured a sparse assortment of odds and ends, including several men's hats and cameo brooches with faces forever frozen in white silhouettes. Nothing about the shop looked magical and Izzy's hopes began to fade.

Then she caught sight of the wiry man in front of the velvet curtains that lined the back wall. He wore a brown bowler hat pulled low over his forehead and had his feet propped up on the display case. The man didn't look at them but she didn't think he was asleep either.

"Hello?" Tom called.

Izzy had a bad feeling about this. She glanced at Emma, who had gone pale and still beside her.

The man sat up and his feet hit the floor with an audible *clump clump*. His bushy mustache hid his upper lip and made his expression hard to read. "What can I do for you, ladies and gent? Come to buy or to sell?"

"Are you Bilk?" Tom asked, and Izzy was impressed that his voice didn't shake.

The man narrowed his eyes and strolled around the display case. He was taller than Izzy had guessed.

"That depends on who's asking."

"We don't have time for games," Izzy said, feeling impatient. "Are you him?"

"Well, aren't you a saucy little mouse." The man smiled, but it didn't reach his eyes. He picked up a lock of her red hair off her shoulder and rubbed it between his fingers. Izzy recoiled, but she was too shocked to knock his hand away.

Emma stepped between them and the man glared at her. "We were told to speak to Mr. Bilk. So if you aren't him, we're leaving."

The man brushed his hand on his shabby vest. "Pushy little mice. Yes, I'm Bilk. What's it to you?"

Emma looked to Izzy and Tom before she spoke. "We heard that you sold items for magic." Her voice trembled and she barely managed to squeak out the last words.

Bilk strolled back around the display case like he hadn't even heard. Izzy expected him to pull back the curtain, but instead he pounded his fist on the display case and his wristwatch winked with magic.

In the blink of an eye, the entire room changed. The dust disappeared, revealing a sparkling and clear display case filled with velvet cushions. Items sprouted from the velvet like flowers while red wallpaper rolled itself down the walls of the shop. Izzy found herself standing in front of a display of pairs of silk ladies' gloves, each labeled with the enchantment they carried. One pair said it could stop the wearer from fidgeting. Izzy looked down at her own hands, twisting with nerves.

"See what you're looking for?" Bilk grunted. He stood behind the display, sizing each of them up while they made their way down the row.

Emma paused in front of a display of gems, studying the price tags. Izzy kept moving and her heart caught in her throat when she saw the magicked musical instruments. There, resting between a flute and a set of cymbals, was a fiddle. It looked like Da's had before the mice nibbled the magic out of it.

Tom tapped her on the shoulder and whispered, "Do you see the flints?"

Izzy collected herself and shook her head. They had a mission here and she couldn't get lost in memories and forget it.

"Did I hear you say flints? As in kindling flints?" Bilk asked, crossing his arms. His eyes never seemed to stop moving as he watched each of them warily.

Tom widened his stance and crossed his arms right back. "Yes, sir. Can you help us?"

Bilk laughed. "Help? Get one thing straight, boy. I don't *help* anyone." He dropped back into his seat. "Yeah, I got kindling flints, but they're not going to be cheap."

"What are they worth to you?" Izzy demanded. "Sir," she added as an afterthought.

"I highly doubt poor mice like you could offer me anything valuable enough." Bilk glanced around his shop like he was taking inventory.

Izzy longed to hiss at him like Figgy.

Emma drew herself up. "Let us see the flints, and we'll show you what we're willing to pay."

His dark eyes gleamed. "Don't work like that, missy. You show me first."

Emma glanced at Izzy and Tom and gave them a stiff nod. "All right."

"Em, I don't know about this," Tom whispered.

"We don't have a choice."

Emma reached into the interior pocket of her coat and drew out a handkerchief-wrapped bundle. It wasn't one of the embroidered silk handkerchiefs she'd had when she was a pupil, but one of the greasy and dirt-stained hand-me-downs from the servants' hall. Inside was the ruby ring, looking every bit as dazzling as Izzy remembered it.

Oh, how Izzy had hated that ring the first time she

saw it. It had represented everything she didn't have—money, magic, and a family that loved her. But seeing Emma in her ragged dress in the middle of the Tarnish, her heart ached at the loss of it.

Emma's hand shook as she held the ring up so that Bilk could see it. "Will this be enough?"

TWENTY-SIX

The Ring

Emma

It took all of Emma's *grace and poise* not to flee.

Everything about this expedition to the Tarnish made her angry. She'd had no idea that people lived so magicless and packed in together like this—that *Izzy* had lived like this. Emma had longed to kick over every single snuffing bucket she saw, but feared that might do more harm than good in the long run. Then there was this man, this slimy man, staring at her ruby ring with greedy eyes.

Bilk leaned forward, licking his lips.

"Where'd you get a gem like that?" He drew back, looking wary. "I don't deal in stolen goods, you know."

"It's mine." Thanks to Izzy's discovery of Miss Posterity's jewelry drawer, it had been easy enough to pluck it from the headmistress's office this morning. She reasoned that Miss Posterity had stolen it. Emma had only taken back what was hers.

Still, Emma knew how it must look. She'd caught a glimpse of herself in a shop window on the way down there. She was ragged and worn-out looking. Her eyes had become too big and her cheekbones were sharp angles. Papa wouldn't have recognized her now—she hardly recognized herself. This ring was the last piece of her past, but she could and would trade it for the flints that would secure her future. She held the ring higher.

Tom looked back and forth between Emma and the ring. For the first time, she wished he hadn't come. Now he was going to find out who she really was.

But Bilk didn't take his eyes off the ruby. "Is that a real gem? It ain't a fake?"

Emma concentrated her magic into it. The ruby glistened with magic and Izzy's coat shifted into a plush ermine fur.

"Oh," Izzy gasped in surprise. Her hands flew to the soft fur at her chest, but it was only there a moment before it shifted back into stiff boiled wool.

Bilk ran a hand through his hair. "How have you got a real gem when you ain't got flints too?"

Emma shook her head. Despite her rags, despite looking like she belonged in the Tarnish, she used that crisp grand-lady voice that commanded attention. "That's none of your business. Now, you promised to show us the flints."

The shopkeeper turned, muttering to himself, and pushed aside the velvet curtains at the back of the shop. "Wait here."

They couldn't tell how far back in the shop he'd gone, so they had to whisper.

"Even for the Tarnish, this guy gives me the creeps," Tom said with a shudder.

As soon as Bilk had gone, there was a rustle and a squeak behind them. Emma turned around to see two mice with beady red eyes watching her from by the door. She shuddered. "I have a bad feeling about this."

"What do we do? Should we leave?" Izzy watched the mice as they crept along the side of the display case. Their pink noses sniffed the magic in the air.

"Let's get the flints and get out of here." Tom crossed his arms. "But then one of you is going to tell me where that ring came from."

"It's hers," Izzy insisted. "From before."

Confusion flickered in his eyes. "Before what?"

Emma glanced at the velvet curtains. "We can't talk about this here."

It was just as well, because Bilk chose that moment to reappear. The mice skittered back into their hole as the curtains swung into place.

"Well, here we are then." He set a leather roll down on the display case. For some reason, he seemed jittery now, and he kept glancing at the window behind their heads. "Made of the finest magical flint," he said with a showman's flourish as he unrolled the parcel. "'Course, they can't get you a kindling license, but that ain't my problem."

Emma watched with a growing sense of awe as the leather roll exposed two golden orbs, about the size of eggs. The kindling flints. They looked like the ones from Miss Posterity's but without the showy diamond *P* in the middle. She felt like she was staring at her future.

"Now you seen 'em. May I?" Bilk asked, gesturing at the ring.

Emma's fingers felt cold when she handed it to him. She couldn't watch him inspect it. Instead, she kept her eyes on the flints.

"How do we know these are real?" she asked. It was hard to tell in the dim light in the shop.

Bilk tore his gaze from the ring to glare at her. "Don't impugn my honor, girl."

Emma wasn't sure what *impugn* meant, but she wasn't about to do it. "Then how do we put the magic in them?" She examined the flint.

Bilk glanced over her head at the window again. What was he looking for? "I'm selling you the flints. That's bad enough. You won't catch me telling you how to use them."

Emma picked up one of the kindling flints. It was heavier than it looked. A hum of anticipation filled her mind. They were going to kindle. She imagined riding home in a carriage with Tom and Izzy. She had built them a beautiful house that they shared and they were wearing fine clothes and had full bellies from lunch at Delmonico's, one of the finest restaurants in the city.

The fantasy felt so real. Before she realized what she was doing, she channeled a little bit of magic into the flint.

"Ouch." She dropped it back onto the satchel. "That's hot."

Bilk gave her a perplexed look. "You satisfied with your purchase, little mouse?"

"Do we get to keep the leather roll?"

"For an extra charge." He eyed Emma's pocket. "What else you got?"

Emma picked up the flints again. They were heavy, so she handed one to Izzy and slid the other into her dress pocket. "Thank you," she said to Bilk, and turned to go.

"Wait," he called out. "Don't you want to see what else I have in the shop? I've got lots of things that might interest young ladies such as yourselves." He grabbed a glass perfume bottle and held it up.

"We must be going," Emma said.

Bilk came around the counter and Izzy flinched.

Emma walked faster toward the door, but he was right behind them.

"Stop!" He reached out a hand to grab them, but Emma threw open the door. She rushed outside with Tom and Izzy.

Then she saw what Bilk had been waiting for. Two uniformed policemen were making their way down the alley, thick wooden batons in hand. The golden *R* badge of the Registry's magical enforcement unit glinted on their chests.

"They're trying to get magic!" Bilk shouted, pointing at Emma. "Selling stolen goods!"

He'd reported them to the Registry. How could she have been so naive? She'd wanted the flints so badly she'd overlooked the warning signs. *Mice*, he'd called them and mice they had been. It was an elaborate trap, and they had sprung it.

A policeman reached out to grab her by the arm. She ducked around him.

"Run!" Izzy shrieked, and they did.

"After them! I deserve my reward!" Bilk hollered at the policemen.

Emma sprinted as fast as she could along the icy street, her boots threatening to skitter out from under her at any moment. The three of them dashed down the alley, rounded the corner, and nearly collided with a man pushing a cart of secondhand hats. The kindling flint in Emma's pocket banged against her leg with every step.

The people of the Tarnish stepped aside without even glancing at them. Ragtag kids being chased by the police weren't any cause for concern down here.

Emma hoped they might lose the policemen in the crowded streets, but they had no such luck. Icy air sliced into her lungs and she took great gasps of it, running as fast as she could.

The policeman closest behind them shouted, "Stop! Thieves! You're under arrest for attempting to gain magic!"

The energy on the street changed at once. Heads turned in their direction as they darted through the crowd in front of a Greek grocery. A boy about their age shot angry red sparks out of his fingertips. He picked up the nearest snuffing bucket and threw the water at the police officers. It had little effect on them—they were grown men and this wasn't the kindling—but his anger spread like wildfire to the other residents of the Tarnish. A girl too young to be sparking picked up a potato and threw it at the police officers. When she missed, another brave girl threw an onion. It hit the first policeman right above his knee and he stumbled and fell on the ice. A cheer went up around the street.

Izzy was ahead, Tom in the middle, and Emma trailing. She felt herself slipping farther and farther behind her friends and the second policeman getting closer to her.

Tom glanced over his shoulder and saw her struggling. He dropped back and grabbed her by the elbow. "I've got you!" His speed propelled her forward, but still the remaining policeman was closing in on them as they neared the corner.

Then a teen boy tugged the reins of his wagon. His horse stepped directly between them and the officer, forcing him to stop and go around. Emma looked back and the boy tipped his cap at her.

Izzy tugged her forward by the arm. "What just happened?"

Before Emma could answer, two girls wrapped in shawls beckoned them from the opposite corner.

"This way," the older girl said, pointing down an alley. "We'll distract them."

"Good luck," her younger sister called as they ran by. Hopeful gold sparks danced on her fingertips.

"Do we have a plan?" Tom called from the rear as Izzy led them onward.

"Yes. We'll head toward Canal Street and catch the uptown train," Izzy replied over her shoulder.

"Which way's Canal?"

"That way." A small boy pointed from his perch on a

fire escape. The whites of his eyes seemed to glow in the dirt that streaked his face, and he too had sparks glistening at his fingertips.

"Thank you," Emma called back.

He cupped his hands over his mouth. "I hope you get your magic."

Emma grinned through her gasps for breath. The people of the Tarnish were helping them!

They ran another block in the direction he'd pointed. Behind them, the noise of a crowd grew, punctuated by the sharp blasts of police whistles, but this block was empty.

Emma's lungs burned. She wasn't used to running like this. "I need to stop."

"Over there." Izzy pointed.

They ducked behind a building and paused next to a stack of barrels to catch their breath. Emma inhaled and then wished she hadn't. The barrels reeked of dead fish.

"What was that back there?" Izzy demanded. "Why did they help us?"

"It's the magic." Emma panted. "They want us to succeed. Figgy was right. They're not content to snuff out their magic anymore."

All three of them grinned. Even though the police were chasing them, even though carrying the flints was enough to get them thrown in jail, they couldn't help it.

"If we get split up, meet Uptown at the Fifty-Ninth

Street station. No point in standing around at the subway entrance here where they could catch us," Tom said, and the girls nodded in agreement. He glanced down the street where the shouts and sounds of the crowd were still growing. "Um, I think we may have started a riot."

"Then we'd better get out of here," Izzy said.

"There they are!" a policeman shouted. There were three of them now. One was soaking wet and another had a trickle of blood on his forehead. They looked angrier than ever. The policemen raised their clubs, intent on using them this time.

"Run!" Izzy, Tom, and Emma shouted in unison.

Emma couldn't breathe, couldn't think. The piercing bursts of the police whistles bounced off the brick walls and lodged in her bones. She became the pounding of her feet on the pavement and the thump of the kindling flint in her pocket against her leg. Blocks went past in blurs of dirt and despair.

She turned a corner and her foot skidded on a patch of ice. Emma fell, landing hard on her side. Something banged against her leg painfully and she cried out.

She lay on the ground, panting as the world came back into focus. Gray clouds above, brick buildings on either side, and Tom and Izzy nowhere in sight.

TWENTY-SEVEN

A Single Flint

Izzy

Izzy paced back and forth in front of the Fifty-Ninth Street subway entrance. Her heart hadn't stopped pounding for a single moment since she'd lost Emma and Tom. With her knowledge of the Tarnish, it hadn't been hard to lose the police officer following her, but her friends were strangers there.

A passing lady and her small dog stared at her with curiosity. Izzy ducked her head politely, but her mind was racing. Her *friends*. The word felt as natural as breathing. They had to be safe, they just had to.

She blew on her hands to warm them and hunger gnawed at her stomach, but still, she waited. The ground shuddered as a train stopped underground. Moments later, Tom emerged from the subway looking haggard.

"Finally," Izzy said, and sighed.

"Where's Emma? Is she here?" Tom asked when he saw her.

Izzy's blood ran cold. "I thought she was with you."

"We got separated. Should I go back down to look for her?"

"In the middle of a riot?" Izzy clasped her face in her hands. "She knew the plan was to meet up here. We'll wait."

Tom glanced into the park. "She'll be here soon. I'm sure."

They sat in silence as a train rumbled into the station, and then another, and another until Izzy lost count. The sky darkened and the magic-light streetlamps flared to life as if lit by a single spark. At some point, it began to snow. Tom tried to fill the silence by talking about an article he'd read about the magic that ran the subway. Normally, she would have been fascinated by new information about magic, but right now she didn't care. She let his words drift around her like the snowflakes coating the ground at her feet. Tom's story stopped abruptly as another handful of people climbed out of the train station. With each face that wasn't Emma, Izzy worried.

"They can't have caught her." She stuck her hand into her pocket and squeezed the kindling flint. A single flint was useless without its partner.

Tears slipped down her cheek. She'd been so worried about saving her own neck she'd failed Emma. Just like she'd failed Maeve. Would she ever stop being so selfish?

"It's my fault," Izzy said.

Tom patted her on the shoulder with a gentle hand. "No, it's not. It'll work out. It has to, right?" His face darkened. "But if she did steal that ring . . ."

"She didn't!"

Izzy told him about how Emma had come to the school as the golden pupil and her fall from grace. She told him about the attic and how she'd hated her at first, but how now Emma was as dear to her as her own family.

As she spoke, Tom looked dumbfounded. His mouth hung open at a crooked angle.

"You saw her in that shop today. She's meant to be a great lady. It's who she is no matter if she's scrubbing pots or wearing rags." Her shoulders slumped.

"We'll get her back." Tom stared at his hands in his lap. "Why did she lie to me?"

"She thought you would hate her if you knew who she really was because of what you said about rich people being horrible."

Tom ran a hand through his hair. Somewhere during the chase, he'd lost his cap. "I wish she'd told me."

They sat in silence. Izzy watched a pigeon strutting in

a circle, but her thoughts were far away, with two girls she'd left behind.

Another train rumbled below, and this time Izzy didn't even dare to hope. Not until she saw the ragged little figure hauling herself up the stairs through the gently swirling snow.

Izzy's breath caught in her chest.

Tom leaped to his feet. "Em? What happened to you?"

Emma's face was streaked with dirt, clean only where tears had trailed down her cheeks. She clutched something in her right hand as she limped toward them.

"I didn't mean to. I fell, and—you see."

She opened her palm and Izzy's breath caught in her throat. Balanced in Emma's hand were the two jagged halves of the kindling flint.

"It's a fake," Emma cried.

TWENTY-EIGHT

A World in Which There Are Sunflowers

Emma

It wasn't a kindling flint. It was only two hunks of hardened tar, painted gold on the outside. Emma held it aloft so that her friends could see what she'd already discovered. Tom grimaced like he'd been punched in the gut. Izzy simply stared.

Emma let the pieces fall from her hand to the ground. They stuck out like black bits of rot in the soft white carpet of snow. She held her breath, waiting for her friends to reassure her that they'd still find a way to kindle.

Then, with a cry, Izzy pulled the other flint from her pocket and hurled it at the ground. Tom jumped out of the way as it cracked at his feet.

"What'd you do that for?" he shouted.

"They're useless." Izzy stared at the broken flint, her face hard. "It's over."

"Maybe they'll still work. We could get some glue." Tom picked up the two halves and tried to fit them together like a puzzle. Bits fell away like crumbs.

"Glue won't help anything. They're made of tar," Izzy snapped.

"We can get other flints. Real ones."

"Other flints?" Emma demanded, her voice cracking with utter hopelessness. "How? I've lost my papa, my dreams, my magic. That ring was all I had—and now it's gone too."

"Izzy told me everything." Tom's voice dropped and his words burned with hurt. "I wish you'd told me, Em." He shook his head. "I always suspected you were too fancy and too good to be friends with the likes of me."

The pain in his voice amplified her feelings of loss. She'd traded the last beautiful thing from her life with Papa for useless tar. She took the broken halves of the kindling flint from him and squeezed them. "You're the one who's too good for me. I offered you everything and gave you nothing."

To her surprise, Tom smiled. "Nothing? I met a house dragon and spent my evenings in the space between rooms. I learned the whole kindling dance." He took a step toward her. "We've come so far. There has to be a way."

She turned away from him. "I've got nothing left to give. You heard Izzy. It's over, Tom. I didn't mean to lie to you. Please don't hate me when our magic snuffs."

She felt Tom's eyes on her, but she was too sad and ashamed of their failure to meet his gaze.

"I could never hate you, Em." He stuffed his hands into his pockets, but still she couldn't look at him. Soft flakes of snow drifted down around them. When at last he turned away, her heart threatened to crack as thoroughly as the flints. "Well, I guess I'd better get home. I'll see you around."

When she looked up, Tom was gone and the snow was already filling in his footprints.

Izzy scooped up the flints and pressed them into Emma's hand.

"I don't want them," Emma protested. "I lost everything for them."

"That's why you have to keep them," Izzy insisted.

With reluctance, Emma put them in her apron pocket. A clock tower down the street chimed. Six loud bongs, each sounding more like a funeral bell.

"We need to go," Izzy said quietly. "We're horribly late and we're sure to get our ears boxed now."

For once, the threat of ear boxing felt hollow. Nothing could be worse than what had already happened today.

They walked east along the southern edge of the park in silence. The lit windows of the houses they passed looked warm and inviting. She thought again of her fantasy about them living in one big, magical house together. There would be no magic, no new life for them. Izzy might still leave to find her sister and Tom would have his family, but without her papa or her magic, Emma would be alone forever.

New York City felt muted and strange in the snow. As they walked up Fifth Avenue, the only sound was the crunch of their boots. A handful of people passed by, heads bowed and shoulders hunched against the storm. In the lamplight, the bare trees reached toward the sky.

Emma stared at her hands, wondering if she'd recognize them after her magic snuffed. She tried to remind herself of the little flower girl, and that her life could be worse, but it didn't help. She'd never felt so miserable.

Then through the silence: A sound. A tiny voice, shaking with cold.

"Flowers for sale, ma'am. Won't you buy a flower?"

As if Emma had summoned her, the forlorn figure of the little flower girl appeared on the sidewalk ahead of them. She stood in a yellow pool of light from a streetlamp. A ragged shawl covered her head and shoulders, but she wore no coat. Her usual basket hung from one arm with half a dozen wilted daisies inside.

Emma ducked her head, hoping the girl wouldn't notice her, but it was too late. She looked at Emma like she saw her, like she knew her deep down and could see the pain the day had brought. The girl walked across the circle of light and held out a flower.

"Here," she said simply.

Emma tensed. "I don't have any money. I can't help you."

She offered the flower again and it drooped toward Emma's heart. "It's all right."

Emma took the flower. "Thank you," she said, though her voice shook.

The girl bobbed her head. Snowflakes glistened on her eyelashes like tiny diamonds.

Tiny diamonds.

Emma stopped.

"What is it?" Izzy tugged at her arm but Emma ignored her.

"I think—I need to—" But Emma couldn't put it into words. A thought was forming, something she'd been trying to understand for weeks. She thought about the flashes she'd seen in the glass and the water. Their flint, though only tar, had warmed with magic when she touched it. She'd read that people used to kindle with stones, but she hadn't believed it. It had seemed too simple, but maybe it was supposed to be that way.

But what if over time, people had come to believe the worth of the object was in its monetary value—just like they believed of people? The more Emma thought about it, the more it seemed to fit. When Rosie was struggling to kindle, Miss Posterity hadn't told her to use any of the fancy tools, she'd told her to concentrate. What if kindling schools and expensive tools were merely a way for the rich to keep magic for themselves? What if they'd designed an elaborate process to something that was actually very straightforward? *Focus on the magic. It's all that matters*, Figgy had told them over and over. What if it really was as simple as that?

An idea seized her.

There, on the ground—a patch of ice. She stomped on it with her boot and picked up a shard. It was icy and slippery between her fingertips but crystal clear. With her other hand, she grabbed the remaining wilted daisies from the girl's basket.

With the precision she'd practiced as a pupil, she focused her magic through the ice. It melted immediately.

She had to try again. Emma knelt in the snow without a second thought, concentrating so hard she barely noticed the cold and wet seeping in around her knees. She put one hand on the patch of ice and grasped the flowers with her other.

Anger at the unfairness of the world surged through her as she thought about the ragged child watching her. Emma longed to wield her anger like a club and break something, but the world was already broken. She had always thought her anger was something she should avoid and she had shoved it aside in favor of *grace and poise*. Now she saw she'd been wrong. There were things in the world that deserved her anger. For the first time in her life, she didn't care what Mama or Papa would have done. The only thing that mattered was what she was going to do.

Emma closed her eyes, concentrating.

It was hard to work with the ice, harder even than with the cloudy school crystals, but the magic surged through her. She felt warm, blissfully warm like a summer day. Papa had always said it was hard to be unhappy in a world in which there were sunflowers. She knew he'd been wrong about so many things and she was sorry that she'd never get the chance to show him that the world could be better.

Behind her, Izzy gasped.

"Oh my stones," the flower girl breathed with wonder.

Emma opened her eyes. The ice and snow had melted from the heat of the magic, forming a ring of dry paving stones around her feet. Her tights too were dry. Instead of wilting daisies, Emma held five beautiful sunflowers at the peak of their bloom.

Izzy stared. "But you said you left your crystal in the attic?"

Pride swelled in her chest as she shook her head. "It was an idea I had—"

"What's that you've got there?" A gentleman with a waxed mustache and wearing a long wool coat stopped next to them in the lamplight. He stared at the flowers in Emma's hand. She drew back, expecting him to be angry with them for doing magic, but instead, he smiled. "Are they for sale?"

"They're sunflowers." Emma stood, holding them out for his inspection. They looked like a bit of paradise in the snowy world of New York City. "They're done with flickerings though, so they won't last."

"That's all right. I can fix the enchantment permanently on the way home." He flashed a small garnet ring and smiled kindly. "How much?"

Emma raised her chin. "Five cents each."

The flower girl inhaled sharply at such a steep sum and Izzy nudged her to keep quiet. She watched the man like she was afraid he might lash out at Emma for demanding such a price.

The man pulled out his wallet. "I'll take them." He handed her a quarter. "I've got a daughter about your age and she's very sick. She'll like these even more when I tell her about the clever girls that made such exquisite summer flowers on such a cold day. Worth the price, if you ask me."

He hurried away in the snow, clutching the yellow bouquet like a torch against the dark.

Emma handed the quarter to the girl. "Here."

"I couldn't." The girl shook her head. "You made 'em."

"But they were your flowers." Emma pressed the coin into the girl's palm and wrapped her fingers over her hand. It was as cold as the ice. "Keep the money. And this." She pulled off her coat and wrapped it around the girl's shoulders. "What's your name?"

"Mary," the girl answered. Her eyes were wide at the luxury of having twenty-five cents and a wool coat, however worn.

Emma looked her in the eye. "Do you know how to use magic, Mary?"

She shook her head. "A sparking here and there."

"Did you see what I did with the flowers?" Emma

quickly demonstrated how to focus magic on the clear bit of ice. Focusing magic through a gem was like threading silk through the eye of a needle. Using the ice was clumsier, like trying to thread a whole strand of yarn at once, but it was possible. "Practice it every day, and you should be able to do it on your own soon. If you need help, come and find me." She gave the address of the school and told Mary to knock at the back door.

Mary covered her face with her hands, completely overwhelmed. "Thank you, miss. Oh, thank you," she cried. Then the girl hurried off into the night, Emma's coat trailing behind her like a cape.

Izzy gawked at her. "What you said about the ice and the magic—did you figure that out by yourself?"

Excited, Emma explained about how she'd accidentally channeled magic through the wash water and the piece of glass and how it had given her this idea. "I wasn't sure it would actually work, but I had to try. You have to really know how to focus magic properly to do it. I think that's how it's been kept a secret for so long. Figgy said more people used to have magic and this is how. You don't need fancy gems or special tools, you just need something clear to focus the magic."

Izzy stared at the dry paving stones with an unreadable expression on her face.

Emma's breath hitched. "I know you said I shouldn't involve anyone else, and that you think I'm wrong to trust people, but I had to help—"

Izzy cut her off, leaping at her and throwing her arms around Emma's neck. She hugged her tightly. "You're incredible," she said. "I can't believe you figured that out."

"I couldn't have done it without Figgy." Emma practically glowed with pride. "Come on. I can't wait to see the look on his face when we tell him."

They hurried down the alley toward the back stairs of the school. Her magic felt like it was burning especially bright and warm inside her and she hardly noticed that she was cold without her coat. Her hunger, however, was impossible to overlook. It was likely well past seven thirty now and there was sure to be trouble, but the prospect of the cozy kitchen and warm food kept her feet trudging onward.

As if someone had heard her thoughts, the kitchen door swung open, golden light spilling from inside.

"You're late," the silhouetted figure in the doorway said in a voice colder than the ice on the back stairs.

Emma looked up into the furious eyes of Miss Posterity.

TWENTY-NINE

The Diamond Girls

Izzy

Miss Posterity stood in the doorway, barring them from entering.

"Where were you?" she demanded.

"We got lost," Izzy said, which wasn't too much of a lie.

"Get in here, this instant."

The headmistress grabbed them by the shoulders and pulled them roughly inside. Izzy's arm banged against the doorframe and Emma stumbled. It was so warm in the kitchen that Izzy's cheeks ached. She took off her coat and hung it on the peg by the door.

Cook hurried toward them. "I was so worried," she blubbered. "I thought something happened to you girls. I told her you were on a long errand—"

"Hush, Cook," Miss Posterity snapped.

Cook had tried to cover for them! Wonders might never cease tonight. But Miss Posterity was still there, pointing at the stairs.

"This way," she commanded.

As she followed her into the main hallway, Izzy tried not to panic. If Miss Posterity wasn't going to box their ears, they were in worse trouble than she'd anticipated.

While Izzy shuffled along, Emma kept her head held high. Melting snow crystals dotted her skirt, leaving uneven black circles.

Miss Posterity stopped in the middle of the foyer. The electric lamps buzzed and her shadow on the wall stood tall and menacing.

"Turn out your pockets," she demanded.

Oh stones. This was bad. Izzy and Emma didn't dare look at each other. Emma held the jagged lumps that used to be the kindling flints. With a trembling hand, Izzy held out three pennies, a bit of spare thread, her crystal, and her beloved letter from Omaha.

"This is worse than I thought." Miss Posterity grabbed the crystal from Izzy. "I should report you for this."

"I found it and was going to put it back." Izzy's heart was pounding so loudly she was sure Miss Posterity could hear it. *Don't read the letter*, she silently pleaded. *Punish me for the crystal and let that be all.*

But the headmistress was in such a fury, even the discovery of the crystal wasn't enough to distract her. She pocketed Izzy's crystal and seized Emma's wrists, yanking them over so she could see the tops of her hands. Emma cried out as the fake kindling flint pieces fell and clattered across the tile.

"Where is it?" the headmistress demanded. "I know you stole it."

"Stole what?" Emma squeaked.

Someone coughed. Izzy risked a glance upward and wasn't surprised to find the rest of the school peering between the banisters. Of course Miss Posterity was doing this here. She wanted to be overheard. The cross-stitch on the wall read, *Sometimes an example must be made.*

"The ring, you foolish girl. The ruby ring that was in my office. Do you have any idea what it was worth?" Miss Posterity searched Emma's fingers, then grabbed Izzy's hands. Maeve's letter fluttered to the ground, landing at Miss Posterity's feet. Izzy stood frozen, wanting to dive after it, but too terrified to draw the headmistress's attention.

Emma's hands curled into fists. "You mean *my* ring? My papa gave that to me. You're the one who stole it."

The backhanded slap was so swift that none of them saw it coming. Emma cried out and staggered back a step. Her hand flew to her cheek and stayed there, covering where Miss Posterity had struck her.

"I kept that ring as a reminder to never make a foolish gamble on someone like you again." Miss Posterity raised her hand like she might strike her again.

Izzy looked at the letter one last time and made her choice. She wouldn't lose Emma again, not without a fight.

"Leave her alone!" She leaped at the headmistress, but Miss Posterity sent her crashing to the floor with a shove. The breath left her lungs in a whoosh and she gasped for air.

"How dare you. You have nothing and you are nothing," Miss Posterity seethed.

"No," Emma said.

If Izzy had had air in her lungs, it would've been sucked right out again by the fury contained in that single word. She looked up. Emma's hand was still clasped to her cheek and her eyes were narrowed with anger. It was that simmering anger that Izzy had seen Emma smooth over with her mantra of *grace and poise*, but this time she let it burn.

Emma took a brave step toward the headmistress. "That gem belonged to my mama and the gold was from my papa. They intended for me to kindle my magic with it. I've learned a valuable lesson at this school, but I didn't learn it from you."

Emma lowered the hand that had been clasped to her cheek. Miss Posterity had struck her with the back of her hand and the giant diamond in the headmistress's ring had left a jagged cut. Blood ran down Emma's cheek.

"Having money doesn't make you worthy of magic. True worth comes from here." Emma placed her right hand over her heart.

Though she was still struggling to breathe, Izzy pushed herself to her knees. She put her right hand over her heart like Emma and glared at Miss Posterity.

Emma stared down the headmistress. "I am worthy of magic, and no one, especially not you, will ever take that away from me. Like my ring, it's out of your hands."

"So you think you know everything now?" Miss Posterity sneered. "I'll throw you both out into the snow. See how much you're worth when you're frozen."

Izzy's hand slipped from her heart. It was so cold and Emma had given away her coat. They'd die out there.

Above them, Frances climbed onto the first rung of the banister and clasped her right hand over her heart. "Don't turn them out! Let them stay," she cried. It was either the stupidest or bravest thing Frances had ever done.

For a moment, no one dared breathe, and Izzy was

leaning toward stupidest, but then the twins placed their hands over their hearts too.

"Let them stay," they repeated in unison.

Izzy watched in shock as the call spread down the row. One by one, the girls Izzy thought would never help someone like her placed their hands on their hearts and pledged their support. Even Beatrice Scorn looked back and forth between the cut on Emma's cheek and Miss Posterity's snarl, until she too put her hand over her heart.

Izzy wanted to hug them. It was a very strange feeling.

Miss Posterity looked at the girls above them and her face went as pale as her hair. She took a step toward Emma, then appeared to think better of it. Her gaze fell on an easier target, already on the floor. Izzy tried to crawl away, but sharp fingers dug into her hair.

"How dare you disrespect me and turn my students against me," she shouted. "I want you out immediately!"

Izzy shrieked as the headmistress pulled her by her hair toward the door. She kicked her feet and twisted, but the grip on her hair was too strong. Her eyes watered from the pain, but still she fought.

"Emma!" She wouldn't let them be separated. Not now. Not ever. Izzy wasn't going to lose another person she loved. She kicked Miss Posterity in the shins and the headmistress screamed.

"Little brat! I'll throw you out!"

"Enough!" Miss Clementine roared.

Izzy froze, as did Miss Posterity. The silence in the hall was deafening.

Miss Clementine stood partway down the stairs. Her hair was half in curlers and she wore a lilac dressing gown, but every inch of her was a force to be reckoned with.

"Enough," Miss Clementine repeated in a lower tone. She advanced down the stairs toward Miss Posterity. "For too long I've bitten my tongue while you treated these girls horrendously, Petunia. But I won't stay silent anymore. You and your greed are the only things to blame for the school's financial situation. Do not take it out on these girls."

Miss Posterity staggered back a step, releasing Izzy's hair. Izzy took the opportunity to scramble away as fast as she could, and managed to grab one of the fake flints in the process. It would come in handy if Miss Posterity tried to seize her again. For a moment, Izzy dared to hope she and Emma might escape unscathed, but she should have known better.

Miss Posterity drew herself up. "Clem, you're fired. I want you out first thing tomorrow." She glared at the balcony. "Everyone go to your rooms at once! If I catch anyone out of bed tonight, they will be expelled and sent home with a report that they are unworthy of learning magic."

Izzy watched with a sinking sensation as one by one their supporters disappeared until the balcony above was empty. Only Miss Clementine stood her ground, looking at the headmistress with a stern frown.

"I don't care what you do to me, but have a heart, Petunia. They're children."

"I do have a heart, thank you very much. I'm not going to throw them into the snow," Miss Posterity snapped, though she had just tried to do that very thing. "I'll lock them in the attic tonight." She stuffed her hand in her pocket and her eyes lit up as she drew out Izzy's crystal. "They've been attempting to gain illegal magic. Tomorrow I'll report them to the Registry. At least then I'll get my money's worth."

Snow tonight, police tomorrow. Izzy wasn't sure which option was worse.

Miss Posterity turned to Izzy and Emma, still standing in the foyer. "Well, what are you waiting for, you ungrateful thieves? You heard me."

Emma's hands balled into fists. "One day I hope you look back on this and are horrified by your actions. The time will come when the world will see what you're truly worth."

"Yeah, you're the worst," Izzy added.

It was impossible to miss Clem's sly grin of approval.

Miss Posterity trembled with rage. "Upstairs! Now!" She shouldered her way past Miss Clementine. "Pack your things and get out."

As she marched them up the stairs, Miss Posterity's bun came loose so that her long white hair streaked behind her. The sight of her so unraveled was terrifying, as were the angry lines on her face.

"Don't bother trying to get your little friends to help you again. I'm locking everyone in their rooms tonight," she said as they rounded the third-floor landing.

Izzy kept her eyes on the stairs, but she was already working out a plan. They'd have to leave tonight. It wasn't ideal, but it was the only option.

"Inside, both of you," Miss Posterity demanded when they reached the attic. She raised her chin. "When the Winds start to blow, I hope I get to personally shove your hands in the snuffing buckets."

With that, she pushed them inside the darkened room and slammed the door. A lock that had never existed before magically appeared and clicked. Izzy pulled at the handle, but it wouldn't budge.

"Go get your crystal from the drawer, Em. We'll break out," Izzy said, but when she turned around, they weren't in the attic.

They were standing in Emma's old bedroom.

THIRTY

The Attic Shifts

Emma

Emma looked around her old bedroom in wonder. The furnishings felt so fancy to her now, she almost didn't recognize them. But there was the painting of white roses over the bed and there was the dove-gray carpet that she had loved to wriggle her toes in. A white, ornately carved dresser took the place of the attic's old broken one, the mirror whole and the washbasin new.

The games and books were gone—sold, most likely—but Emma hardly noticed. She was too focused on the warm fire crackling in the grate and the feast laid out across the tea table. Her mouth watered at the sight of the steaming roast beef, buttery mashed potatoes, and piles of green beans dotted with almonds. Real food and not a Blanding among them.

"Oh!" Izzy gasped and clapped her hands over her heart. "But how?"

A slow smile spread across Emma's face. Her cheek still hurt where Miss Posterity had struck her, but her heart felt happy. "I think the house is on our side."

"Or Figgy and Cook." Izzy's smile slipped as she looked at the lock on the door. "So what are we going to do?"

"Eat first, obviously."

"Good idea."

They dug into the meal with relish. Everything was delicious. Cook really should have been working at a fine restaurant. As she ate, Izzy kept touching the top of her head, like she was checking to see if her hair was still attached.

"How's your head?" Emma asked.

"Not so bad." Izzy crammed bread in her mouth. "Your cheek's stopped bleeding."

"I can't believe she—" Emma set her fork down and pressed a hand to her stomach. She suddenly felt a little sick about everything that had happened downstairs.

"Eat this. You'll feel better." Izzy buttered another slice of bread and offered it to her. "You were amazing tonight. I've never seen Miss Posterity shake like she did when you stood up to her."

Emma took the bread. "I should have said that a long time ago."

"And the girls stood up for us too!" Izzy shook her head in disbelief.

"I do feel bad for Miss Clem losing her job, though. I wish there was something we could do to help her in return, but there's no time."

Izzy helped herself to more potatoes. "Are you thinking what I'm thinking then? That we should leave tonight?"

Emma nodded. "No sense in waiting around until Miss Posterity drags us to the police."

She took a big bite of the bread. The butter melted in her mouth and she had to admit she did feel better. They dove into the food in earnest, eating until they came to dessert.

"Cook made my favorites!" Izzy held up a sugar cookie with little frosted flowers on it. She nibbled on it. "I always thought I'd be excited when it finally came to leaving, but . . ." Her voice trailed off.

A lump rose in Emma's throat. She stared into the fire. "Tom and Frances will miss us."

"So will Figgy. Do you think we'll have time to say goodbye?" Izzy brushed a crumb off her cheek. Or maybe it was a tear. It was gone before Emma could tell.

"Probably not." They gazed into the fire as it crackled and popped, each lost in the thoughts of what they would leave behind.

The flames reminded Emma of what would happen if they didn't find real kindling flints before the Winds began to blow. Her magic had felt extra bright and wild since she'd done that enchantment with the snow. All at once, her skin felt too warm and she pushed her chair away and went to stand by the window.

"Wait. How will we get to Omaha? We haven't any money for train fare."

"I'm impressed." Izzy's eyebrows rose. "The old Emma wouldn't have noticed until we got to the station."

Emma winced at the accuracy of that assessment. "And?"

"Well." A flush rose behind Izzy's freckles. She jerked a thumb toward the door. "You know how the top stair squeaks? The board's loose and I keep my wages under there. It's not much, but it's enough to get us to Omaha."

Emma stared at her in amazement. Izzy was offering to share everything she had—her plan, her family, even her life savings.

Izzy must have misunderstood Emma's look because her eyes widened.

"We can make more money. I'm sure somebody in Omaha needs something scrubbed."

Emma threw her arms around Izzy. "You're my best friend in the whole world."

Izzy shrugged like she was trying to scrape off the

hug. "You're not so bad—I mean"—her voice cracked—"you're my best friend too." She threw her arms around Emma and hugged her back.

When they broke apart, Emma yawned. She wasn't used to feeling so warm and full and it made her sleepy.

"Maybe we should take a little nap before we go," she suggested. "It's been such a long day."

"It would be such a shame to waste a nice bed," Izzy agreed with a look at the thick mattress and down covers. "Just a short nap."

They washed their faces and settled into bed in their shifts. Emma's body sank into the soft mattress. Perhaps the greatest luxury was that they each had a pillow of their very own.

Emma meant to stay awake and make plans for their escape tomorrow, but she drifted off almost immediately, the horrors of the day and worries about tomorrow replaced by dreams of puddings and cakes and Figgy chasing butterflies in a field of flowers.

While she slept, strong Winds picked up. They made the windows tremble in their frames and alarms ring throughout the city, but the girls in the lovely bedroom were too deep asleep to hear them.

The next time Emma opened her eyes, it was an hour before dawn and Izzy's hands were on fire.

THIRTY-ONE

Focus on the Magic

Izzy

Izzy's hands glowed like torches in the darkened attic.

Outside, the Kindling Winds blew. For the first time, Izzy could hear them calling to her. It sounded like the loveliest piece of music she'd ever heard and seemed to sing, *Now. Now is your time.*

"Emma. Wake up," she said. "It's happening."

Emma's eyes went from sleepy to wide in half a heartbeat.

"The Winds. I hear them." Emma gasped when she saw Izzy wearing bracelets of flame. She started to rub her eyes, then pulled away like she'd been burned. But her hands were still only hands. "Mine hasn't started yet."

"But you hear it, right? It'll happen."

"We have to go to the classroom and get crystals." Emma leaped out of bed and ran to the still-locked door. "We're trapped." She looked around the room. Their notes and Emma's crystal were in the real attic, wherever that was now.

Izzy swallowed, understanding what that meant. She was going to have to kindle here and now—or die trying. The flames flared up to her elbows.

Emma held up a hand. "You have to keep calm before we do the grounding or the flames will get out of control." She rummaged around in Izzy's apron, which was hanging on the hook next to the mirror. It was the same hook Izzy had hung Emma's dress on that first day. It felt like a different lifetime.

"Use these." Emma pulled out the two lumps of the broken kindling flint.

Izzy recoiled. "But they're fake!"

"Remember what I showed you with the ice and snow? Focus on the magic, Izzy. That's what Figgy's been telling us all along. The objects don't have to be fancy to work. We can do this."

Emma sounded so sure, but Izzy was terrified it wouldn't work. She was going to burn up. She'd never make it to Omaha.

"Oh, and you need something in place of a gem,"

Emma said. Without warning, she took one of the flints and smashed it against the washbasin mirror. Izzy flinched as glass rained down around the pitcher. Emma selected the largest shard and held it up. It glistened, clear and sharp in her hand. "It's clear like the ice but glass won't melt."

Izzy could feel herself starting to panic. "How can I hold the flints and the glass at the same time?"

Emma tore the sash off her apron and tied the glass to Izzy's arm with trembling hands. "You're ready now. You can do this. No fear, right?"

"No fear," Izzy repeated, but everything inside her screamed, *Fear.* The flames were starting to burn in a less-than-comfortable way. "I need you. Help me."

"I'm here." Emma's gaze was strong and steady. She placed half a kindling flint into each of Izzy's hands. "Hold on tight."

Izzy took a deep breath. She brushed the flints together like she was ringing a gong, just like they had practiced. She concentrated, infusing the stones with her magic, and the bits of tar warmed in her palms.

"Together?" Emma asked, holding out a piece of glass.

"Together," Izzy agreed.

She touched her shard of glass to Emma's.

Lumen quod intus lucet qui nos verey simus ostendet, they recited. *The light that shines from within reveals us for who we truly are.*

The grounding was more powerful than either of them had imagined. Energy surged through Izzy, and Emma let out a soft *oof*. Izzy had to concentrate to keep her magic from whooshing up in a giant column of flame.

"Start the dance, Izzy!"

They'd practiced the moves so many times, Izzy's muscles knew them as well as her brain did. She didn't care how graceful she looked, only that she kept her focus on the magic. Still, it was a constant battle to keep the flames under control and Emma had been right that using the glass was much harder than refracting her magic through a crystal. Every time she got nervous, the fire flared up, but then she saw Emma next to her, leading her safely through the dance.

She kept thinking about what this would mean to the world, that a girl like her was going to kindle. Izzy pictured the hopeful faces of the kids in the Tarnish, how much better their lives could be if they got to keep their magic. She thought about the selfish people who kept magic for themselves. If this worked, if she kindled, she would do something about it.

Magic sang within her veins. She felt at once that she was a tiny speck in the whole of the universe, and at the same time infinite, like she was a part of everything, and everything was a part of her. She was soaring and swimming, climbing and falling. This was magic and she was free.

Izzy reached the final steps. She knocked the broken flints together one final time and the flames whooshed out, plunging the room into darkness. The sweet, terrifying scent of smoke filled her nose.

"Did it work?" Her heart hammered in her chest. She stared at her hands, or at least where she thought her hands should be. Her eyes hadn't adjusted yet. Green and red ghosts of the flames still rippled across her vision.

"Try something," Emma whispered, reverent.

Izzy concentrated on the bit of glass still tied to her arm. The lamp flickered to life. Her magic felt better than it ever had before, like slipping on a glove custom-made for her hand.

"It worked!" they both shouted at once, and flung their arms around each other. They jumped around in a circle cheering, not caring if Miss Posterity or the whole school heard. Nothing could dampen their joy in that moment. Let them hear. Let the whole world know what they'd accomplished.

"I am worthy of magic," Izzy cried into Emma's shoulder. Then she pulled back. "But what about you? Why haven't you started?"

Emma bit her lip and looked at her still-flameless hands. "Miss Clementine said it doesn't always happen at once." She tilted her ear to the window. "I still hear the Winds."

Izzy gripped Emma's hands, willing magic into them. "It will happen."

A girl's scream ripped through the night from downstairs.

"The other girls," Emma said, her face going pale. "They're igniting—and they're locked in their rooms. We have to help Frances."

Izzy thought of the vow she'd made during her kindling. She was done being selfish. It was time to make good on her promise. "We have to help everyone," she said.

THIRTY-TWO

The House Dragon

Emma

Emma took a shard of the mirror. With it gripped in her palm, the Winds grew louder, like a band marching steadily toward her. Still, her magic did not ignite.

She shoved at the door, rattling the hinges. Nothing. She screamed in frustration.

"Let me try." Izzy narrowed her eyes and made a series of pushing motions with her hand. The lock clicked and the door swung open.

Emma gripped the glass harder, feeling the sharp edge against her palm. Why was her magic hiding again?

They pulled on their shoes and paused only long enough for Izzy to pull up the board of the creaky top stair and grab a beat-up purse that was missing half its beads. She tucked the kindling flint pieces inside and slipped the strap over her shoulder. "Let's go," she said.

Together, they stumbled down the stairs. A haze of smoke hung below the ceiling of the third-floor hallway.

Izzy covered her nose and mouth with her sleeve. "Where's Figgy? Can't he stop this?"

"Help!" a voice shouted behind a door, followed by a cough. "Help us!"

Emma raced toward the door but Izzy was faster. She rushed down the hall to unlock the room with her magic. Hannah and Anna tumbled out through thick black smoke, coughing. Fire ringed their hands.

They looked shocked by the identity of their rescuers.

"No time to explain," Emma told them. "Go get the kindling supplies ready for everyone."

Hannah coughed into her hand, then remembered it was on fire and started to scream. The flames flared up around her.

"Hurry!" Emma shouted.

They disappeared down the stairs while she and Izzy set to unlocking the other doors. They sent the flaming pupils within to the parlor to join the others.

As they disappeared down the stairs, Emma couldn't escape two terrible, nagging worries: If everyone else had ignited, why hadn't she? And where was Frances? If her old bedroom had shifted up to the attic, Frances could be anywhere.

"Frances?" Emma shouted. "If you can hear me, answer!"

"Emma?"

She couldn't tell which of the two remaining doors it had come from. The corridor was getting hotter and the smoke thicker.

The next door was harder to open. Izzy frowned. "I think they've messed it up, trying from the inside."

Emma banged on it. "Who's in there?"

"Who's out there?" came a haughty reply.

Beatrice.

Izzy scrunched her nose in concentration. The door swung open with a groan.

Beatrice's face was red and sweat was beaded on her forehead. Lucy coughed behind her, her face blackened with soot, though her eyebrows were still intact. Neither of them said anything when they saw their rescuers' faces.

"You're welcome," Izzy said dryly.

"Everyone's meeting in the parlor," Emma told them.

Beatrice doubled over as coughs racked her body. Lucy hesitated by her side for a second before she ran for the stairs. Emma watched with pity. At some point, she had come to understand that Beatrice had never really been her friend. Izzy had taught her that a true friend stuck by you, no matter what. In truth, she felt sorry for Beatrice for not understanding that.

"Come on. You can do it." She urged Beatrice toward the stairs.

"Why are you helping us?" Beatrice coughed. Flames spread up one of her arms and she held it out at an awkward angle from her body like a broken wing.

"Because you need help and no one else is going to do it."

Beatrice looked at the flames on her arm and her eyes went wide. "Emma, I'm so scared—"

She barely got the last word out. Flames flared up to the ceiling. Beatrice screamed a second before the lamp exploded, showering them with glass. Fire spread down the wall like a terrifying tapestry.

"Beatrice! Go downstairs right now!" Emma shouted.

To her surprise, Beatrice listened. She fled, trailing flames behind her. The wallpaper blackened and peeled as the hallway itself began to burn. They had to get out as soon as possible.

"Frances!" Emma screamed. "Where are you?"

A streak of black fur raced down the hall. "Here, she's here!" Figgy scratched at the last closed door. The air around him shimmered more than ever, like his feline body was the hottest part of the fire. Emma understood that this was his magic, fending off the flames.

"Where have you been?" Izzy shouted.

"Getting reinforcements!"

Cook and Miss Clementine charged up the back stairs with the fire buckets, tossing water onto the fire. Parts hissed out, but other flames burned determinedly a few feet away.

"Is everyone out up here?" Clem shouted.

Izzy unlocked the final door with a loud click. "Everyone except Frances, but we'll have her out in a minute."

"Good work, girls." Cook grinned at them and wiped her forehead with her sleeve.

"Get Frances and go. We'll take care of evacuating the second floor," Clem said, and then she and Cook went charging back down the stairs.

Izzy pushed Frances's door open and Emma hurried inside, coughing from the smoke. Frances was slumped in the corner by the window. Flames no bigger than match heads dotted her entire body. Figgy dashed over to her and jumped on her.

Her eyes fluttered open. "The house dragon's come to rescue me."

"Finally someone gets it right," he said, and sighed. "Come on, we have to get out of here."

They threw Frances's arms over their shoulders and the three of them stumbled toward the main stairway. The back stairwell was now a raging inferno.

"Can't you stop the fire?" Izzy coughed at Figgy.

"I'm doing everything I can." His pointy ears twitched in distress. "The house won't burn fully as long as I'm in it, but I can't hold it much longer. This fire's too powerful."

The front door was wide open and the fresh air from outside beckoned. But another set of double doors at the back of the house caught Emma's attention. From inside, she could hear chanting and frightened whimpers.

"Izzy, take Frances outside. I'll meet you there."

Ashes fell from the ceiling as she dashed through the foyer and into the parlor. The older girls were in various stages of burning, shouting the Latin words in panic and flinging their arms around in a desperate attempt to start the kindling. Clearly they had been relying on Miss Posterity to lead them, because they were skipping steps in their panic. Emma wondered where the headmistress was and when Clem would be done evacuating the second floor, but then decided there wasn't time to wait.

"Everyone needs to get out now! The house is on fire!" Emma shouted, but no one could hear her over the chaos. "What do we do, Figgy?"

Figgy leaped onto the piano. His shadow flickered

on the wall behind him, huge and not at all catlike. The pupils' eyes widened at the sight of the shadow's scales and massive talons. A dragon indeed.

"Everyone out now!" Figgy roared.

There was a stunned moment of silence before the girls stampeded for the door without hesitation.

"Good job, Figgy," Emma said.

"Thanks." He flicked his tail and his shadow swung its heavy, scaled tail on the wall. "Now let's get out of here and kindle that magic of yours before we die. Sound good?"

They hurried out into the foyer. Emma was about to run past Miss Posterity's office when she saw the headmistress's hand on the floor inside. She shoved the door open to find the room filled with smoke and the woman who had taken everything from her sprawled on the carpet. A box lay on its side next to her, jewels and cash strewn from when she'd fallen. While Emma and Izzy had rescued the students, that was what Miss Posterity had tried to save.

"Hurry. I can't hold the fire back much longer," Figgy pleaded. His whiskers were drooping.

Still Emma hesitated. She didn't even want to touch Miss Posterity but she couldn't let her die. The headmistress coughed and muttered groggily, as if to confirm that she was indeed still alive.

"Emma?" Izzy shouted from the front door, just as Frances shouted, "Emma, where are you?"

"In here! Help me!" She made up her mind. Grabbing Miss Posterity under one arm, she pulled. Seeing what she was doing, Izzy ran in and grabbed the headmistress's other arm. Frances joined in, hauling the headmistress by her ankles. Together, they dragged their heavy burden into the hall.

The house let out a terrible groan. Figgy sprinted behind them with a shout of, "Everyone's out!"

They burst through the front door and cold air rushed into Emma's lungs. Her muscles ached, her back screamed in protest, and one of Miss Posterity's shoes fell off, but she and Izzy and Frances kept pulling her until they reached the safety of the snow-covered sidewalk.

Emma let go, gasping for breath.

"What's wrong with that cat?" Hannah pointed, and Emma turned around.

Figgy stood alone on the ash-strewn front lawn, the last creature on the school grounds. "No . . . more." He arched his back, staggered, and collapsed in a heap on the paving stones.

Emma's scream was drowned out by the deafening crash from the building as, behind Figgy, the school caved in upon itself and collapsed.

THIRTY-THREE

Shards of Glass and Garden Stones

Emma

Emma watched, heart in her throat, as Izzy rushed through the gate and scooped up the limp form of Figgy. She kept her head down, dodging the sparks and falling debris from the fire, clutching the house dragon to her chest.

"Did I do it?" Figgy wheezed when they had made it to the sidewalk.

Izzy kissed him between his ears. "You were brilliant."

The three of them joined the group of pupils gathered around the prone form of Miss Posterity. The faces of those who should have been kindling by then looked pale and worried in the light of their flames. Some of the eleven-year-olds hadn't thought to put on shoes before fleeing their rooms, and they hopped back and forth on the icy sidewalk in their bare feet.

"How are we supposed to kindle without her?" Lucy nudged the teacher with her foot, but she didn't wake.

Several of the girls began to whimper and their flames grew brighter from their fear. Emma looked around for Miss Clementine, but she was nowhere to be seen. One of the younger girls said she and Cook had gone to fetch the fire brigade. Time was running out and there was only one option available.

Emma turned to her best friend. "Izzy, we need you to lead the kindling."

"Me?" Izzy looked around at the crowd of girls and they looked back at her just as skeptically.

Emma took the broken kindling flint pieces out of her pocket and gripped them tightly. "It has to be you, Izzy. You're the only one of us with kindled magic," Emma insisted.

"Go," Figgy said, jumping down to the sidewalk and shaking off the soot in his fur. "It's time to show them your true worth, Isabelle."

Izzy swallowed and took the flint pieces from her purse. The gold paint had almost entirely flaked off them by this point. She pressed her lips together and turned to the assembled school.

"Has everyone got a gem? We're going to kindle and we're going to do it right now."

Emma pocketed the flints and carefully picked up glass from the blown-out windows of the school for the girls who hadn't brought their rings or necklaces. "It will work. Focus on the magic," she told them.

Beatrice took a shard and stared at it. The ends of her curls were on fire. "The kindling can't be led by a servant."

Izzy sighed. "If you'd prefer to see your magic snuff, then be my guest. The rest of you, grab two rocks from the garden and line up."

Beatrice muttered something under her breath, but she dutifully collected two garden stones from under the snow along with everyone else.

As the girls lined up, Emma stared at her hands. Her fingers still weren't so much as smoking. She reached for her magic, but it shrank away from her. It was hiding, waiting for something, but what?

The kindling began, and not a moment too soon for some of the girls. Izzy went down the line, touching her mirror glass to the girls' gemstones and window shards. Together they murmured the incantation and Izzy grounded the start of each girl's magic as it rose up around them in a burst of energy. As they followed Izzy in the dance, Emma longed to join them.

As the sky began to lighten with the approaching dawn, a crowd gathered on the street, drawn by the noise and the flames. The Gem Row residents watched in their silk pajamas right next to the milkmen and coal-delivery boys in their flannel. In the flickering light of the kindling, their faces all looked the same—enthralled and awestruck. They gathered together, shoulder to shoulder, without regard to their stations, and watched the kindling dance.

Yes, watch and learn, Emma thought. *This is how the world catches fire.* She looked at her unlit hands again and felt sad that she wouldn't be a part of it.

Tom ran to her, with Mrs. Sabetti red-faced and panting close behind.

"I came to find you." Tom held up his hands to show the flames ringing his wrists.

"He says he knows how to kindle. I tried to talk sense into him—" Mrs. Sabetti protested.

Emma handed him two garden stones and shoved him into line. "Go! Show her. Show them all."

Tom lined up with the students from Miss Posterity's and Izzy hurried over to ground his magic. Emma watched with a mix of pride and sadness as Tom danced through the steps she knew so well. What was her magic waiting for? She stepped back, feeling awkward, but then heard Izzy calling for her.

"Emma! Emma Harris, where did you go? You have to kindle too!"

Hope fluttered in her chest. Maybe her magic would ignite now.

"I'm here!" Emma shouted, stepping forward.

Still dancing, Izzy turned toward her voice. When she spotted Emma, her eyes widened in terror. "Emma, run!"

A strong hand grabbed Emma by her shoulder, spinning her around. Icy fear shot through her entire body as she came face-to-face with the tweed coat of Inspector Conduit.

"At last. Mr. Horace has had me looking for you for a long time, young lady. Come with me."

With a firm hand on her shoulder, he propelled her toward a shiny black car parked down the street. Emma tried to dig her heels in, but it was useless. This wasn't fair. After everything they'd accomplished, she couldn't believe it was ending this way. She'd been so close.

She could hear Izzy shouting for Tom and Frances to help, but they were kindling and couldn't stop now.

The inspector reached the black car and flung open the back door.

This was it. She closed her eyes and braced herself to be tossed inside.

"Mr. Horace, sir?" the inspector called into the carriage.

"How many times must I correct you, Inspector?" The man inside sighed wearily. "Well, what is it?"

It was a voice she'd thought she'd never hear again.

"I've found her, sir."

Emma opened her eyes. The man in the back seat wore a crisp navy blue suit despite the early hour. There were dark circles under his eyes like he hadn't slept for months. His legs were stuck out straight in front of him in thick plaster casts. He'd grown a beard and his shoulders slumped, but she would know that beloved face anywhere in the world.

"Papa," she whispered.

Her hands burst into flame.

THIRTY-FOUR

The Light That Shines from Within

Emma

Time seemed to slow. Papa stared at her through the open car door. He was pale and worn out, but alive. Amazingly, miraculously, her papa was alive.

He doesn't recognize me, she thought with a sinking feeling. She'd changed so much in the months they'd been separated. She stood in her ragged servant's shift, hands on fire, praying that he would know her.

"Papa?" she said again, taking a step toward the car.

He searched her face like she was the answer to a long, painful question. The shadows on his face lessened as a light of recognition came into his eyes. "Emma!" he cried.

She wanted to leap into the car and throw her arms

around him to make sure he was real, but her hands were torches. "You're alive?"

"I'm alive," he repeated as tears filled his eyes. "Oh, Emma, where have you been? I've been looking for you everywhere."

"Here, I've been here. How is this really happening? You're not dead!" Her voice quavered. She felt so happy she thought she might cry.

Emma wanted to hear his story and to tell him everything that had happened to her. She had so many questions. One thing was clear though, Papa was back and she would never let him go again. She didn't want to leave him for even a second, but the flames in her hands stretched out like long question marks and her skin prickled with heat, reminding her she couldn't delay. They would have all the time in the world for hugs and telling tales. Now it was time to kindle.

"I have to do this, Papa," she said, holding up her burning hands. She had to kindle before it was too late.

He reached out a hand to help her, but she shook her head.

"I'll be all right," she said, echoing her words from the day he'd brought her there. This time, she knew in her heart it was the truth.

For a moment Papa looked like he was going to

protest, but then his hand dropped into his lap and he gave her a nod. "Go, my girl. I'm so proud of you."

Emma's heart swelled as Izzy hurried toward where she stood by the car. Izzy handed her the flints and Emma gripped them tightly. It was time to take her place in the world.

"Together?" Izzy asked.

"Together," Emma agreed.

She struck the broken pieces of kindling flint and touched her broken glass to Izzy's. Magic swelled up from inside her and it was bright, and brilliant, and blissfully hers. She stepped into line between Tom and Frances.

Then, alongside her friends, with her papa and the rest of the world watching, Emma kindled her magic.

THIRTY-FIVE

Illuminate the World

Izzy

Izzy stroked Figgy's head and watched as golden flames arced around Emma. Her own dance had been clumsy, every step deliberate, but Emma moved like she'd been born to do the kindling.

Which, in a way, Izzy supposed she had.

Emma knocked the flints together and the flames went out. The crowd cheered and Izzy joined in, but she felt more like crying. Emma had her magic and her papa back. Her life would return to the way it used to be, full of rich people, things, and notions. Soon, the attic, their plan, and Izzy would be distant memories.

Dreams of she and Emma finding Maeve together billowed away like the smoke still pouring from the house behind her. She turned to look and saw the empty air where their attic turret used to yearn toward the sky. Miss Clementine had returned with the firefighters in their horse-drawn fire wagon. Despite the firefighters' best efforts, the building was destroyed. There was no going back now. The only way was forward.

She hugged the house dragon tighter. "What's going to happen to us, Figgy?"

"You're crushing me." He wriggled in protest. "Put me down. I want to see what's happening over there."

Izzy set him down. He trotted past the ankles and hems of the crowd over to where two men were lowering Emma's father into a wheelchair. Mr. Harris had plaster casts straight up to his hips and his legs stuck out in front of him. Emma was talking a mile a minute, gesturing with her hands at the house and the street. When Figgy stopped in front of him, her father bowed his head respectfully while Emma introduced them. Izzy doubted he'd smile like that if he met her. He'd probably be horrified that Emma had been spending her time with a servant.

The sky was now the bright blue of morning, but no one was leaving. The street had the buzzing energy of a festival. A kind Gem Row neighbor draped a blanket over her shoulders. "Congratulations, dear," she said, giving Izzy's shoulder a squeeze.

"Thank you." She wondered if the lady would snatch

the blanket back if she knew Izzy was a servant at the school.

The bright warmth of her magic still filled her and she didn't need the blanket, but she hugged it tight around her shoulders anyway. Maybe things were better this way. She had her magic and now she could follow her original plan. It was time to disappear from this place and find her sister. Goodbyes were too painful. She would slip away into the crowd. But when she glanced back at Emma one last time, she saw her friend was gesturing her over.

Against her better judgment, Izzy changed course and headed toward her. *Things will be different now*, she reminded herself.

Emma grabbed her by the hand and pulled her into their circle. "I have to introduce you—Papa, this is Izzy." Her voice was breathless like she couldn't believe this moment was happening.

"That was a very impressive display, Izzy," Papa replied.

Questions raced through her mind, but Izzy kept her gaze respectfully downcast. "Thank you, sir."

"From what my Emma has been telling me, it is I who should be thanking you."

Izzy looked up in surprise. Mr. Harris had an eyebrow raised and a smile on his face.

Before she could reply, someone grabbed her by the

elbow and spun her around. She looked up and the fury in Miss Posterity's eyes sucked the breath from her lungs. The headmistress reeked of smoke and her pupils were uneven, which only made her more terrifying.

"Here they are," Miss Posterity wheezed. She jabbed a finger in Izzy's face. "Fetch the police and have them arrested at once."

The firefighter next to her nodded and pushed away through the crowd.

Mr. Harris wheeled his chair directly in front of the headmistress. Any trace of his smile was long gone. "Miss P., we meet again. George Harris. Perhaps you remember me?"

Miss Posterity looked back and forth between Emma and her father. Her forehead wrinkled in confusion and she released her grip on Izzy. "Mr. Harris? But you're supposed to be dead!"

"And for a time, I thought I was." He didn't flinch under her disbelieving gaze. "Rubble from the building broke my spine. I was pinned beneath it during one of the aftershocks and I'm told they didn't find me for several days. After that, I was in a hospital in a coma. When I woke, I was too weak to remember my own name and no one there knew who I was. By then, my Emma had disappeared. I arrived in town last evening to search for her myself."

Miss Posterity adopted that overly sweet voice that turned Izzy's stomach. "This is wonderful news, certainly, but why didn't we hear from you? The newspapers made it quite clear you were dead!"

"They did, and they printed an embarrassingly small retraction when I alerted them to their error." Mr. Harris reached for Emma's hand. "I tried to contact you sooner, but it took weeks before I was well enough to move even the tiniest bit, and weeks longer before I could speak well enough to dictate letters."

"You sent a letter?" Emma paled and Izzy didn't have to wonder why. Had a letter from Papa been among the bills that they burned in the stove? They would never know.

"Yes, but I failed to obtain a reply and my doctors still wouldn't allow me to travel. That's when I hired Inspector Conduit to search on my behalf."

"*You* sent the inspector?" Miss Posterity's face puckered like she'd eaten a sour Blanding.

Inspector Conduit stepped forward, consulting a notebook stamped with *Pinkerton Detective Agency* across the front. "Yes, Miss Positively. When I visited your school twice and both times you stated that the girl was not here, I told you I was working for Mr. Horace."

"Harris!" everyone shouted.

"He really is terrible with names," Izzy muttered under her breath.

Miss Posterity's face turned purple. "Clearly there has been a terrible misunderstanding. I fear I am but the victim of a cruel situation."

"A cruel situation?" Emma echoed. She seemed to grow two inches taller. "You took everything away and sent me to the attic. You boxed my ears and made me go without food, long before the letters or the inspector arrived. You had every opportunity to be kind and you chose not to be. The only thing cruel about this situation is you."

Miss Posterity blinked and began to back away. "I—I should go check on the rest of the school."

"Before you go—" Mr. Harris began, but they were interrupted again.

This time it was by a very important-looking man with a very serious mustache. Or perhaps he was a very serious man with a very important mustache. If someone had asked Izzy what a politician looked like, she would have described this man, right down to the way his slicked-back hair was as shiny as his shoes.

The crowd parted before the politician. Four police constables in navy blue uniforms stood behind him, nightsticks at the ready.

"Is that them?" he asked in a booming, official voice.

Izzy and Emma drew back in fear. Each threw an arm out, trying to shield the other, so they wound up in a half hug. Then a familiar figure appeared next to the politician. Her long black hair hung down over the bright blue blanket thrown around her shoulders.

"Yup," Frances said. "That's them."

"Mayor Slight. Thank goodness you're here." Miss Posterity pointed at Izzy. "This girl, this *servant girl*, has illegally obtained magic!"

"What are you waiting for, officers?" Mayor Slight ordered. "Arrest her."

Izzy clung to Emma. She dug down into her magic and readied herself to fight. *I'm sorry, Maeve*, she thought. *I tried so hard to get to you.*

But to her surprise, the officers grabbed Miss Posterity.

"What is the meaning of this?" Miss Posterity looked around at the horrified faces in the crowd. "I've done nothing wrong!"

"That's not what I've just heard from my daughter. Such a tale of scandalous abuse and neglect of a pupil left in your care. I can see the evidence of it on that girl's face right there." Mr. Slight pointed at the still-raw cut on Emma's cheek from Miss Posterity's diamond.

"This is a misunderstanding," Miss Posterity sputtered. "I am an esteemed member of society, sir. My reputation—"

"Is ruined," Papa finished for her. "We'll see you in court, Miss P."

Izzy and Emma watched in disbelief as the officers led the still-protesting Miss Posterity away.

Frances spotted their shocked expressions. "You didn't know that my father was the mayor of New York?"

They shook their heads, too stunned for words.

"You liked me anyway?" Frances cried with delight, and hugged both of them.

The sun rose higher, painting the morning sky in brilliant shades of magenta and orange. Despite the cold, the atmosphere on the street was one of a party and no one was inclined to leave. Then, as suddenly as they'd begun, the Kindling Winds stopped, like an exhalation that had run out of breath. A cheer rose from those gathered closest to the students and spread up and down until everyone was applauding the newly kindled.

Izzy's heart skipped a beat. Her magic hadn't snuffed, but it was still illegal and she was surrounded by politicians and policemen.

She tried to inch away, but Frances ushered them over to meet her father. Mayor Slight shook Emma's hand, but held on to Izzy's.

"My Frances tells me that you saved her life twice tonight. In fact, I hear you saved the whole school."

Izzy felt like she was still on fire. "I suppose I did."

"How did you manage it?" The mayor took one of the garden stones out of his jacket pocket and turned it over in his hand. "You're only a servant and these are only garden stones."

"And I'm only the kitchen cat," Figgy called from his place on Papa's lap.

The mayor's bushy eyebrows shot upward. "*Great gems*, did that cat just talk?"

"House dragon," Izzy, Emma, and Frances said in unison. Figgy beamed at them.

"This night is full of surprises." Mayor Slight turned his powerful gaze to Izzy. "Tell me, Isabelle O'Donnell, how did this happen? And you best not leave anything out."

So Izzy told him the whole story, every last bit of it, from the time Emma arrived at the school, to the terrible turn of events that had brought her to the attic. She told them how Frances had been an incredible teacher and the mayor smiled at his daughter with pride. Whispers raced through the crowd when she got to the part where Emma discovered that the kindling objects didn't need to be fancy gems or golden flints.

Emma listened with a smile, her shoulder pressed

against her papa's. The girls from the school drifted over to listen and Tom and a relieved-looking Mrs. Sabetti stood right next to them. By the time she got to the fire and freeing everyone, at least fifty people had gathered around. Gem Row millionaires stood shoulder to shoulder with their non-magical neighbors, listening to the red-haired servant who had kindled her magic.

When she finished, the mayor stared at the garden stone in his palm. Izzy's heart drummed a worried beat. Maybe she should have run when she had the chance.

"You got up to all that without telling me?" Mrs. Sabetti thumped Tom on the back of his head. Then she burst into tears and threw her arms around him. "I'm so proud of you."

Her outburst broke the spell that had hung over the crowd and people began speaking in excited tones.

Izzy held out her wrists to the mayor. "I suppose you have to arrest me now."

"Arrest you? I don't think so." He cleared his throat. "I have an announcement to make." The crowd turned to him in expectant silence. "You may know that magic has been a growing issue in our fair city. Despite the objections of the city council, I am sympathetic to those who wish to legalize the teaching of magic to anyone who proves themselves worthy of its study, regardless of their financial circumstances." He gestured at Izzy.

"After what I've witnessed here this morning, I am using my authority to create a special license that will allow such a school to open in this city. I'll call it the Isabelle O'Donnell License, in honor of the incredible young lady here in front of me. Any school that wishes to apply will be considered as soon as I sign it into law."

Izzy's breath caught in her chest and tears sprang to her eyes. *Wait until I tell Maeve*, she thought with pride.

The mayor continued speaking, something about them having witnessed an incredible event together and hoping he could count on their votes come election time, but Izzy was distracted when someone tackled her from the side in a hug. It was Emma, followed by Tom and then Frances, with Figgy in her arms. Before she knew it, the whole school was there, hugging her and crying out their thanks.

Above their heads, the sun rose, illuminating the world with its golden rays. It was the start of a new day, a new life. One that would be filled with magic.

From the Ashes

APRIL 1907

The house was a big one. It had to be to hold the number of students that would fill its halls starting tomorrow.

It rose like a four-story phoenix from the ashes of the former Miss Posterity's Academy. Wide windows gave it an airy appearance filled with light, and Emma had personally designed the colorful interior.

Papa had received a substantial contract to help rebuild the city of San Francisco, which also rebuilt his fortune and reputation once people learned he was not, in fact, dead. Since it was hard for him to travel, he sent his representatives—with very specific letters of introduction and names triple-checked—to oversee the construction. This allowed him plenty of time for his favorite project: the school. Whispers around the city had made it the most talked-about magitectural design in New

York. Articles appeared in newspapers about the school's unusual origin story in last year's kindling and the new Isabelle O'Donnell License. But that wasn't what made Emma so proud.

The wooden sign wobbled in Tom's grip. "Does it look straight, Mr. Harris?"

"It's hard to tell with you standing in front of it," Emma teased. Tom grinned as he looked at her over his shoulder and the corner of the sign dipped. He'd made it himself with some coaching from Papa. Golden letters three inches tall glimmered on a black background.

She wheeled Papa's chair back a few inches on the sidewalk so he could get a better view.

Papa tilted his head. "Up a little on the right, I think. There. That's good."

Tom waved the glass ring he wore on his right hand and the sign fused itself to the post.

THE MANHATTAN SCHOOL FOR MAGIC the sign read, and Emma thought it was as simple as that. Manhattan was the place and this was a school for magic. No exclusions or limitations. They would teach as many students as they could.

Best of all, there was no attic in this new building, and there would be no servants forbidden to learn. In fact, there would be no servants at all. The students would pitch in to keep things running. They would help one another.

Inside, Miss Clementine and Frances were preparing lessons for the new pupils. Antonia Sabetti and Mary the flower seller, students now themselves, were exploring the new library while Cook joyfully concocted a restaurant-quality and Blandings-free welcome feast in the kitchen. Figgy snoozed in a sunbeam on the stoop and Izzy was in the back garden, gathering flowers to display in a vase in the front window. All Emma's and Izzy's families and friends were here—almost.

"I'm glad that's done. Our new pupil will be here any minute," Emma reminded Papa.

Tom steered Papa's chair toward the house. "Let's not wait on the street. She's had a long journey and we don't want to overwhelm her."

Emma grinned one more time at the beautiful building and then hurried to catch up. It wasn't what she'd drawn in her sketchbook—it was so much better.

"I'm still so happy our letters found her, Papa," Emma said as they made their way up the paved front walk. "Do you think Izzy suspects?"

He winked. "I think she hopes."

Tom pushed the chair up the ramp next to the stairs. "Come on, I smell cookies baking."

As they reached the front door, a carriage pulled up in front of the school. Emma turned around, her heart in her throat as a freckled girl with bright red hair climbed out. She wore a brown dress the color of prairie dust and carried a cardboard suitcase. Maeve stared up at the front of the school, grinning like she couldn't believe her luck.

Izzy came out the front door carrying a beautiful bouquet of flowers. "There you are, Emma. I was wondering—" Her voice cut off in a choked cry.

Emma held out her hands for the flowers and Izzy passed them to her without taking her eyes off her sister.

Then she dashed down the path, running as fast as the wind to embrace Maeve. Emma shared a smile with Tom and squeezed Papa's shoulder. This was better than she'd ever dreamed.

Izzy took Maeve's suitcase and held out her hand. Then, together, they walked up the steps to their magical new home.

ACKNOWLEDGMENTS

If I had one of Miss Posterity's cross-stitches, it would read, "An author may write a story, but it takes many talented people to magic it into a book." This story would never have reached your hands without:

Brooks Sherman, thank you for seeing the potential in this story early on and for inspiring me to grow as a writer. Your guidance and support are worth more than gold. I owe you one for coining *Miss Posterior*.

To my amazing editor, Janine O'Malley, thank you for championing Emma and Izzy's story and for loving Figgy even though I know you're more of a dog person. Your notes are gems and you've enchanted this book into something better and brighter than it was before.

My thanks go out to the incredible team at FSG BFYR. Melissa Warten, thank you for your crystal-clear line edits and for the publishing magic you perform behind the scenes. Thank you to Hayley Jozwiak, Lelia Mander, and Chandra Wohleber for saving me from myself with your astute attention to detail. Many thanks to Aurora Parlagreco for the positively delightful design. Brittany Pearlman, Jordin Streeter, and Melissa Croce, thank you for your enthusiasm and expert guidance, and for helping this book find its readers.

To Geneviève Godbout, thank you for bringing the girls and Figgy to life so beautifully on the cover.

Thank you to the team at Janklow & Nesbit for your support. A special shout-out goes to Roma Panganiban.

To my writing group, The Guillotine Queens, who know that writing is all in the execution. I am grateful every day for Tracy Badua, Jessica Bibi Cooper, Kat Enright, Sam Farkas, Jenn Gruenke, Jessica James, Kalyn Josephson, Ashley Northrup, and Brittney Singleton. Please keep the cat pictures coming.

To Jessica Kim, Julie Abe, and Melissa Seymour, thank you for your sharp eyes and gentle hugs. I adore you all.

Jessica Cluess, thank you for being Figgy's first fan and for literally holding my hand when this book sold. I am ever grateful for your friendship.

Alexa Donne, thank you for always being right and for changing my life by choosing me as your Author Mentor Match mentee.

Gretchen Schreiber and Victoria Van Vleet, thanks for your enthusiasm, the writing dates, and for letting me borrow your last names.

Thanks to Melanie Thorne, who taught me how to write my first novel and suggested I try middle grade for the second. I am forever grateful to our original workshop group, including Ben, Christina, Jamie, Jeff, and Jim, whose feedback shaped me as a writer.

To Lorelei Savaryn, I feel like fate (a.k.a. Sam) brought us together at the perfect time. Thank you for being a shining light in a dark place.

To my writing community: Stephanie Brubaker, Erika Cruz, Karina Evans, Erika Lewis, Lindsey Meredith, Brian Palmer, Bill Povletich, Austin Siegemund-Broka, Emily Skrutskie, Whitney Vendt, Emily Wibberly, and Whitney Wyckoff: You are all gems and I am lucky to have you in my life.

Many thanks to Mary Pendergraft, professor and chair of the department of classical languages at Wake Forest University, for making kindling possible with the perfect Latin incantation.

Thank you to the Tenement Museum in New York for giving me the opportunity to walk in Izzy's shoes and for guidance on what Tom's family may have eaten.

Because this is a book featuring a truly terrible teacher, I have to thank the wonderful teachers in my life.

Thank you to Mr. O'Hara, who taught me the elements of style and was the first teacher to encourage my writing. I'm eternally grateful to Mrs. Gesek, Mr. Cooper, and Ms. Moran at Montgomery and to Mrs. Steel at Brywood for sparking my love of history. To Mrs. Vail, my eighth grade English teacher: I vowed that one day I would write a book and include a note saying that you weren't allowed to ruin it with vocabulary exercises. Well, here you go.

Caroline, Dave, and Shasta, thanks for always listening, your friendship, and all the tennis balls.

Julie C., Melissa G., Matt G., Julia H., Herman S., Kathleen S., Lauren V., Steve V., Ben W., and Matt Z.: It's thanks to you that I know how to write about true friendship.

To Bonnie, Emily, Jane, Lindsay, and Teddie, thank you for your unceasing enthusiasm. I hope this lives up to your expectations!

Mom, Dad, Jessie, Drew, Kara, Zac, Quincy, and Mom-Mom: I feel blessed to have such a wonderful family. Thank you for loving me and putting up with my need to run away and write.

To Cora and Margaret, your smiles are my greatest inspiration.

Last but certainly not least: Dan, I would be lost without your love and support. Thank you for being my strongest advocate, my toughest reader, and my best friend.

The adventure continues . . .

Keep reading for a sneak peek of *The Tarnished Garden*!

The Snuffing

DECEMBER 1902

NEW YORK CITY

Maeve hadn't sparked magic yet, but she knew how to effectively disappear. She hurried toward her best hiding spot as the counting began. Though hide-and-seek was a frequent pastime for the kids on Rust Street, no one ever found her crouched behind the snuffing bucket on the corner. On a cold December day like this, the steam rising from the magically warmed water was either too much of a threat or a promise of snuffed magic for anyone to get too close. But for Maeve, there was no better place to hide.

Jimmy Pickett counted loudly behind her. *Twenty-eight, twenty-nine . . .* Maeve had until the count of fifty to get to her spot but couldn't risk running on the slick, frozen pavement. The tread was nearly gone from her too-big boots, and the rags stuffed into the toes poked out through the holes.

She ducked around a display of half-frozen turnips in

front of Murphy's Grocery. A glance behind her revealed a handful of other kids fanning out to their hiding spots along Rust Street.

A hand shot out from behind the turnip display and grabbed Maeve's skirt.

"Hide with me," her older sister, Izzy, said as she tugged Maeve down next to her. Their knees knocked together, but the thick stockings that Mam had knit protected them from pain.

The street vendor on the curb leaned over his push-cart full of men's hats. "Well, if it isn't the O'Donnell sisters."

Maeve put her index finger to her lips. "Don't tell any-one we're here, Mr. Green."

Their downstairs neighbor didn't take the hint. "I didn't know Murphy's was getting in a shipment of red hair and freckles this morning!" He put his hands on his hips and laughed at his own joke. Fortunately, two women with shopping baskets came over to browse the hats and Mr. Green shifted his attention to bargaining with them.

"Ready or not, here I come!" Jimmy Pickett had the loudest voice in the Tarnish.

Maeve looked out at the street. "We're too exposed here." She hesitated. Did she dare reveal her best hiding place? For Izzy, she decided she would. "Come on, I know a better place to hide—"

"Stay with me." Izzy swept her hand to indicate the bustle in front of them. "We get to be entertained by everything happening here. Besides, hide-and-seek is for little kids and I get bored."

"Jimmy's twelve and he still plays," Maeve pointed out.

Her older sister rolled her eyes. At eight years old, Izzy fancied herself very grown-up. Too grown-up, Mam often said with an exasperated shake of her head. But Maeve was six and not only did she want to play, she wanted to win. She could see the corner with her snuffing-bucket hiding spot from here. Right behind it, there was a little cranny in the wall that perfectly fit one small-for-her-age girl. Maeve bit her lip, torn between staying with her sister, her favorite person in the whole world, and moving on to the best hiding spot in the whole world.

Down the block, Jimmy shouted. Maeve tensed. He'd probably found Josie Kern. Everyone always found Josie first because of the bright blue coat she had received from some Uptown charity. It was the kind of color that either came from money or magic, and it stuck out in the Tarnish.

A breeze whistled down the street, tugging at shawls. A strand of Izzy's hair blew across Maeve's face, casting the busy street in a rosy hue.

Maeve pushed the hair out of her face. "Izzy, we should—"

But Izzy's attention was on the tiny gold sparks dancing between her fingertips. Maeve's eyes widened at the sight of her sister's magic. Even a year after Izzy had started sparking, Maeve still hadn't gotten used to seeing it.

"It's the Kindling Winds," Izzy said in a reverent tone.

As if to prove her point, a second and stronger gust

whooshed through the block, flinging icicles from awnings and sending ladies' skirts swinging.

Jimmy shouted again. But it wasn't a cry of triumph.

Mr. Green glanced away from his customers. Lines of worry appeared on his dark brown forehead. "Jimmy Pickett's ignited."

"Come on." Izzy stood up. She grabbed Maeve's hand and pulled her to her feet. "Let's go watch."

Maeve knew that twelve-year-olds' magic either snuffed or kindled when the Winds began to blow, and that no one in this neighborhood knew the secrets of kindling. But she'd never witnessed a snuffing before.

Down the block, there was a thin pillar of black smoke above dark-haired, blue-eyed Jimmy Pickett. He stood in the middle of the street and stared at the rings of flame around his wrists. Izzy gasped with awe, but Maeve felt sick to her stomach. She and Izzy had pretended they were kindling so many times, but Maeve had never fully understood that when the Winds blew, she would be *on fire*.

"It's beautiful," Izzy whispered.

It's terrifying, Maeve thought.

"Clear the way to the bucket for the lad," Mr. Green shouted. His customers clutched their baskets and stepped aside.

But Jimmy wasn't heading toward the bucket. Instead, he swung his arms through the air.

"He's going to try to kindle his magic," Izzy said, right before the people around them started shouting.

As Jimmy pumped his arms, the flames grew into whorls

as big as barrel hoops and the crowd that had gathered stepped back, forming a circle around him.

"Does he know how to kindle or is he making it up?" Maeve's knuckles were white from clutching her hands together so hard. Neither sister could take her eyes off the flames.

"Dunno," Izzy whispered. "Maybe he's an Ember."

Maeve recoiled. "Mam says the Ember Society's not real."

The skin of Jimmy's fingertips had reddened like he'd touched a hot stove. He coughed and smoke came out of his mouth.

"Get to the bucket, boy!" Mrs. Murphy shouted from the front door of the grocer's. "The longer you wait, the worse the burning gets!"

"I don't wanna snuff. I love my magic too much," Jimmy said through gritted teeth.

Maeve watched, and wished the world was a different place, one where love didn't have to hurt so much. She whimpered. Izzy's face softened and she wrapped her arms around her little sister.

The crowd rippled as someone pushed their way through. It was Jimmy's father, with a snuffing bucket tucked under his arm.

The water sloshed as Mr. Pickett held out the bucket. "It's time, son. I know it ain't fair, but neither's the world."

The girls clung to each other.

"There you two are," Da said, and Maeve felt his hand on her shoulder. He gently spun his daughters around and

Maeve looked up at his bright red beard and worried eyes. "You're too young to see this."

"But I want to watch," Izzy protested. Behind them, there was a splash and a sizzle.

Maeve felt nauseated and she was thankful when Da led them away to where Mam was waiting on the outskirts of the crowd. Their mother must have run downstairs in a hurry because she wasn't wearing her shawl.

Mam put her arms around the girls' shoulders and gave them a quick squeeze. "It's scary, I know. As long as we have each other, we'll be all right."

Maeve's mind raced as she and Izzy followed their parents toward the front door of their tenement building. Izzy would suffer that horrible burning when she was twelve and it would happen to Maeve not long after that. Behind them, she heard Jimmy's da consoling him. The ghosts of flames still danced a sickening green in Maeve's vision when she blinked.

"That's never going to happen to me," Izzy whispered to Maeve.

"Me neither," Maeve agreed, relief pouring out of her like a too-long-held sigh.

"Yeah, when we kindle, we'll do it right," Izzy said.

Maeve slipped on a patch of ice and fell. She was too stunned for it to hurt. How could Izzy see things so differently?

"You all right?" Izzy offered Maeve a hand up. Gold sparks flickered at her fingertips.

Maeve stared at the hand but didn't take it. How could

Izzy want to kindle after what they'd witnessed? Could magic ever be worth going through that?

Maeve burst into tears.

"Oh, Maevers. Let's go inside," Da said, scooping her up.

She wrapped her arms around Da's neck and pressed her face against the boiled wool of his coat to block out the world.

Maeve thought again of her hiding spot. When the Kindling Winds blew for her, she'd head straight for the bucket—even if she had to do it on her own.

ONE

The Rotten Egg

MAY 1907

Maeve

Maeve slipped her feet into the stiff ankle boots of her school uniform. She'd been in New York and at the Manhattan School for Magic for two weeks, and everything about her new life pinched worse than the boots.

She tied the laces and let her heels clunk against the wooden bed frame. How long could she dawdle before Cook expected her downstairs for her shift on kitchen duty? She looked around the room for an excuse. Her roommate, Antonia Sabetti, was brushing her glossy black hair for what Maeve estimated was the third time that morning. Antonia's older brother, Tom, was friends with Izzy. Apparently, this meant that Maeve and Antonia were supposed to be friends too.

Antonia caught her eye in the mirror and Maeve pretended she'd been looking at the pink paisley wallpaper. There was far too much pink in this room. Both of the beds had pink and cream bedding, and the pink wardrobe that stood in the far corner contained a bunch of new dresses for Maeve—some pink as well.

Maeve was uncomfortable here, and not only because she didn't like pink. She didn't feel like she deserved any of this. Not the lovely study desk—thankfully, cream colored—or the textbooks with their new, store-bought scent. She felt guilty every time she put her school-issued crystal into the pocket of her pinafore to go to class because she knew the terrible truth: She shouldn't be at the Manhattan School for Magic at all.

Maeve was terrified of magic.

She raked her fingers through the tangles in her red hair and wove it into a single braid down her back. It wasn't the tidiest braid she'd ever done, but her mind was distracted. She wanted to love her magic the way that Izzy did, but every time she tried to do magic, the word *dangerous* sizzled in her mind. Yesterday, their teacher Miss Lawrence had given each pupil a glass of water with the instruction to channel her magic into the water until it steamed. When Maeve had searched down inside herself and felt the raw edges of her magic, she'd panicked and dropped her glass. It shattered into so many pieces even Miss Lawrence couldn't magic it back together.

The school year had started in April instead of January because the new school had still been under construction. The headmistress, Miss Clementine, was always reminding the students that the shortened school term meant they needed to work extra hard. But working harder was exactly what Maeve was afraid of, and she knew today would be no different.

At the thought of trying to do magic again, fearful silver sparks shot from Maeve's fingertips.

"*Bleeding stones*," Maeve cursed, as a few of the sparks fell on the pink paisley carpet.

"You should be more careful." Antonia paused her hair brushing. She eyed the spot on the carpet where Maeve's sparks had landed. "You know what happened to the last school that was here, don't you?"

"Right. Sorry." Of course Maeve knew. Everyone she met here told their own rendition of the courageous Isabelle O'Donnell's dramatic kindling amid the burning of Miss Posterity's Academy for Practical Magic. It had been an amazing story the first two dozen times Maeve heard it. Izzy had saved the students at Miss Posterity's when the school caught fire during last year's kindling in December. The mayor of New York had been so inspired by her actions that he'd enacted a law that permitted new kindling schools to open, and that allowed anyone to apply, no matter whether they were rich or poor. He'd named the law the Isabelle O'Donnell License after Izzy, who wasn't afraid of anything. Izzy, who was incredibly brave and had learned to kindle against the odds. Izzy, who everyone loved and Maeve could never match.

"I've got kitchen duty this morning. See you at breakfast," Maeve said to end the conversation as she opened the door.

Antonia stood up. "We're *both* on kitchen duty this morning. It's Wednesday, remember?"

With no option to escape Antonia's presence, Maeve led the way out into the hall.

There were seven other bedrooms on the second floor, their varnished doors identical and matching the wood-paneled hallway. The other half of today's kitchen crew, Ida and Minnie, came out of the door opposite theirs. Ida was Black, tall, and carried herself in a graceful way that made her seem even taller. Minnie was even paler and shorter than Maeve and had already busted a hole in the knee of her stockings. Both girls greeted Antonia warmly and mumbled hellos to Maeve before they all started down the hall.

"It's a good thing we don't have to do magic on kitchen duty if *she's* on our shift," Minnie whispered to Ida, but everyone heard her.

"Shh. Don't be rude! She's Izzy O'Donnell's sister," Ida shushed her.

Maeve's shoulders rose up to her ears. She wondered what the penalty would be for missing kitchen duty if she turned around now.

"We should probably hurry," Antonia said, a little louder than was necessary. "Hey, last one down to the kitchen is a rotten egg!"

The other girls took off, laughing as they ran toward the stairs. Maeve hesitated only a split second before she raced after them. Two weeks at the school had taught her that she did *not* want to be the rotten egg. Zuzanna had been the rotten egg heading to their Everyday Enchantments class two days ago, and it had made her dress smell so bad they had to open every window in the classroom.

Maeve's heart pounded in time with her boots down the stairs. *Not last, not last, not last,* it said.

The main hall on the first floor was lit by a huge magicked skylight. Despite the fact that there were three more floors of the school building between the skylight and the actual sky, it always accurately displayed the weather. Gray clouds drifted in the glass above as Maeve and the others ran past the library toward the dining room. She could see the closed kitchen door at the end of the hall.

She gained on the others, her residual strength from farm work winning out over their head start. But as she was about to reach them, her shin twinged where she'd broken it last summer and her new boots skidded on the floorboards. She lost a length and then another behind the girls. When she made it to the doorway, the other three were panting and pointing at her.

Last.

"You're the rotten egg!" Minnie declared. She gripped her crystal and pointed at Maeve's uniform.

Instinctively, Maeve thrust her hands into her pockets and ducked. Her fingers brushed against her own crystal and she felt her magic surge at the same moment Minnie's enchantment hit her.

The stink was immediate and unbearable. The other girls danced away from her, shrieking while pinching their noses in disgust. Maeve had somehow deflected the enchantment and had made the whole kitchen reek of rotten eggs.

Ida gagged. "Why did you do that?"

"I—I didn't mean to," Maeve protested.

She wished she knew a good invisibility enchantment, but she'd undoubtedly mess that up too. Every time Maeve tried to do the pretty magic they taught at the school, it came out wild and uncontrollable. *Her magic is dangerous,* a dozen voices whispered in her memory.

Cook chose that moment to enter through the door from the dining room. She peered at them through the silver-framed spectacles perched on her pointy nose. "Morning, girls. Are you ready—*Stones alive,* what is that smell?"

Minnie pointed at Maeve with the hand that wasn't holding her nose. "She did it."

"It was an accident." Maeve took her hands from her pockets, determined not to touch her crystal.

"Go and open the windows. Thank goodness you're unkindled and the smell won't last long." Cook pointed first at the row of windows near the stove and then at four aprons hanging on pegs by the doors. "Put those on, the rest of you. We're making eggs this morning." She winced. "On second thought, toast sounds better."

"No more rotten eggs when Maeve's around," Ida whispered to Minnie.

Minnie wasn't very good at keeping her voice down. "It's not my fault. You would think Izzy O'Donnell's sister would be good at magic but she's . . . not."

Maeve ducked her head so no one could see how much those words stung. She opened the first window. Spring-morning air rushed in, smelling of motorcars, carriage horses, and the faintest hint of the flowers blooming across the street in Central Park. She reached into her other pocket and rubbed the embroidered sachet again. It made her feel calmer.

After all, she was used to being on her own. Maeve didn't like to talk about her time out West, and there were parts of it she didn't like to think about either. Years earlier, when Mam and Da had died and Maeve was sent away, the matron on the Orphan Train had predicted that her sparks would make her tricky to place. The harder Maeve tried to hide her sparks, the worse the consequences got, right up until she sparked in surprise when a goat butted her and she almost burned down the Taylors' barn. *She's dangerous. Magic is a liability on a farm,* they said as they dumped her back into the matron's frowning care. Maeve had tried her best to never make a mistake and let her sparkings show, but with few options left, Matron dropped her off at a stockyard where the rancher gave orphans room and board in exchange for work. Maeve hated it from the first moment. The cattle were huge and their frightened lowing kept her on edge. The other orphans there were mostly older boys. When they saw Maeve sparking, they told her to meet them in the back field after supper and they'd teach her how to hide her magic. Maeve had gone, but she'd found the field empty—or so she'd thought.

Now, whenever she closed her eyes at night, she smelled the salt and grass scent of the bull. She felt the rush of air as it tossed her up high, and heard the *crack* of her leg as she came back down. The rancher sent for the doctor and

Matron, and Maeve spent the next three weeks alone in a hospital room with only a bouquet of prairie roses for company. One of the nurses gave her a spare bit of fabric and embroidery thread to pass the time, and Maeve made herself a small sachet filled with the dried prairie roses from the bouquet. As she stitched, she told herself she was better off on her own. She kept the sachet to remind herself whenever she doubted it. Like now.

By the time Maeve got the kitchen windows open, the other girls were occupied with the toasting bread and frying sausage. The *thump* of boots overhead signaled the other students were awake. Maeve busied herself with the breakfast preparations and when Cook said it was time, helped carry the food through the swinging door into the dining room.

One long rectangular table with twenty chairs took up most of the space, but the pressure of where to sit wasn't the only thing that made Maeve uncomfortable. The robin's-egg-blue-and-white frescos on the wall, depicting exotic flowers and women in Grecian gowns, gave Maeve the impression that she was standing in a cameo brooch. It was elegant, but the frescoes could be bossy.

As if on cue, a voice from a figure in the closest fresco, a woman with a water pitcher, whispered, "Stand up straight."